Piece
of
Work

Also by Laura Zigman

Her
Dating Big Bird
Animal Husbandry

Piece of Work

Laura Zigman

WARNER BOOKS

NEW YORK   BOSTON

Warner Books
Hachette Book Group USA
1271 Avenue of the Americas, New York, NY 10020
Visit our Web site at www.HachetteBookGroupUSA.com

Printed in the United States of America

First Edition: September 2006
10 9 8 7 6 5 4 3 2 1

Warner Books and the "W" logo are trademarks of Time Warner Inc. or an affiliated company.
Used under license by Hachette Book Group, which is not affiliated with Time Warner Inc.

Library of Congress Cataloging-in-Publication Data
Zigman, Laura.
    Piece of Work / Laura Zigman.—1st ed.
        p. cm.
    Summary: "A mother is forced to return to work as a celebrity publicist and deal with clients
and a boss who are more immature than her three-year-old son"—Provided by publisher.
    ISBN-13: 978-0-446-57838-7
    ISBN-10: 0-446-57838-X
  1. Mothers—Fiction. 2. Press agents—Fiction. I. Title.
    PS3576.I39W55 2006
    813'.54—dc22   2005035569

Book design by Charles Sutherland

For Brendan, and Benji, and Sarah.
And for Colleen.

Acknowledgments

I am deeply grateful to Rich Green for agent-matchmaking. And to Theresa Park, who had me at hello and whose guidance and friendship since has made all the difference. And to Amy Einhorn at Warner Books for her smart suggestions and skillful editing.

I am also very grateful to Shannon O'Keefe and Julie Barer at The Park Literary Group for reading multiple drafts; to Laura Brett and Patty Horing for sharing their insider-knowledge of Larchmont; and to Jamie Raab, Peter McGuigan, Kirsten Neuhaus, Francoise Le Clerc, Emily Griffin, Abigail Koons, Linda Lichter, Diane Luger, Jeff Springer, Madeleine Schachter, Charles Sutherland, Tareth Mitch, Jen Romanello, Emi Battaglia, Lisa Sciambra, and Deborah Dwyer for their efforts on my behalf.

Thank you to Marian Brown, Elisa D'Andrea, Patrick Dealy, Mike Denneen, Ivan Held, Wendy Law-Yone, David Leibowitz, Barbara Lietzke, Ed Schaeffer, Jen Trynin, Glen Weinstein; Micki Avery, Patrice Thornberg, Marion Kearney, Nancy Cunningham, and Lydia Kim from the Preschool Experience; my book group: Deb Klein, Nancy Leslie, Kathleen Olesky, Elizabeth Smith, Mimi Bergson, Jan Cannon, Liza Dundes, and Andrea Hauser; and Nia Vardalos and Playtone Productions.

And very special thanks to my Blog Moms—Lisa Goodman, Pinar Kilicci-Kret, Monika Mitra, and Hilary Monihan—who got me through.

Author's Note

This is a work of fiction. Characters, places, and events are the product of the author's imagination and are not to be construed as real. Any resemblance to actual events or persons (living or dead) is purely coincidental. Although some celebrities' names and real entities and places are mentioned, they all are used fictitiously.

Piece
of
Work

The common idea that success spoils people by making them vain, egotistic, and self-complacent is erroneous. On the contrary, it makes them, for the most part, humble, tolerant, and kind. Failure makes people cruel and bitter.

—Somerset Maugham, *The Summing Up*

According to the American Humane guidelines, no animal actor should have to work like a dog. For instance, if an ape is on set for more than three consecutive days the production must provide a play area or a private park where the ape can exercise and relax. When a bear is working on a film, anything that produces smells that might bother the bear—cheap perfume, strong liquor, jelly doughnuts—must be removed from the location. Only cats that like dogs should be cast in cat-and-dog movies. No individual fish can do more than three takes in a day. Also, under no circumstances can a nonhuman cast member be squished. This rule applies to all nonhuman things, including cockroaches.

—Susan Orlean, *The New Yorker*

— 1 —

On a day just like any other day, Julia Einstein—onetime big-time publicist turned full-time stay-at-home mom—was standing in the kitchen, trying to figure out what she was going to make for dinner that would require the least amount of time and energy. She hated thinking about dinner: what they should have, what they shouldn't have, what kind of takeout she could get that she could disguise as homemade, what excuse she would give Peter when he got home to explain why, yet again, it was six-thirty and she was still staring into the refrigerator without a clue. Meal preparation was her least favorite part of her "job," and for almost four years she'd done almost anything—except going to the gym—to avoid it.

It was around ten-thirty that bright April morning and, as usual, Julia was allowing herself to be bossed around by a three-year-old. She liked to think of it as a choice since it gave her the option of maintaining a shred of dignity in the face of frequent humiliation and subjugation. Toddlers, she remembered hearing someone say, were like big tyrants of tiny countries, and judging from the way Leo had her running around most of the time, she couldn't have agreed more. He wasn't half as bad as most three-year-olds she knew—monstrous little beasts who could have sprung up whole from the pages of a Maurice Sendak picture book—though Julia wouldn't have cared if he were. She loved him more than life itself and couldn't think of anything she'd rather do after spending ten years getting pecked to death by celebrity clients than cater to his every whim. Demanding, insatiably needy, and all ego and id, he was still by far the best boss she'd ever had.

It was while she was happily catering to several of those very whims simultaneously, "multitasking" as she heard it was now called in the actual "workplace"—getting him a small bowl of white cheddar Cheez-Its, flipping the channels with the remote to see if *Little Bear* or *Arthur* or something besides that annoyingly cloying *Caillou* was on any of the public television stations that came with their one-hundred-dollar-a-month extended cable package, and finding his once-white now-gray and shredded baby blanket—that Peter suddenly appeared in the living room out of nowhere. He was wearing a spotless navy wool suit, a crisp white shirt, and a boring red tie. Not a hair was out of place on his handsome blond head, and had he not been holding a near-empty bottle of Heineken, she might not have thought twice about what he was doing home in the middle of the day.

"Who died?" she said, remote in hand and several white cheddar Cheez-Its in mouth. Like any normal Jew, Julia assumed unexpected events and behaviors were signs of death or disaster.

"No one died." He laughed, or tried to, anyway.

"Then what are you doing here?"

"I live here." He forced a smile and took a swig.

"I know you do, but you don't usually live here before dinner-time." Which, by the way, she'd completely forgotten about. "Not to mention drink."

"Well, today's a special day." Another forced smile, another swig.

Julia swallowed her Cheez-Its, put the remote down, and led him gently by the arm to the kitchen. Then she stared into his face, hoping he wasn't going to announce that he was leaving her for another mother who had a job and didn't wear elasticized pants.

"Why is today a special day, Peter?"

He finished what was left of his beer, put the bottle down on the counter, and braced himself with both hands on the kitchen island. Then he looked up at her and forced his biggest smile yet.

"Because today I got fired."

Julia tried to grasp the full meaning of the words but she couldn't. Peter had never failed at anything since she'd known him.

"But why?"

"I don't know. They said something about restructuring my department but I stopped listening when they started talking about my 'package.' Two months of pay, a year of medical coverage, plus the use of an executive placement office to help me find another job."

She shook her head. "Who else got fired?"

"No one."

"It was just you?"

"It was just me." He picked up the empty Heineken bottle and started picking the label off. "I guess that makes me special."

"You *are* special, Peter," she said, hugging him. "You're really, really special." They both laughed a little but Julia could have kicked herself for pointing out that he was the sole recipient of the company pink slip. He rested his chin on her shoulder and for a minute they were quiet. When they stopped hugging they were quiet again.

"So how do you feel?" she asked finally. It was a stupid question, she knew, the kind local newscasters ask people when their house is on fire and they've just lost everything, but somehow it was the only thing she could think to say that made sense.

He shrugged, then sighed. "Actually, I feel pretty good."

"You do?"

"I do. I feel"—he looked up at the ceiling as if the perfect word to describe what it felt like to be him at that exact moment in time was hanging from an invisible little string—"free."

She knew that people who experience traumatic loss go through distinct stages—Denial, Anger, and Grief were three she could recall—and now she wondered if Delusional Positivity was another. Even if it wasn't, she knew whatever phase he was in she was going to have to support him one hundred percent.

"That's great."

"I mean, maybe it's a good thing. Maybe it's for the best and I'll find a better job."

Julia couldn't imagine Peter finding a better job than the one he'd already had—he'd been a management consultant for one of the most prestigious management consulting firms in the world, with great pay and benefits—and though the whole concept of seeing how bad things that happened to good people sometimes ended up being good things that weren't so bad was completely alien to her, she was glad he could see the situation that way.

"So how do *you* feel?" he asked.

She was too stunned to know how she felt, but she knew how she didn't feel—free. But before she could come up with something hopeful and optimistic and completely false to say, she saw her parents' faces suddenly materialize at the back door.

"Shit," she said.

Peter, who just thought she was expressing her feelings about the situation, since he'd had his back to the door and didn't see her parents, moved toward Julia and put his arms around her to comfort her. "Don't worry. It'll be okay."

"No." She shook her head and extracted herself from his embrace and the misunderstanding and went to the door. Tuesday was Costco Day and Julia had forgotten that her parents—Len and Phyllis Einstein, who lived one town over in New Rochelle and had an uncannily bad sense of timing—often stopped by her house in Larchmont to share their bounty—toilet paper, cashews, salmon fillets as big as clown shoes—on their way home. Living ten minutes away from them was a blessing—the free babysitting, the holidays they got to celebrate together, the grandparent-grandchild love affair that blossomed the minute Leo was born—but sometimes she could do without the bulk food drops.

Her mother came in first, holding a giant rotisserie chicken showcased in a clear poultry-shaped plastic take-out container, and then her father came in carrying a four-pound bunch of bananas which Julia knew her mother would split in two to share since *who in the world could eat four pounds of bananas before they went bad.* They'd obviously seen Peter through the door because now their eyes were as big as saucers and they didn't say anything about the food.

"What's wrong?" her mother asked, still clutching the chicken.

"Nothing," Julia and Peter said in unison.

"Is somebody sick?" her father said, looking straight at Peter. "Are your folks okay?"

He nodded. "Yes, they're fine."

"We should send them an Easter card, by the way," her father said, turning toward her mother.

"We did."

"I don't remember signing it."

"I forged your signature."

An awkward moment of silence passed during which Julia relieved her mother of the chicken and her father of the bananas.

"So what are you doing home in the middle of the day?" her mother finally asked, unable to hold in the Anxiety of Not Knowing any longer.

Julia looked at Peter and for a split second she knew they were thinking the same thing, that they should make something up to spare themselves the third degree. But a second later she knew they were thinking the same thing again: Just get it over with.

"Peter lost his job," Julia said, instinctually taking on the role of Official Mouthpiece and using as passive a phrasing as possible to clarify that this was something that had happened *to* Peter, not something he'd done to himself.

Once a publicist, always a publicist.

Her mother, never one for subtlety, put both hands up to her cheeks. *"Oy."*

"It's okay," Julia said, spinning the facts. "We'll be okay."

"What do you mean it's okay? He has another job already?"

"No, but he *will.*" She spoke slowly while raising her eyebrows up and down, as if signaling a child who didn't know any better to stop staring at whoever they weren't supposed to be staring at.

"A lot of layoffs at the firm?" her father asked.

"Yes," Julia said before Peter could tell them the truth and make things worse for himself. "A lot of layoffs."

"How many?" he asked.

"How many?" She shrugged. "The whole office."

Peter stared at her. "Julia?"

"What do you mean the whole office?" her father said.

"They shut down the whole New York office," she said. "You know, downsizing."

"Uhm, Julia?" Peter tried again.

They both ignored him.

"What kind of firm shuts down their New York office?" her father continued. "Wouldn't they shut down one of their smaller offices? Like a branch office? Doesn't your firm have a branch office in Chicago?" He tried to look over Julia's head directly at Peter now, but Julia moved to block his view.

"They don't call them branch offices anymore," her mother said.

"What do they call them then?"

"Satellite offices."

Her father shrugged, unimpressed, then waved her mother away with his hand as if he didn't care what she thought even though they all knew he did.

"What makes you such an expert on Peter's business anyway?" her mother said.

"I never said I was an expert. But I think I know something about his business."

"How could you know about his business? You were an accountant."

"An accountant *deals* with business."

"An accountant deals with *money*."

"Money *is* business."

Julia could tell the situation was getting out of hand like a hostile news conference, and she knew if she didn't put a stop to it soon, her parents would eat her and Peter—and then each other—alive.

"Anyway," she said, interrupting another round of bickering that was about to erupt. "Like I said, we'll be fine."

Her mother made a face. "Well, you're very cavalier."

"I'm not cavalier. I'm trying to be optimistic."

"Being optimistic so soon seems cavalier," she said, shaking her head again. "But maybe it's just me."

Whenever her mother said *Maybe it's just me* it really meant *Maybe it's just you,* which was her way of not saying that she was right and Julia was wrong and which always made Julia go a little crazy.

"Can't you ever just pretend to be positive?" Julia said, trying to look above her father's head directly at her mother, but he was blocking her view.

"It's okay, Julia. Really," Peter said.

"Don't you see," Julia went on, pointing to Peter, "that he's in an incredibly fragile emotional state?"

"I'm not in a fragile emotional state," Peter said.

"Yes, you are," she said, patting his cheek.

"No, I'm not."

"Yes, you are," she said again, her voice rising. "Not that there's anything wrong with that. I mean, I certainly would be if I were the *only person in my entire office to get fired!*"

Her parents looked stricken. So did Peter. Julia bit her upper lip with her lower teeth and wished Leo would come in already and make a few demands to distract them all.

"Look, I know this is a stressful time for everyone," Peter said, spreading his arms like wings and putting them over her parents' shoulders, "but we're going to get through this."

Her parents nodded and Julia looked at the chicken and the

bananas on the counter. She wondered if, for as long as she lived, those two foods would forever remind her of the day, the moment, the strange instant when life as she and Peter had known it suddenly ground to a halt. But her childhood was filled with moments such as this—when negativity would flood the room and no one could breathe—and she couldn't think of anything she had stopped eating because of it.

She touched the domed top of the chicken container with her finger, and, as usual after she lost her temper with her mother, she felt like a big baby. Her parents had grown up in the Depression and had lost a child. It wasn't their fault that fear and worry and concern were almost all they knew.

"Do you want to stay for lunch?" she said, wishing she could make it up to them and hoping, actually, that they would stay.

"Lunch?" her mother said. "It's ten-thirty in the morning. We'll say hello to Leo and then we'll leave."

"The last thing you need to worry about at a time like this," her father said, patting Peter on the arm and kissing Julia on the head, "is us."

It was still light out when Julia and Peter and Leo went to bed that night. They'd turned the clocks ahead only the week before and already the days were longer. Or maybe after the strange day they had, sitting around the living room in shock for most of the afternoon and early evening, it just felt that way.

"Can you imagine living in Norway or Sweden or Alaska during the summer?" Julia said, staring up at the ceiling as the dusk finally fell. "How can you fall asleep if it never gets dark?"

"Imagine living there during the winter," Peter said. "How can you get up if it never gets light?"

Lying on top of the covers with Leo between them, Julia wondered out loud what it would be like the next morning when they woke up and Peter didn't go to work.

"It'll be nice," he said. "We'll go out for pancakes. Then we can spend the rest of the day together and do something fun."

Ever since they'd first met, Peter was always talking about having fun—fun things they could do and fun places they could go—and even though back then they almost never went anywhere except each other's apartments, she had never had more fun in her whole life. She closed her eyes and her mind reeled back to the night they first met: when she told Peter what she did, he told her he wanted to see where she worked since he didn't know anything about entertainment public relations.

"It'll be fun," he'd said.

She wasn't sure whether or not he was really interested in her company's corporate culture as he'd claimed, or whether inviting himself to her office was his way of arranging a low-anxiety first date—not that she was sure he even considered it a date—and she didn't really care. He was tall and strong-jawed with a full head of straight blond naturally streaked hair cut in a conservative chop that was so intoxicatingly *other* and unlike any head of hair she'd sat behind during all those years of Hebrew School. Seeing him in Creative Talent Management's opulent reception area on the twenty-seventh floor that day and prying the drooling receptionist and two male assistants waiting for the elevator off of him, she panicked. He was way better looking than she remembered and way better looking than anyone she'd ever gone out with.

"God, I'm *schvitzing* here," he'd said, peeling off his overcoat and navy pin-striped suit jacket. "I literally just ran over from a meeting on Fifty-seventh and Sixth. I didn't want to be late. Especially on our first date." He handed her a white plastic bag. "I got one chopped liver and one corned beef. I figured we could share."

Julia was suddenly *schvitzing,* too, and she wasn't sure if it was because he'd used and pronounced a Yiddish word correctly and with the authenticity of someone who had grown up speaking the language (which, of course, he most certainly had not), or because he'd brought lunch for them—two sandwiches the size of bricks from the Carnegie Deli. Not only had he paid for lunch, which most men under the age of fifty seemed genetically incapable of doing, but he'd also brought a good lunch. She remembered trying to explain to a guy she'd gone out with a few times the year before why sandwiches from Korean corner delis or from supermarkets should be mocked, not eaten.

She and Peter talked that day for over three hours, and seven years later, they were still talking. They talked about different things now than they did then—what Leo said, what Leo did, what Leo had done one day that he hadn't done the day before—and she suspected the topics of their conversations were about to change again, to the mortgage and car payments and savings accounts and credit card bills and spending within their means and all the other things couples talked about when their future seemed suddenly uncertain.

Peter reached for Julia's hand in the dark and held it.

"It'll work out," he said, barely above a whisper, which is when she knew he was as scared as she was. "It'll work out."

Neither of them was anywhere close to falling asleep when Julia moved Leo toward the footboard of their bed and tapped Peter on the shoulder.

"Remember when we first met and you told me you wanted to see my office?" she asked. "Did you really want to see my office or was that just an excuse to see me?"

"What do you think?" Peter said.

"I don't know. That's why I'm asking."

"Of course it was an excuse."

"Why did you need an excuse?"

Peter rolled onto his side to face her. "Because you were a hottie. And I was afraid if I asked you out and you said no, I'd be crushed."

Julia rolled onto her side, too. "You thought I was a hottie?"

"You were a hottie. You're still a hottie." He nudged her on the hip and kissed her lightly on the lips. "Hot. Hot. Hot."

"But you were a hottie, too," she said. "So wouldn't you have assumed that I'd say yes?"

Peter traced the outline of her jaw and chin with his finger, then shook his head. "You can't assume anything when you're hunting the big game."

"And that's what you were doing with me?"

"That's what I was doing with you."

— 2 —

It was the first Saturday in September—Labor Day weekend, an uncomfortable irony that wasn't lost on either of them—and Julia was racing around the house trying to get ready to meet her friend Patricia Fallon in the city for dinner. She was, of course, running late, and the fact that there were Thomas the Tank Engine trains all over the living room and the stairs and unfolded laundry all over her bed wasn't helping. It was hard enough imagining what she was going to wear—Patricia was taking her to some new supercool one-syllable restaurant of indeterminate cuisine—but having to navigate the obstacle course of clutter that had gone unchecked in the five months Peter had been home and out of work only made things worse.

Not that it was all his fault. Even before he'd lost his job, Julia was organizationally- and neatness-challenged, unsure of how to stop the suburban sprawl of toys from the living room into the dining room. Her "desk" in the kitchen consisted of a narrow landing strip of counter space near the back door and two drawers just underneath it which were barely wide or deep enough to hold much of anything besides elastic bands, broken toys she was trying to hide from Leo while she tried to fix them, and all the brochures from preschools she'd pored over the past year before deciding on the Preschool Experience in the center of Larchmont. But now that she had Peter's crap to deal with as well—his shoes and sneakers and newspapers and books and magazines all over the house—she felt like a lab rat whose cage kept getting smaller and smaller.

Early on in his unemployment, Julia had the ridiculous fantasy that he, a professional organizer who had made his living re-organizing disorganized companies, would use the time he now had on his hands to help her get a grip on things: that after, say, the fifth or sixth time he wondered aloud why there was only one pair of scissors in the whole house and why it always seemed to be in the upstairs bathroom instead of with the paper clips and the glue stick and the Scotch tape in one of the stupid little draw-ers in the kitchen, he would either buy another pair of scissors or label the existing pair "Kitchen." But as weeks turned to months and Peter's many trips into the executive placement office and oc-casional lunches with contacts proved fruitless, Julia could tell not only that no such help would be forthcoming, but that it was more important for her to try to focus on keeping his spirits up than the house neat. So she didn't harp. She just let him do His Thing.

While His Thing used to be getting up and leaving for work while she and Leo were still asleep and coming home right before Leo went to bed, now His Thing was getting up with Leo and Julia, eating breakfast with them, and then sometimes going into Manhattan to the executive placement office and sometimes not going—he didn't tell her much about his job search after the first month or two, and she didn't ask him; if he had something to tell her, she figured he would. On the days that Peter didn't go into the city, which, as time went on, became the norm, he seemed perfectly content to be home with time on his hands: he'd go to the gym after breakfast, take Leo to the park or to the playground after lunch, and even work on a variety of hobby-like projects he kept enthusiastically starting but never finished—building Leo a bird feeder and a clubhouse and a set of electric train tracks in the basement. To preserve his fragile ego, she hadn't asked him to help with the housework, and she'd even asked him to stop helping with the cooking, since whenever he microwaved Leo's chicken fingers or microwaved the macaroni and cheese, he ended up using almost every kitchen utensil they owned and producing a huge mess which she would then feel obligated to clean up since he'd been so "helpful." To preserve his own ego, he hadn't asked her to help him with the bills that he insisted on keeping in a gigantic stack, along with the checkbook, on the dining room table—a constant reminder to them both that they were heading down the slippery slope of credit card debt. Numbers didn't lie and she knew it wasn't easy for him those nights to stare down the truth, once a month, all by himself.

Like the bills, the clutter didn't go away, so that Labor Day Saturday she drove to Scarsdale for the grand opening of the Container Store. After making her way through the crowds and filling out a raffle form for a free merchandise giveaway, she carefully selected one color-tabbed mail and bill organizer, two clear plastic under-the-bed storage containers, and several closet shelving units that looked easy enough for Peter to install. But when she pushed her cart to the front of the checkout line and handed the overly excited "sales associate" her Visa card, Julia got an unexpected surprise: her card was denied.

Julia could have tried another one of her credit cards—she knew they weren't maxed out on all of them—but she didn't bother. She'd gotten the message loud and clear—*We have no income*—and it wasn't just embarrassing, but a wake-up call, too. Leaving her cart and walking back to her car through the busy parking lot, Julia decided to call Patricia to see if she was free for dinner the following week. Patricia had opened Pulse, her own P.R. firm, the year after Julia had left the business to pursue "other interests"—permanent maternity leave—and Julia thought maybe she could start taking on some freelance work from home.

"This is your lucky day." Patricia was at her office finishing up a few things before closing up shop for the rest of the weekend. "I've just had a cancellation. Want to get together tonight?"

Julia slid behind the wheel and strapped her seatbelt across her chest. She almost said that she'd just had a cancellation, too—*her credit card*—but she was careful not to let Patricia see past the façade she and Peter had up until now successfully maintained— that they were fine, that it was only a matter of time before Peter found a job, and that when he did, everything would go back to the way it was before he was fired.

But the truth was that they weren't fine. It was hard finding a job at his level, and at this point—after almost five months of his looking for work—neither of them knew how much longer it would take for him to start bringing in a paycheck.

Back home, Julia found Peter in the living room. He was lounging on the couch watching a Yankees game.

"Where's Leo?" she said, looking down at the pile of sports

pages and sneakers that had re-accumulated during the hour and a half she'd been gone.

"At your parents' house."

"Again?" She was hoping to see him before she left for dinner.

"They came and got him because they said they were going through withdrawal. It's been almost three days since they've seen him." He looked away from the television set reluctantly—baseball was, she'd been told over and over again, an exciting game— and then tried his best to ignore it. "So you didn't find anything at the Container Store?"

"I found lots of stuff at the Container Store but when I went to pay for it my credit card was denied."

He muted the sound and shook his head. "Shit. I'm sorry."

"It's not your fault. I shouldn't have been shopping."

She stepped over a gigantic pair of black suede Pumas and sat down at the end of the couch. "So what about that job you were talking to that guy about?"

Peter shrugged. "He hasn't offered me anything yet. We're still just talking."

"Does it sound interesting?"

"Not really."

"But if they offered it to you, you would take it."

"I guess."

"You guess?"

"It's just not the right job."

Julia tried to be understanding but every time Peter heard about something even remotely possible, he seemed to talk himself out of it, and here he was, doing it again.

"But maybe you should take it anyway."

"But it hasn't even been offered to me."

"But if it does get offered to you, doesn't the fact that you have *no* job trump the fact that it's not the *right* job?" she said. Not to put too fine a point on it.

He shut the game off and sat up. "That's the shortsighted way of looking at it."

"Well then, what's the long-sighted way of looking at it?"

"I want the next move I make to be the right move. I don't want to just take something out of desperation."

She nodded, trying to be reasonable, but they *were* desperate, weren't they? His two months of "severance" were over and every month he wasn't earning was another month they were dipping into their savings. The longer he waited for the perfect job to fall from the sky, the more it prolonged his reentry into the workplace.

She shrugged and made a face. "I think you're being a little cavalier."

He rolled his eyes. "Is that what your mother thinks?"

"I don't talk to my mother about this."

Which was completely true. Just because her mother talked to Julia about Peter's unemployment didn't mean Julia talked back.

"Then you're scared," Julia said, finding another more likely explanation for his excuses.

"Scared of what?" Peter snapped. Clearly, she'd touched a nerve.

"Scared of failing again. I mean, getting fired does a job on anyone's self-esteem, especially a man's. Maybe you're feeling gun-shy, afraid to get back on your horse." She could have thought of a dozen more clichés to go along with the first two, but Peter bolted from the room and headed for the hallway.

"Thanks for reminding me that I failed!" he yelled as he went up the stairs.

"That's not what I meant!" she yelled back. But when she ran to the stairs and looked up, all she saw was the last of him right before he slammed their bedroom door and disappeared behind it for the rest of the afternoon. Which gave her plenty of time to ponder the imponderable:

She was becoming her mother.

Twenty minutes later, when Julia went into their room, Peter apologized. He always apologized first, which was one of the many reasons Julia had always believed he was a far better person than she would ever be since she always found it hard to say she was sorry even when she really was sorry. It was one of the many ways—including his ability to do math and his innately non-Jewish lack of the Fear of Death gene regarding water sports and winter sports—that she hoped Leo would take after him instead of her.

"No, I'm the asshole," she said, full of shame for saying what she'd said and for not apologizing more quickly.

"Well, I'm the asshole, too. I'm the one who got us into this mess. And I'm going to get us out of it."

She nodded and smiled and almost asked, *How?* But she didn't want to sound pushy.

"You were right. The next time a job even comes close to being right—even if it's not right at all and even if I really, really don't want to take it—I'm going to take it. Because that's what people who are out of work have to do. Take jobs they don't want until they find something they do want."

She nodded and smiled again but her heart wasn't in it. She hated the thought of Peter taking some shitty job that was beneath him and suffering in silence just so he could continue to win the proverbial bread, but the last thing she was going to do was argue with him—or tell him that one of the reasons she was meeting Patricia for dinner was because maybe she'd ask her for some work—she didn't want to risk emasculating him any more than she already had today—so instead she kissed him and threw on the first thing she saw in her closet since now she was extremely late: a plum-colored Eileen Fisher sweater and a pair of plum-colored Eileen Fisher slightly cropped linen pants.

Just before she could have taken a good look in the mirror and had the opportunity to rethink her nonblack matching-top-and-pants Garanimals-type outfit, the phone rang. Assuming it was Patricia, Julia leapt for the phone without looking at the Caller ID display.

But it wasn't Patricia.

It was Bob, from the Container Store, calling to congratulate her.

"Congratulate me for what?"

"Congratulate you for winning our Grand Opening Travel Package Raffle containing a gift certificate and more than twenty Container Store items especially designed for the well-organized traveler!"

Despite the fact that she almost never went anywhere anymore, Julia was beside herself as she left the house—she couldn't wait to get her hands on her big raffle prize and use her gift certificate. She got in her car and headed into the city—she would have taken the train into Manhattan instead of driving, but when she did the math, train fare and taxis were practically the same as tolls and parking. It was only after she had sped down 95 South and across the Bruckner Expressway to the Triborough Bridge that she realized she had forgotten to figure in the cost of gas, which meant that no matter how hard she tried to save money, she would end up spending more than she planned.

Even though she was relieved that she and Peter had made up, she didn't think it was fair that it was entirely his responsibility to support the family, especially when, before they'd had Leo, she'd brought in a very respectable portion of their joint income. Zipping down the FDR Drive and getting off at the Twenty-third Street exit, Julia wasn't sure what she was going to say to Patricia but she did know one thing: it was time for her to start making some money.

When Julia walked into Spruce, Patricia was waiting for her at the bar. She was wearing black trousers and a black cashmere shell, and her short blond hair was pulled back in a tight ponytail. Her taut muscular arms were such a gorgeous shade of brown that Julia couldn't stop staring.

"It's fake," Patricia whispered into Julia's ear as she kissed her hello.

"What's fake?" Julia asked.

"The tan. I get it sprayed on once a week." She took a step back from Julia to look at her arms and admire them for herself. "It's pretty realistic, isn't it?"

"Very realistic."

"It's a total pain in the ass—you have to stand there in a bikini while they spray you—not to mention that it's a fortune, but it's worth it. No tan lines and no wrinkles."

Julia could barely process the fact that she'd actually come to a place like Spruce, a restaurant that had its entire perimeter lined with potted spruce trees—wearing a monochromatic outfit that wasn't black, let alone fathom standing around in a bikini in some

Upper East Side salon getting a spray-on tan. Obsessing all the way to their table as she followed Patricia and the hostess, Julia couldn't help explaining her choice of clothing.

"I was kind of in a rush."

"You look great," Patricia said, moving her eyes from sweater to pants before Julia sat down. "You look very—purple."

"Yes, well, it's fake," Julia said, trying to quip. "I got it sprayed on before I left the house."

"Funny," Patricia said, sitting down, too.

Julia and Patricia had worked together at Creative Talent Management for four years—during most of which Julia was single just like Patricia still was. They'd always made quite a striking pair when they went out together—Julia with her long brown hair and black eyes, Patricia with her short blond hair and green eyes—and she couldn't help getting a pang of nostalgia for the old days when they used to date with much weirdness and little success and talk about boyfriends and clients for hours on end.

"So I know you think nothing exciting ever happens in the suburbs," Julia said, snapping her white cloth napkin onto her lap and covering up as much of her purple pants as she could. "But something really amazing happened to me today."

Patricia's eyes widened. "Did the Cute Butcher ask you out?"

Julia laughed out loud. "The Cute Butcher is married!" she said, referring to the guy who owned the Italian Meateria in New Rochelle and who everyone she knew referred to as the Cute Butcher. "As am I."

Patricia laughed, too. "So?"

Ignoring her, Julia smiled and leaned forward with her fabulous secret. "I won a raffle."

"You won a raffle?" Patricia said, her voice an octave higher. "Like from a church?"

"No—from the Container Store. A special 'travel package raffle,'" she explained, describing the large nylon tote bag Bob said was waiting to be picked up, filled with special suitcase inserts and nylon zippered pouches and plastic shampoo and toothbrush containers and mini folding umbrellas and decks of cards. Just as she was getting to the best part—the hundred-dollar gift certificate slipped right into the tote itself!—she noticed that Patricia's face had fallen. Then one eyebrow went up in concern like a road flare.

"Hey, Jules," she said, with a withering look. "You really need to get out more."

Julia felt herself redden instantly. She looked down at her napkin in her lap as if it needed something—smoothing or lint-picking or crumb-flicking—and wished she could have beamed herself home and away from Patricia, who was still staring at her with that who-have-you-become? look of horror.

Can't ask for a job now.

"God, you're *so* right," Julia said, rolling her eyes with great exaggeration and deciding her best recovery strategy was to blame her grand mal seizure of nerdiness on Peter. "I think I have a bad case of cabin fever. Too much togetherness."

Patricia nodded. "I mean, I love the guy, but all joking aside, it must be annoying to have him around all the time."

"Very annoying." Her strategy, though successful, was making her feel extremely guilty, so she tried to change the subject.

Ask for a job.

"But enough about me," she said, right after the waiter came and they both ordered. "Give me some Juice already."

"Juice" was shorthand for gossip, something Patricia was never short of. Even when they still worked down the hall from each other, Patricia always seemed to get more of it than Julia ever did:

finding out that a certain rock star and his wife were well-known "swingers"; how a certain middle-aged comic actor insisted on having a hairdresser present at photo shoots even though he had no hair; or that one of the former Monkees had refused to get out of his solo band's tour bus in front of a concert venue because he "didn't want to get mobbed" by fans even though there was no one waiting outside.

Patricia shook her head. "I don't have any Juice."

"No Juice?" Julia couldn't help being disappointed. She'd come all this way and was looking at a menu she couldn't make heads or tails of—What the hell was truffle foam?—and now she wasn't going to have anything good to tell Peter when she got home.

"Well, I did just sign a big client."

Julia's eyes widened. "Who?"

"I can't tell you."

"You can't tell me?"

"I had to sign a confidentiality agreement."

Julia laughed. "Oh, come on."

"I'm serious. I can't tell anyone."

"Not even me?"

"Not even you."

"But I don't know anyone anymore! Who am I going to tell?"

"Peter."

"He doesn't know anyone either!"

Patricia laughed. "Sorry!"

"Come on!" Julia said. She couldn't believe she was begging like this, but she felt like her life suddenly depended on whether or not she could manage to extract something—anything—out of the Master Sphinx. "Just give me a hint. Male or female?"

"Male."

"Film or television?"

"Film."

"Married or single?"

"No comment."

Julia nodded instantly. "Someone who's getting divorced and wants you to help him look like he's not the asshole."

Patricia laughed again. "No comment."

Julia nodded again. "Or someone who's married but who's really gay and needs you to help him continue to look straight."

Patricia picked up the wine list and hid behind it. It shook a little because she was still laughing even though, as Julia knew, this was serious business. She remembered what it was like keeping other people's secrets; figuring out the puzzle of a famous person's problematic personal or professional life and finding a way to fix it. But the part of the job Julia had always perversely loved the most was the challenge of managing the most unmanageable clients: a skill that had distinguished her during her thirteen years at CTM.

She had always wondered why she was so enamored of this particular kind of ego gratification—she didn't think it was because she enjoyed the abuse or because she had some sort of pathological low level of self-esteem which made her enjoy being shamed and ordered around and treated, generally, worse than a farm animal. It was actually the opposite, she thought. It was the excitement she craved, the adrenaline rush, the same terrifying thrill she imagined lion tamers felt when they entered the cage or when bullfighters entered the ring with just their red silk capes and tight little pants—the fact that everything could be reduced to one simple idea: eat or be eaten; kill or be killed.

Very few people seemed to have this strange counterintuitive desire to tame the beast, and in the business of celebrity public relations, Julia came to see that she had it in spades. When it was time for the toughest clients to be taken to premieres for films that already had bad word-of-mouth, or to be walked down the red carpets of award ceremonies they weren't nominated for or were certain not to win, or to be accompanied during difficult post-rehab interviews, it was Julia who got those difficult assignments. When the toughest clients had chewed up and spit out a long line of publicists, it was Julia who was sent in to take over. For a brief moment at the table after they'd ordered, she was surprised: there was a teeny tiny part of her that missed a teeny tiny part of the work, but it was just big enough to push her over the line of indecision.

Say it now.

"So I was going to ask you," Julia said, starting slowly and not really finishing her sentence.

"Ask me what?"

"About a job. Peter hasn't found anything yet and I figured maybe I could help you out with a project or two, either from home or from the office. Since he's around now and Leo's in preschool, it wouldn't be a problem for me to, you know, go back to work, even temporarily."

Patricia's face fell for the second time that night.

"Oh God, Julia, I'd love to hire you! Really I would! But there's nothing right now and I couldn't bear to have you sitting up front making coffee until something opens up."

"Of course," Julia said, feeling completely humiliated. She waved her hand at Patricia and wished she'd never brought it up. "Just because you have your own business doesn't mean you can give everyone a job."

"No, wait. Let's think for a minute. Where would be good for you?"

Julia shook her head. "No, it's stupid. No one's going to hire me. I haven't worked for three years, which in this business is a lifetime. Plus, I don't even really want to go back to work. I'd probably miss Leo too much and have to be sent home after the first day."

Patricia stared at her. "How do you know no one will hire you? Have you tried yet?"

"No." Not except for just now.

"I mean, you're definitely at a disadvantage for having been out of the game so long. Not to mention the fact that jobs are tight now. But we'll find you something."

The waiter arrived and set their plates down on the table. Patricia looked at hers and she looked at Patricia's.

"Yours looks really good," Patricia said first.

"Yours looks really good, too," Julia said back.

It was an old joke: they always ordered the same thing— tonight it was salmon—whenever they went out together.

"What about Susie Thompson?" Patricia said, slicing an asparagus spear in half. "You could give her a call."

Julia shook her head. "I hate Susie Thompson. She always used to pretend that she had no idea who I was even though we'd been introduced about fifty times."

"What about Doug Bradley?"

Julia shook her head again. "He's a nice guy but I don't know the first thing about promoting pharmaceutical companies."

"You'd learn. Plus, it's all the same anyway. You just pick up the phone and start lying."

They both laughed, then Patricia put her fork down and shrugged.

"I still don't see why you don't just call CTM. I'm sure they'd hire you back. I mean, you left on good terms, didn't you?"

"Sort of." Julia winced when she remembered the face that Marjorie, her über-boss, had made when she finally told her she'd decided to make her upcoming maternity leave permanent. "I think she lost all respect for me. She's one of those women who thinks you're a total loser if you don't take calls from the delivery room."

Patricia was quiet.

"I don't know," Julia continued. "It would be too humiliating to beg her for a job now." Patricia nodded as if her logic made sense, which only made Julia feel worse.

"Well," Patricia said, "there's always John Glom Public Relations."

Julia recoiled. "John Glom Public Relations? The firm that handles desperate has-beens?"

"They have an incredibly high turnover rate and they're always hiring," Patricia pointed out. "The only problem is, the guy who runs things now is someone I worked with a long time ago and he's kind of an idiot. His name is Jack DeMarco but we used to call him 'Jack DeWack' because he was so annoying." Patricia sighed as if she wished the door to this unfortunate hellhole had never been opened, even though she was the one who'd opened it.

"Aren't they really, really small?" Julia said, stalling for time. She thought she remembered hearing how, unlike Peter's firm, they actually *had* downsized their New York office a few years ago in favor of their L.A. office, and the idea of working in a tiny sweatshop without any hustle and bustle and glamour and excitement was too depressing to contemplate.

"Let's see," Patricia said, counting on her tan, well-manicured fingers. "There's Jack DeWack."

Finger.

"His assistant."

Finger.

"His deputy Janet who I know left recently because she just applied for a job with me and I don't think they've replaced her yet."

Finger.

"And Janet's assistant, who stayed on."

Finger.

A four-finger operation. Julia poked at her salmon, then glanced at her watch. Even though it was barely nine o'clock and Leo was already asleep, she couldn't wait to get home, not only because her conversation with Patricia had taken such a grim turn but because her piece of salmon had been the size of a small child's foot and she was already hungry again.

"Well, I guess you should e-mail me Jack DeWack's contact information in the morning," Julia said, not even bothering to try to hide her reluctance. "At least I'll have an in there."

"Okay, but when you get in touch with him, don't mention my name," Patricia said quickly. "The last thing I need is for him to track me down and hit me up for a job."

— 3 —

As soon as Jack DeMarco opened his mouth a week later, Julia remembered why she had been so secretly relieved not to be a celebrity publicist all those years.

Because she hated celebrities. And people like Jack.

"We screen our senior staff very, very carefully," Jack said that morning in mid-September when she met with him, his voice barely above a whisper as if he were a partner in the agency, which she knew he wasn't. "Discretion. Competence. Creativity. These are the tools of our trade, the goals of our particular mission."

She smiled politely, then stared earnestly at the yellow legal pad she'd brought with her and which, unused, was starting to feel like a prop. She kept meaning to write something down but found she simply couldn't bear to—so much did she not want this job. This position she was interviewing for was, after all, a demotion from the last one she'd had, and if she hadn't been so desperate for a job—any job—they both knew she would never have even been considering it.

But she did need the job. Badly. So there she was, wearing a too-tight too-short black skirt and suit jacket that she'd squeezed herself into like a sausage, trying to look as if it hadn't been almost four years since she'd worn panty hose.

"And our particular mission is dealing with celebrities who have, in the past, been used to a certain measure of fame but who now, for whatever reasons—bad career choices, substance abuse problems, general mismanagement—find themselves below that measure of fame."

Listening and nodding, she finally forced herself to put pen to paper:

Jack DeMarco is impressed with himself.

"Our mission is to advise them on strategies which will allow them to reclaim that level of fame and give them a new life in the public eye."

Jack DeMarco loves to hear himself talk.

"In other words," he said before pausing to clarify the concepts he'd just laid out and before she could make another note, "we manage celebrities *in transition.*"

Jack DeMarco is a year—maybe two—away from complete baldness.

She nodded, but in those few moments that she had let her mind wander, she'd missed the gist of his speech.

"That's a euphemism. A euphemism for what we specialize in."

He smiled at her and lowered his voice. "What we specialize in are *has-beens*." Then he spelled the word for comic effect.

She laughed, and so did he, and after a few unexpected moments of mutual empathic eye rolling about the business they were in, she looked around his sad-sack office. It was drab with the sort of cheap faux-cherry furniture—big desk, credenza, shelving wall unit—and oversized leather "manager's chair" that were always hallmarks of loser companies and loser executives. The rugs were gray and they smelled vaguely of old cigarette smoke and french fries, and she wondered whether Jack spent a lot of time smoking and eating french fries in his office or whether she was just having some sort of stress-induced olfactory hallucination. On the near walls hung framed and signed publicity headshots of former "has-beens" who'd had hugely successful comebacks—Burt Reynolds. John Travolta, and Cher. Smaller, dustier photos hung on the far walls.

Jack noticed Julia squinting across the room. She suspected that those were his actual clients—not the actors on the near wall.

"Kathie Lee Gifford. Justine Bateman. Billy Baldwin," he said, squinting, too, before he looked away in disgust. "Some people just aren't meant to come back."

She looked back down at her pad and took her first real pretend-note of the meeting:

Some losers: losers forever.

"Certain people should never have become famous in the first place," he added. "But that's another story."

Except for Justine Bateman, whom she had always loved in *Family Ties* and felt had great comic timing and enormous potential, she was in complete agreement. Here they were, two people—*two publicists*—speaking the same language. Despite herself she couldn't remember the last time she'd met someone who truly understood how undignified and unseemly this work could be.

"They're terminal cases, these has-beens," he'd continued. "Former stars who have virtually no public profile, no stock in the entertainment marketplace anymore. Which is what makes it so challenging." He pulled his chair closer to the desk, then leaned back in it—seemingly his preferred position for informing and edifying. "The American public is incredibly fickle. But there's nothing it loves more than watching a has-been make a comeback. It's the ultimate success story."

"Like CPR," Julia said, trying to get the metaphor right so Jack would see that she was smart. "Bringing someone back from the proverbial dead."

Jack smiled, deeply satisfied. "Exactly."

It was clear that she got it, and it was clear that *he* got that she got it, and even though it didn't seem to her to be that hard a thing to get, she couldn't help basking in his approval and in the coconspiratorial way he smiled and lowered his voice:

"There are certain things only other publicists can understand."

Julia nodded.

Jack DeMarco fancies himself a philosopher.

Jack drummed his fingers on the desk and flashed her a smarmy smile. She got a weird feeling, suddenly, like he was going to make googly-eyes at her, so when all he did was wink and make his fingers into a gun she was repelled but relieved.

"So. Who's your favorite actor?" he finally asked.

She tried to remember who had been on *Entertainment Tonight* the night before when she was microwaving Leo's fish sticks even though according to the box in order to maximize crispiness they weren't supposed to be microwaved: "Sean Connery."

Jack nodded. "Who else?"

And the night before that. "Johnny Depp."

Jack drummed his fingers on the desk again. "What's your favorite movie?"

"I'm not sure. I haven't seen one in about two years."

Jack stopped drumming. Whatever momentary attraction he may have felt seconds before was clearly gone.

Julia laughed. "That's what happens when you have children." *You become so detached from the real world that when you finally try to reenter it you're not allowed to because you scare people off with how dumb and detached from the real world you sound.*

He stared at her. "Two years. That's a long time," Jack finally said.

Julia waved her hand at him dismissively, dropping her pen in the process.

"I was exaggerating," she said as she struggled to pick it up, her skirt so tight when she bent down that she almost lost consciousness. "It was probably only a year." She could feel her eyes blinking rapidly the way they always did when she lied. "A year and a half tops."

He nodded, registering the big hole she had dug for herself.

Shut up.

Jack shrugged, stared down at her resumé for what seemed like the first time. "So, is that why you left Creative Talent?" he said, pausing to do the lapse-in-employment math. "Three years ago? Because you had a baby?"

She closed her eyes, hoping she hadn't completely blown it. "Yes."

"And what did you have, a boy or a girl?"

"A boy."

"What's his name?"

"Leo," she said, even though they sometimes called him Scooby.

Or Scooby-Doo.

Or The Scoob.

As Jack continued to scan her resumé, an image of Leo's soft-cheeked face that morning—wet with tears, twisted with the agony and betrayal of unexpected abandonment, pressed up against the living room window pleading for her to *Come back, come back* as he watched her make her way out the front door and into the car and drive away—popped into her head. She winced at the memory of her own quick-dissolve on the drive to the station, and felt her throat start to seize up again. On Tuesday mornings the two of them usually went to the Whole Foods in Scarsdale to get fleeced on organic produce and Pirate's Booty—the rich man's Cheetos—and then to the Food Emporium for everything else. Sometimes they even went all the way to the Cute Butcher's for marinara sauce. Though she'd been away from him for only a few hours, she missed Leo like a lost limb, which made her worry about how she would survive much longer separations when and if she went back to work full-time.

"And who's your husband?"

"Peter Morrissey."

"What does he do?"

"He's a management consultant," she offered quickly without embellishment.

"Let me ask you something else," Jack said, putting down her resumé and clasping his hands on top of his desk. "What do you think of Mary Ford?"

Despite trying to stay focused on the interview, she couldn't help being completely distracted by whether or not Leo had found the battery-powered Thomas train that he had misplaced right before she was leaving the house and which had added to the intensity of the misery of her departure since she didn't have the time or the wherewithal to conduct a thorough search. Maybe it was under the couch. Or inside his Thomas lunchbox. Or stuck behind the booster seat of her car that she had driven and parked at the train station — the actual train station with real trains that took people to real places, like into the city for horrible job interviews.

"Mary Ford?" she repeated.

"Mary Ford is a client."

"Right." She should have known that. And five years ago, she would have known that because she would have done actual homework before an interview like this instead of just reading a few back issues of *People* magazine at her parents' house.

Jack smiled. "She's terrific."

Julia smiled back. "Great."

"Terrific" was P.R.–speak for "a real piece of work."

"I was wondering if the opportunity to work with her might be something you'd be interested in."

Julia had, in fact, never seen a Mary Ford movie from start to finish — she had never been much of a film buff or a fan of old movies — but she needed this job, so she forced herself to snap to attention, block everything else out, and concentrate. And lie.

With abandon.

"Absolutely! Mary Ford is one of my all-time favorites!"

"Really." Jack looked quite pleased. Finally.

So she lied again.

"Yes!"

And again: "My mother loves her, too!"

And again: "And so does a good friend of mine!"

"Who's that?"

"Patricia Fallon."

Jack sat back in his chair and smiled broadly. "Patty Fallon!"

"Patricia," Julia corrected. She couldn't help herself—Patricia hated being called Patty.

"She and I go way back," he continued. "We were both assistants at Hill & Knowlton years ago."

Julia tried to stop the knowing smirk from spreading across her face, but she couldn't. Jack swiveled—back-forth-back, back-forth-back, back-forth-back—then started in with the drumming again. "So is Patricia still in P.R.?"

"Yes. She is."

"*Still* in P.R.!" he repeated cheerfully, as if she were as stuck in a dead-end career as he was.

"Actually," Julia clarified, knowing she was going too far, "she started her own firm about three years ago, called Pulse. She handles mostly big entertainment clients: magazines, publishers, film and television people." She paused for a moment, trying to decide whether or not to break publicist-client privilege and reveal to Jack that Oprah considered Patricia not just a publicist but also "a friend." Which of course she did since she was already feeling guilty for blowing Patricia's cover and figured she could atone for her bad behavior by rubbing Jack's nose in her success.

He swiveled a few more times, then cocked his head. "So why aren't you working for Pulse?"

Julia forced a smile and rolled her eyes as if working there was more than someone like herself could ever dream of when in reality it was just an incredibly sore subject.

"No openings."

"No openings for the boss's close personal friend?"

"Nope!" Julia's smile broadened to the point of muscle strain. "Plus," she added, trying to spin Patricia's recent rejection to her advantage, "even if there was an opening, it wouldn't be a very good idea. I wouldn't want to ruin a perfectly good friendship by working together."

Jack stared at her again. "Why? Are you difficult to work with?"

"Sometimes." She laughed, since of course she wasn't difficult to work with, but it was such a supremely stupid time to make a stupid joke that Julia suddenly realized she was unconsciously trying to sabotage herself.

Think. Of. Leo. You. Selfish. Pig.

Jack finally stopped swiveling and went back to Mary Ford.

"Anyway, in about a month the new fragrance created especially for Mary Ford—Legend—will be in stores, and we'll be using Mary Ford to promote and market it through media appearances and personal appearances at select department stores across the country over a four-week period starting in mid-October. Legend is intended as a comeback vehicle for her, so obviously it's an extremely important project for both Mary Ford and John Glom Public Relations." He turned toward his credenza. "I'd let you smell it but I can't find my sample bottle. Anyway, we all have a lot invested in the success of this particular venture. Which is why whoever we hire for this position has to be able to handle a client and a tour of this magnitude."

Julia felt her attention waning yet again but when Jack glanced again at her resumé, this time favorably, she sat up straight in her chair.

"Although I will do most of the traveling with Mary Ford, there will be certain trips I'll need someone else to cover—for the obvious reason that, given my position here, I can't spend all of my time out of the office with one client. As you know, this business is all about perception."

And deception.

"Anyway, it's a plum assignment for the person assigned to it. I mean, how many people can say they've worked with a true Hollywood legend?"

Depending on how loosely one defined the term "true Hollywood legend," hundreds of thousands, if not millions, of unfortunate publicists could make that claim. Including Julia.

"So are you on board?"

She nodded, and Jack sat back in his chair, so deeply relieved that he couldn't help grinning from ear to ear. And before they started to discuss particulars, Julia made one more note on her pad:

Just sold my soul for $$.

— 4 —

Having accepted the job she didn't want, all Julia wanted to do was leave Jack's stupid office. She was dying to go home already and see The Scoob, who had, just the day before, discovered his penis (which he called his "peanut") and who needed—according to two different books she referred to only in emergencies and at crucial developmental milestones because she found them so excessively child-centered she feared following their instructions would produce a Chia Pet of a child narcissist—to have his discovery "acknowledged and validated."

Not to mention the fact that she couldn't wait to get out of her interview suit, which was, by now, cutting off circulation to her limbs and internal organs.

Taking the commuter train from Grand Central back to Larchmont, then driving the half mile from the station, she arrived home in the late afternoon to find her parents' bright blue Ford Taurus parked in front of her house.

She pulled her "preowned" black Volvo wagon that still wasn't paid off and that needed a tune-up into the driveway and turned off the engine. Sitting behind the wheel in silence, she stared at the house—a modest, slightly shabby Tudor, half an hour outside the city, that she and Peter had moved into about a year after Leo was born. The paint was worn and some of the gutters were sagging and even though they couldn't afford now to do any of the work on it that they'd intended on doing when they'd bought it—a new kitchen, a second full bath, maybe even an addition with a family room and an outdoor deck—she still loved the house.

And the neighborhood.

Though she had always been too embarrassed to admit it to most of her single urban friends like Patricia, she and Peter, both coddled products of the suburbs (Westchester and Long Island, respectively), actually liked the suburbs. They couldn't imagine raising children in a concrete jungle; there was too much noise and traffic, too much sophistication and not enough bad taste. They wanted Leo to grow up going to malls, playing in finished basements and playrooms, and learning—the way native New Yorkers don't—how to drive before the age of thirty.

Her eyes moved to the lawn. They'd had to let the landscaper go at the beginning of August and now it was obvious that it needed cutting and edging. She wondered what would become of it if they never bothered to hire the landscaper back and continued to let the grass grow—how high it would get, how quickly into the fall it would become covered over with leaves, how long it would take for Rita Janeway, the neighborhood watchdog, avid horticulturist, and committed conservationist and recycler with the fake British accent (she was from New Jersey) who lived across the street, to threaten to sue them if they didn't tend to their property properly. But then she remembered: her parents were there and she had to go into the house and explain to them that just because she was going to be working for a third-rate public relations firm when she used to work for a first-rate one didn't mean that they were complete failures as parents.

But still she didn't move.

The car windows were all rolled up and the unexpected heat and humidity of the mid-September Indian-summer day seemed to be rising audibly—cicadas hissing in the trees, insects dropping onto the windshield and walking silently across the glass, children's bicycle bells ringing in the distance. She had grown up less than five miles from where she sat now, and when she closed her eyes she remembered what it was like playing alone in the backyard of her parents' house after dinner as the sun went down—jumping from one piece of flagstone on the patio to another without stepping on the blades of grass and the little blue flowers that grew in between them. Right before dusk on those long summer evenings she'd always hear the out-of-tune tinkling notes of the ice cream truck make their way through the trees. She didn't get an ice cream sandwich or Popsicle every night, but it wasn't because her parents didn't let her. It was because she didn't always ask. After her brother had died she'd tried not to ask them for things that weren't absolute necessities.

When a bead of sweat rolled down her back, she collected her things—her briefcase, her commuter train and taxi receipts for tax purposes, and the Arts & Leisure section of the *New York Times* (she was going to see a movie this year if it killed her). Then she took what was left of two glazed Dunkin' Donuts—a short stubby elbow curve of dough still in a wax bag—that she'd bought at Grand Central to console herself and got out of the car.

Julia put her key in the door but, as usual when her parents were waiting on the other side of it, it opened before she'd even had the chance to turn the lock.

From the doorstep her eyes readjusted from bright sunshine to dim indoor light, and when they did she saw her parents and Peter looking back at her. For a second or two they all stared at each other—her mother at Julia, her father at Julia, her father at her mother, her mother at her father, Julia at Peter, Peter at her—all trying to gauge each other's mood and figure out what not to say.

"We brought dinner," her mother said nervously as Julia finally squeezed past them all in the foyer and closed the door behind her.

"We figured, after your interview, you wouldn't feel like cooking," her father finished, his voice so heavy with a sympathetic presumption of failure that Julia felt, the way she generally did when her parents rushed in trying to be supportive, like she was being suffocated with a huge white pillow.

Julia was going to say *I never feel like cooking,* but before she could get the words out, Peter pointed toward the kitchen.

"Your mother made chicken! And a salad," he said, with the same sort of desperately forced enthusiasm that she herself had used all that morning during her conversation with Jack De-Marco, and which, she realized now, was a farce. He looked sharp and casually well dressed in his usual weekday khakis and button-down striped shirt intended to create the illusion that he just happened to be home for the day instead of indefinitely unemployed, and Julia still wasn't sure if this was a good thing or a bad thing.

Looking across the kitchen, her stomach sank. Her mother wasn't just a terrible cook, she was the worst sort of terrible cook: *a terrible cook who thought she was a good cook and therefore refused to stop cooking.* She forced herself to smile as she walked to the counter and stared down at the sad little meal her mother had prepared, so well-meaning yet so inedible: once-frozen, now-defrosting boneless skinless chicken breasts sprinkled with paprika, of all spices, stuffed with Uncle Ben's rice pilaf, and lined up like dimpled little fists in a foil-covered rectangular Pyrex glass dish; canned peas or green beans or wax beans or Veg-All on the counter, ready to be opened and emptied into an aluminum saucepan and boiled beyond recognition; and a salad of iceberg lettuce, sliced cucumbers, and supermarket tomatoes with low-calorie Thousand Island bottled dressing.

Though Peter had always gotten along with her parents and had always felt very grateful for all the free babysitting they provided and for the fact that they had never made him feel any worse about being Catholic instead of Jewish than he already felt (growing up in Great Neck and spending his college years and most of his adult life living on the Upper West Side of Manhattan, he had long since felt like a Jew trapped in a non-Jew's body), he could not abide her mother's cooking, leaving Julia to come up with a vast array of polite excuses for why they were never able to eat dinner at her parents' house but were always more than happy to have them over to their house.

She headed toward the kitchen table and took off her unbearably dull black Ferragamo pumps with the two-inch heels and the decade-blurring squarish toe (were they from the early 1980s or the late 1990s?) which she'd always hated and wore only once or twice a year to temple on the High Holidays and the occasional funeral or other family function. Her parents surrounded the table as she pushed and prodded her briefcase into the corner with her nude-colored nylon-hose-covered toes. As always, they were dressed exactly the same, in durable sweatshirts (her mother's maroon, her father's navy blue), pressed jeans, and matching black suede Merrells with skid-resistant rubber soles as thick as tires—postretirement uniforms that were practical, comfortable, indestructible, and ready for almost anything: food shopping, babysitting, or early-bird dinners.

Julia looked up at them and sighed. Though they couldn't possibly have looked any cuter, she dreaded the inevitable:

The questions are coming. The questions are coming.

"So?" her father began again, his voice full of trepidation.

"You didn't get the job?" her mother finished.

Julia went to the refrigerator and turned. "Actually, I *did* get the job."

"*Mazel tov!*" Peter said, coming over to give her a kiss. His cheek was soft and smooth and smelled of Old Spice—another sign that he was either a stronger person than she was in the face of adversity or that he was sliding even deeper into denial. She knew he was happy about the fact that their five months of zero net income would finally be coming to an end, but she also knew that his true happiness had more to do with the fact that now they had a legitimate reason not to eat her mother's food and to go out for dinner instead of staying in to save money: they needed to celebrate.

"Thank God," her mother said, hovering over the Pyrex dish as if the chicken breasts needed to be watched, lest they try to escape. "You'll finally get a paycheck."

"And benefits," her father added, beginning one of their perfectly timed duets of mutual relief for catastrophe averted.

"Now you won't have to sell the house."

"Not that you would have had to, of course."

"Of course not."

"We would have helped you."

"Even if we'd had to remortgage our own house."

"Anything to help you get back on your feet."

Julia looked at Peter and they both winced.

"So this John Glom Public Relations that Peter was telling us about," her father finally asked. "I've never heard of them. Who do they handle?"

"They handle Mary Ford, as a matter of fact," she said. "Which appears to be the main reason they're hiring me."

"Mary Ford?" her parents asked in unison. Their eyes lit up the way they used to when she still worked at Creative Talent. Despite all her years in the business and all her attempts to explain to them that being a celebrity publicist wasn't the same as being a celebrity ("Just because you're *with* famous people doesn't mean that *you're* famous") they never believed her. They were the children of Russian and Polish immigrants, who had grown up in Brooklyn, and to them, doctors were celebrities, and movie stars were gods. Riding around in limousines and staying in expensive hotels with them—no matter how much you had to wait on them hand and foot and get yelled at for things that weren't your fault—was success and excitement beyond all comprehension.

"Mary Ford is a big star!" her mother said.

"*Was* a big star," Julia clarified.

Her father appeared not to hear her. "So what does she have out now? A new movie?"

Julia shook her head. "She doesn't have a new movie."

Mary Ford was a has-been. Has-beens didn't have new movies. They had new "products."

"She has a perfume."

"A perfume?"

"What kind of perfume?"

Julia shrugged. "What do you mean, what kind of perfume?"

"Well, what's it called?"

"Legend."

"What does it smell like?"

"I don't know."

"You don't know?"

"No."

"They didn't let you smell it?"

"No."

"Or give you a sample?"

"No."

"Or even a spritz?"

"No."

Julia turned to Peter. He, too, seemed to be wondering why she hadn't managed to get a whiff of the stuff.

"She's Jewish, you know, Mary Ford," her father said to no one in particular.

"Of course she is," her mother said back.

"She changed her name."

"They all changed their names back then."

"They still change their names."

"The first husband died of cancer."

"So did the second husband."

"I thought he died of a stroke."

"A stroke brought on by cancer."

"What kind of cancer brings on a stroke?"

"Brain cancer."

"The first husband didn't have brain cancer."

"Not the first husband. The second husband."

"Was he Jewish?"

"Of course he was Jewish. So was the first husband."

Julia knew that when the talk turned to Jews and to death and dying, her parents would soon become so engrossed in their conversation that she could finally slip away unnoticed and find Leo.

Backing out of the kitchen and picking up her shoes on the way up the stairs, she found him sitting on their bed watching a Thomas the Tank Engine video, pawing with his right hand through a small plastic bowl of salted peanuts in search of nuts that weren't too big or too small or too brown. The misplaced train was now safe inside his left hand.

For a minute she didn't say anything. She didn't want to disturb the mental photograph she was taking of him at this exact moment in time *which would never come again* and preserve it, commit it to memory, so precious was the sound of his crunching and chewing and the sight of his little body, compact and round and soft, already in his pajamas, listening and watching with such intense concentration the fate of those creepy little trains with their big-eyed faces. Watching him, she almost didn't notice the video's narration (the episodic series featured voice-overs by such noted has-beens as Ringo Starr and Alec Baldwin) and the oddly evil and politically incorrect message that the seemingly endless series of stories—written by a British cleric at the turn of the century—delivered with unabashed frankness and without apology: that hate and rage were inevitable by-products of competition between "cheeky" little engines like Thomas and big "cross" engines like Gordon who were desperate for attention and approval from Sir Topham Hatt, the "Fat Controller."

Once, early on, when Leo was still a newborn, she had come up with an idea to take a Polaroid of him every day and write a caption in the blank white space beneath the picture ("Diaper change: 4 days, 2 hours," "Sleeping: 2 months, 6 days"). And while she had taken hundreds of pictures—rolls and rolls of color and black-and-white film with a non-digital 35-millimeter camera that she dutifully got developed into prints and mailed out to a short list of friends and family—she had not, of course, managed to take a daily snapshot. She'd been too overwhelmed; it had begun to seem unmanageable (Where would she put all the pictures? Wasn't Polaroid film ridiculously expensive?), not to mention vaguely pretentious. But it was moments like this— watching him when he didn't know he was being watched, looking at his hands and feet and legs and wondering how he had gotten so big so fast—when she most regretted not having a stack of photos that she could look through and see the span of his life advance like a sequence of images in a flip-book or a silent time-lapse film clip:

Birth to the present—three years, five months, and seventeen days—in six and a half seconds.

She sat down behind him on the bed and kissed the smooth slope of the back of his neck, then put her cheek to his cheek and listened to the sound of his chewing. He smelled like soap and shampoo and peanuts, and she closed her eyes to take in his essence. Without turning his head away from the television, he reached around her face to touch her earlobe—a strange and slightly compulsive thing he did to her only when he felt great affection or was about to fall asleep.

"You came back."

"Of course I came back," she said, undoing the button of her skirt and sighing with intense relief. "I always come back when I go away."

He ate another peanut, then pointed at the screen.

"Look," he said. "Trains."

She nodded. "Trains."

"Can I get them for my birthday?"

His birthday was seven months away and he had nearly a hundred trains, but instead of trying to explain any of that, she stretched out next to him on the bed and closed her eyes. But he poked her until she opened them.

"What?" she said.

He pointed. "Your legs."

She looked down, confused, then realized Leo had never seen her in a skirt and panty hose. It was a long time since she'd seen herself in a skirt and panty hose, too.

He nodded, and petted her legs as if she were some sort of exotic stuffed animal. "I like your legs."

"Thank you."

"You're welcome."

He turned back toward the peanuts and the trains.

"So, Scooby," she said, about to begin her own round of questions (she was nothing if not her parents' daughter). "What did you do today?"

He grinned. "We had pancakes."

"At Stanz?" (their neighborhood diner) she asked, picking a peanut out of his little bowl and putting it in her mouth.

"No. Daddy made pancakes."

Julia stopped in mid-crunch. "Daddy *made* pancakes?"

Leo nodded.

Even though she couldn't remember buying the frozen kind— organic or nonorganic—she assumed that's what Leo was talking about. "You mean, he made them in the toaster?"

"No. He made them on the stove."

As Leo watched *Tom and Jerry* on the Cartoon Network and Julia watched him, she couldn't help but wonder what other surprises were in store for her. Peter had never let on that he could so much as toast a bagel, but today he had pulled a Dustin Hoffman in

Kramer vs. Kramer and made his motherless son a home-cooked breakfast.

Half an hour later, Leo was asleep. Julia got up, changed into her favorite I-have-no-life-outside-my-house outfit: a pair of stone-beige Gap pants, a black T-shirt, and a pair of brown suede Birkenstocks—shoes so ugly she couldn't believe she'd actually broken her vain youthful vow never to put comfort over fashion and buy a pair—and moved through the room to the door by completing a series of silent and exaggerated tai chi–like movements that she'd perfected after many such escapes from Leo while he was still sleeping. Downstairs she found Peter asleep on the couch in the midst of a room full of trucks and blocks and train tracks. Sitting in the armchair across from him, she wished she could stop wondering why, when he'd been home all day, he couldn't have cleaned up the living room or made their bed or emptied the dishwasher—Isn't that what she did when she was home?—but she couldn't. Before they had Leo she never thought about their household division of labor and who did more, but after they had Leo—and especially after he'd lost his job—she seemed to think about it all the time.

Since everyone was asleep she figured she'd call Patricia and get it over with. While she waited for her to answer one of her phones—work, home, or cell—she opened up the refrigerator and looked in on her mother's chicken breasts. She poked at them and then left them alone in the chilly darkness to think about what they'd done. She'd deal with them later.

Patricia answered her cell phone. She was walking outside and Julia could hear traffic and people's voices nearby.

"Where are you?" Julia asked, sticking her head back in the refrigerator in the hopes of finding something to shove in her mouth.

"On Madison and Sixty-eighth."

"Why?" Julia opened a plastic take-out container and found two half-eaten chicken fingers. She wondered how long they'd been in the refrigerator and whether or not Leo would miss them.

"Hair color and cut, leg wax, bikini wax, manicure, pedicure. I was there for almost six hours."

Julia ate the chicken finger in two big bites. She hadn't had a decent haircut—not to mention everything else—since before the new millennium, but that was neither here nor there.

"How'd the interview go?" Patricia asked.

"Good," she said, trying to swallow. "I got the job."

"How do you know?"

"What do you mean, how do I know? Jack told me."

"You mean, he offered you the job on the spot?"

Julia attacked the second chicken finger. "Yup."

"God. He must have been more desperate than I thought."

"Gee, thanks," Julia said.

"No, no, no. What I mean is he must really be short-staffed. Or maybe he's swamped with clients."

"Never mind," Julia snapped. She went to the long cabinet next to the refrigerator to see what else she could compulsively eat.

"So are you nervous?" Patricia asked.

"Nervous? Why should I be nervous?" She ripped open a sleeve of saltines and shoved one into her mouth whole and felt the points of the square digging into her cheeks. She wondered if the lower part of her face had taken on the shape of the cracker the way Tom's head took on the shape of a frying pan when Jerry hit him with one. "Jack DeMarco is an idiot and John Glom Public Relations is a joke. You basically said so yourself."

"That's true. But Jack is still a new boss and the position is still a new job. I don't know . . ." Patricia hesitated, then cleared her throat. "You must feel a little . . . rusty."

Rusty didn't begin to describe how Julia felt, but she wasn't about to admit that to Patricia. Instead, the way she usually did when Patricia's brilliant career made her weak with insecurity, Julia pretended to be intensely confident.

"Actually, I'm really looking forward to the challenge."

Despite the fact that she didn't have anything to wear.

And that it would probably take her at least a month to figure out the phones.

And the cell phones.

Not to mention the computers.

And the laptops.

And all the other miniaturized electronic communication and data storage devices that had been invented since she'd left the business world.

"That's great," Patricia said with enthusiasm which was actually completely genuine and which only served to complicate Julia's already complicated feelings toward Patricia. If only Patricia were always a bitch instead of only just sometimes, she would be so much easier to dismiss.

— *5* —

In the cool early autumn days that followed—the few that remained in her life as a stay-at-home mom that she loved and didn't want to give up—Julia and Peter and Leo were almost inseparable. When Leo didn't have preschool, they forked over their seriously overtaxed Visa card at Whole Foods, then went to the park or to the nearby beach, had dinner, and gave Leo a bath and read to him before bed. When Leo did have preschool, Julia prepared his lunchbox (a wide-mouthed thermos of Annie's organic macaroni and cheese, a small plastic container of organic cheese curls, a sippy cup of milk, and a napkin and fork) with a ridiculous level of devotion (making the time- and labor-intensive ten-minute stove-top Annie's instead of the two-minute microwave version; tucking the fork into the little pocket of the folded napkin; making sure that everything was right-side-up when she zipped up the lunchbox instead of upside down the way it had been on more than a few occasions during those very first days of school).

She would have folded the napkin into an origami swan or sail-boat and climbed into his lunchbox herself if she could have, but instead she tried to pretend that this week of mornings was just like the other week of mornings and the other week of mornings before that; that she would always be there to drop Leo off at school in the morning and pick him up in the afternoon, even though, in a few days, she wouldn't be.

But Peter—her understudy, her replacement, her own personal *All About Eve*—would be.

Peter would make Leo's lunch, get him dressed, lock the seat-belt around him in the booster seat; Peter would talk to him about trains and school buses and trees and leaves on the way to school and talk to the mothers at the cubbies about the weather and the teachers and the pros and cons of fleece or flannel, mittens or gloves, snow pants or long underwear. Peter would pick him up after school, put his art projects into his backpack, and talk all the way home in the car about his day—who he'd played with; what they'd done; what snack had been served, graham crackers or animal crackers; whether or not someone's mother had brought in birthday cupcakes.

One morning while Peter was shadowing her, staring and watching her every move so that he could copy it later, she stopped zipping up Leo's lunchbox.

"What?" She stared at him from across the kitchen island.

"I'm watching you."

"Why?"

"Because I want to see how you do that."

"Do what?"

He pointed. "That."

She looked down at her hands. "You want to see how I zip up a lunchbox?" She shook her head as if it were the stupidest thing she'd ever heard and then turned away—her eyes were filling up with tears and she couldn't help feeling ridiculous. "Okay. Here's the plastic container of pasta," she said, making a big point of unzipping the lunchbox and opening it up wide so Peter could look in. "Here's the small bottle of water. Here's the snack-size Ziploc bag which today just happens to be filled with Cheez-Its even though they're made with transfat and salt and everything else that cancels out the organic macaroni and cheese I just slaved over. And here is the fork and napkin which I forgot to put in and which I'm now going to squish in over here on the side." She flipped down the soft-sided flap of the lunchbox and found that she couldn't zip it shut. "Shit," she said under her breath even though she felt like screaming it as loud as she could.

Peter leaned across the island and gently slid the snack bag next to the water bottle instead of where it had been, on top of the plastic container of pasta. He then flipped the lid of the lunchbox down and zipped it easily.

"See, if you snuggle the snack into the contour of the water bottle you can make use of unused space."

She stared at him, then started to laugh. "I can't believe you used the word 'snuggle.'"

He started laughing, too. "Neither can I."

"That was disgusting."

He shrugged and they both laughed harder. "I know. I have no idea where that came from."

"Apologize," she demanded, practically doubled over now. "And promise you'll never say that again."

*   *   *

In the evenings, after Leo was asleep, she and Peter planned their new schedule—arranging for her parents to babysit on Tuesdays and Thursdays when Leo wouldn't be in preschool so that Peter could continue to go to the executive placement office in the city twice a week if he wanted to, and making sure all essential household tasks were covered. By the end of that last week home together, Peter, who during most of their marriage had taken little interest in the minutiae of their daily life, was now about to do something he'd never done before:

"I'm going to study our existing domestic organizational structure and analyze our options for a structural reorganization," he said, emptying a large Container Store shopping bag of supplies in the kitchen.

She understood only half of what he said but it was enough for her to get his point: Peter was taking over.

"Great!" she said.

"It's what I'm calling 'The Project,'" he said with a surprising lack of irony.

She grinned. Finally, after all these years of hoping and dreaming, he was bringing his work home with him like all the other husbands did! He was turning his keen eye and considerable analytical skills on their life and using the tools, toys, and language of his former profession to guide them through their upcoming role reversal! Two nights later he created a color-coded flow-chart on a large magnetic presentation board—the kind with movable blocks of time *(Blue: Julia at work; Green: Leo at preschool; Yellow: Gymboree class; Red: Peter Executive Placement Office; Purple: Len and Phyllis babysit; Orange: Leo and Peter free for playdates; Pink: Adam and Lisa free for playdates; Brown: "Tom and Jerry" on Cartoon Network)*—and placed it on a display easel in the corner next to the refrigerator.

She pointed to an unmarked black square. "What's this?"

Peter raised his eyebrows up and down, then made googly-eyes. "Date night."

She blinked. She couldn't believe they'd become the kind of people who had to "schedule" in "dates," but they had. She stared at the rest of the board and forced a smile. "Wow."

"You like it?" he asked, as if his life depended on it.

"Very thorough." She nodded and pointed to the pink squares. He'd even gotten in touch with Lisa Goodman, her shrink friend who lived nearby and whose son, Adam, was Leo's age and who Julia and Peter secretly called "Batman" because he always wore a black nylon cape.

"When I talked to Lisa to find out her playdate schedule, she invited me to have coffee with that group of moms you two just started hanging out with." He leaned over to check a pad of paper—his identity assumption notes—to make sure he got the names right. "Pinar. Monika. Hilary. Actually, tomorrow we're going to Bradley's after drop-off."

Julia blinked. Pinar was a former urban planner, Hilary was a former interpreter at the U.N., Monika was a former magazine editor, and, just as she had been up until now, they were all full-time moms. She had really liked that group of women from the start when they were all squished into the little coatroom those strange first days, putting away backpacks and lunchboxes in cubbies, trying not to cry when it was finally time to leave but all tearing up until Monika—the only one of them who had been through the preschool experience at the Preschool Experience before with an older child—led them around the side of the school and into a tight row of shrubs so that they could look into the classroom and see that none of the kids were sobbing and that they were all having fun. They'd all gone across the street for coffee those first two mornings after drop-off—something they'd planned on doing as regularly as possible.

She'd longed to be part of a group of women like that since her years in Larchmont had yielded only one friendship—with Lisa, who saw patients part-time out of an office in her huge but equally disorganized Tudor two streets away from Julia's. Their bonding, like the bonding of most women who lived in the sub-urbs with young children, took place at the nearby playground, and the issue that brought them together was what brought many women who spent time with their young children at playgrounds together: the mystifying, maddening, and largely ignored socio-logical phenomenon of woman's inhumanity to woman.

When Julia had started going to Turtle Park, Leo was eighteen months old, and whenever she went she always seemed to en-counter among all the nannies the same three aggressively well-groomed (French manicured, hair blown straight and highlighted various shades of brown to blond), Pilates-obsessed (they were al-ways talking about the class they took together) yummy-mummy types. She probably never would have noticed them—they didn't look much different than all the other women she saw every day in and around town who basically ignored her and made her feel like some sort of minimally groomed barn animal—if they hadn't literally turned their backs whenever they saw her coming *and* if they hadn't been extremely friendly to Peter the few times he'd taken Leo there by himself, even going so far as to invite him to their Bikram "hot" yoga class. (Yoga, with its enforced sweating—unlike Pilates, with its odd emphasis on the lower abdominal muscles—seemed to have gender-crossover appeal.)

Julia never knew what she'd done to offend them—she couldn't even remember ever speaking to any of them—or why they never invited her to their fitness classes which she clearly needed far more than Peter did, and she didn't really care, except that now the idea of going to the small, clean nearby park—something she'd fantasized about enjoying when she still lived in the city and had to drag Leo in his stroller over to Union Square Park at Fourteenth Street, which was crowded with people and bike messengers cutting through on their way to somewhere else and which really wasn't much of a park to begin with, or down to Washington Square Park, which was thick with students and drug dealers and noisy little dogs on short leashes—was now fraught with uncertainty and dread: Would the Three Bitches be there? If she stopped going to Turtle Park and started going to Willow or Flint Park, would there be three different but equally bitchy bitches there, too? Were the bitches you knew better than the bitches you didn't know?

Despite Peter's moral support after going with her to the park and seeing for himself how cold they were to her (so cold, in fact, that he pronounced without bothering to soften his message in any way: "They hate you. I don't know why, but they definitely hate you," which she deeply appreciated) she had been on her own.

Until Lisa Goodman appeared one early spring day with her big liberal Jewish hair and her sense of rebelliousness and righteous indignation about almost anything—"What do you mean, Whole Foods has stopped selling Nutella? Who are they to dictate what we eat and why?" "No more free weight-training classes at the Scarsdale JCC? I don't accept that."—and saved her.

"How dare *they* ignore *us*!" she'd said to Julia the first time they'd spoken—a day so important in her personal history of suburban human connection that it had since taken on a magical silvery haze in Julia's memory. Lisa hadn't bothered to introduce herself—she didn't need to, really; they both felt instantly like they'd known each other for years—but she did take the time to explain as Leo and Adam had started to play together in the grubby little sandbox that those same women had never deigned to speak to her either and that her rage at their behavior had known no bounds for almost two years.

"I think it's because I don't straighten my hair," she said, nodding as if she'd just discovered how to split the atom. "Not because I'm not a self-hating Jew, but because I'm too lazy. Only, they don't know that. They probably just think it's some kind of political statement."

Julia wasn't about to admit that she thought Lisa's hair was some kind of political statement, too, so instead she just pretended like she was so highly evolved that a thought like that would never have occurred to her.

"If *anyone's* going to ignore *anyone, we* should be ignoring *them*," Lisa continued, her tone as indignant as a teenager's. "We're far more interesting and intelligent than they are. I can tell that just by looking at you, even though I don't know anything about you." She threw her hands in the air and shook her hair in frustration. "I mean, this isn't Manhattan. This is Larchmont. You relinquish all rights to snobbery when you move to the suburbs."

Though Julia didn't have as much disdain for the suburbs as it seemed Lisa did, Julia still couldn't believe the relief she felt. Finally, someone who was not only validating her suffering but who was actually talking to her!

"It's just like Hebrew School," Julia said. "When you were too afraid to get up from your desk because you knew all the girls were going to make fun of your ass."

Lisa nodded her hair emphatically, and then looked completely confused. "But you don't have a big ass."

"Yes, I do."

"No. You don't." She turned around and flashed Julia her own behind—lifting her short faux-shearling jacket in an attempt to make her point. "*I* have a big ass." She put her coat down over her very respectable-sized backside and returned her attention to Julia and to the matter at hand. "Ass size notwithstanding, they look at us like they hate us," she said, pausing philosophically and with the hurt finally showing in her face. "Why do their hate us?"

Julia was too delighted at that moment with their female-to-female mating ritual—the comparison and discussion of each other's relative fatness, the acknowledgment of their equally miserable experiences in Hebrew School—to come up with an answer. But over the next few months during playdates with their boys at the playground or during quick evening walks to Starbucks, they would "process"—a word they used as a verb to describe a Talmudic level of analysis, deconstruction, interpretation, and explanation—everything from the Three Bitches to Peter's job loss to the pros and cons of living in Larchmont.

But none of that mattered now, on the eve of their official role reversal. Peter forced a smile and sat down at the kitchen table, his khakis and button-down shirt showing just the slightest bit of wear around the front side pockets and the collar.

"Are you nervous?" she asked, with the same slightly taunting tone that Patricia had used with her when they'd discussed her new job. Only, unlike Julia's, Peter's answer wasn't a big, fat ego-sparing lie.

"Of course I'm nervous. There are a million things to remember, and I know I'm going to feel like a total outcast. I mean, sure, the other mothers will take pity on me once or twice and let me tag along, but in the end they're not going to want me hanging around."

Julia sat down, too. He was probably right. Women liked to talk about their husbands and their marriages and their kids with complete impunity—they liked to deconstruct the other mothers and figure out their own place within the pecking order of "working" mothers versus "nonworking" mothers—and there's no way they could do that with a man present. The thought of Peter feeling left out and out of place and uncomfortable made her feel sorry for him and she worried that he might feel even more isolated in his new job than she already thought she would in hers.

She reached for his hand. "It'll work out," she said. "It'll work out."

He forced another smile and shrugged, allowing himself to be convinced.

Leaving him to work on The Project, she went up to bed, full of guilt for feeling so petty and small-minded and insecure and jealous about so many things, including the biggest one of all: the fact that he wasn't going to have to worry about what to wear to his new job like she was.

Sunday evening, the night before her first day, when he was finally finished with it, Julia looked at the chart. It was a vast sea of blue—*Julia at work*—barely broken up by other colors.

She stared at it, and then at Peter, and then she felt tears rolling down her cheeks. Turning the presentation board over on the easel so she couldn't see it anymore, Peter put his arms around her and whispered into her hair.

"It's only temporary," he said, as they made their way upstairs and into bed. "I'll find something soon and then things will go back to the way they were before."

Swallowing half a Tylenol PM so her worry-filled insomnia wouldn't keep her up the night before her big day, she crawled under the covers and into his arms and fell asleep quickly. And though she dreamed of the time Peter had described—the time when he would find a new job and things would go back to the way they were before—she wouldn't, when she awoke early the following morning, far ahead of the alarm clock, have any memory of it.

— *6* —

The red glare of the numbers—*5:45 a.m.*—blinked and flashed for several seconds before Julia, still inside the gauze of her sleep-aid hangover, realized that she was looking at the clock and that she had to get up. But she didn't want to get up, and the sight of Peter still sleeping soundly across the bed only made things worse. All those mornings she'd rolled over with a smug little grin and gone back to sleep after Peter had left for work when it was still dark were finally coming back to haunt her.

She showered and dressed quickly, struggling with a brand-new pair of panty hose that were shorter and nuder than they were supposed to be. Pulling a white T-shirt over her head and throwing on a black skirt, she reached into her closet for a black cardigan sweater and her shoes, and then tiptoed downstairs.

She was just about to pour her coffee—Peter had been thoughtful enough to set the timer the night before—when she heard footsteps on the stairs. She assumed it was him, coming down to see her off, but it was Leo in his fire engine pajamas that were already getting too small for him, wiping the sleep from his eyes and clutching his blanket.

She had tried to explain to him several times the previous week that she would be leaving home every morning to go to work, but each time she'd started to he'd ignored her, either because he didn't understand what she was talking about or because he didn't want to know. Taking two Eggo waffles out of the toaster and buttering them, she sat down at the kitchen table and pulled him onto her lap.

"So I'm going to work today, remember?" She handed him a waffle and took the other for herself.

He bit into his and chewed slowly like a little animal.

"I'm going to go to the station and take the train," she said.

He stopped chewing and turned to look at her. His eyes were big blue discs and she could see a piece of waffle in his half-open mouth. "You're going to take the train?"

She nodded.

"Which train?"

"The big train that takes me into the city."

"You mean, Thomas?"

She smiled and shook her head.

"James?"

She shook her head again.

"Are you working on the railroad?"

She put her waffle down and hugged him hard from behind, closing her eyes and trying not to cry but failing miserably. Yes, she was going to be working on the railroad. All the livelong day.

Julia arrived for her first day of work sweating in the grip of another annoyingly humid late-September morning. Jack was on the phone when she got in a little before nine, still breathless and perspiring from the wrenching mad dash out of the house to the train and from the train to the office, but he waved her in and motioned toward one of his guest chairs.

"Thanks, Vicky," he said to someone who was obviously his assistant. "Send them in."

Jack put the receiver down and turned to Julia.

"Before I show you around and get you started on the Mary Ford project, I want you to sit in on this meeting."

Julia put her bag down on the floor. "What meeting?"

"David Cassidy is here."

She stared at him. *"David Cassidy is here?"* she repeated, louder than she should have but she couldn't help it. She was shocked— both because Jack wasn't giving her any time to prepare for a meeting of such magnitude and because David Cassidy—*Keith Partridge!*—was about to walk through the door. "Why is David Cassidy here?"

Jack shrugged as if it were obvious. "Despite the fact that he does, believe it or not, continue to appear live in concert and that he has had some success in Las Vegas during the past decade, David Cassidy is still perceived as one of the ultimate has-beens in American popular culture. Which, on a certain level, is unfair, given the fact that he was, according to his website, the first television personality—the first—to be merchandised globally, and that at one time the membership size of his fan club exceeded those of Elvis and the Beatles." Jack adjusted his tie, pulled up his pants. "But that was 1971. Thirty years ago. He's essentially been invisible ever since. Which is why he and his manager, Brian Young, want to hear our thoughts."

Julia tried to focus but her mind went blank.

"How old is David Cassidy now?" was all she could think to ask. "I mean, he must be almost fifty."

"He's fifty-four," Jack said. He reached for his suit jacket that had been hanging on the back of his chair and winked at her as if this—the surprise meeting for which she was completely unprepared—was all in good fun.

"Don't be nervous," Jack said, his tone too light to be at all reassuring. "It's not like this is an audition. You already have the job."

She quickly reached into her briefcase for her yellow legal pad and a pen.

Don't remind me.

Julia discreetly tried to catch a glimpse of herself in some reflective surface in Jack's office and collect herself. Though she'd worked for him for less than five minutes, she knew that despite Patricia's assertion that he was an idiot, he was smart enough to know that he wasn't smart enough to wing anything. She was certain he was fully prepared for this meeting with David Cassidy—certain by the way he'd swung his arms into his suit jacket, certain by the way he'd swaggered over to the door with deliberate casualness, certain by the way he'd winked at her again on his way to greet the men who had just appeared.

"David," Jack said, giving him a smile and a firm shake. Then he turned and held out his hand again. "Brian."

Julia couldn't take her eyes off David Cassidy as Jack led him and his manager over to the two facing leather couches and coffee table on the other side of his office. Though he had, of course, aged considerably since playing Keith Partridge, he had aged well—his hair, no longer feathered with bangs and wings as was the style then, but combed back off his forehead and held in place with a bit of mousse or gel; his black suit and white shirt that he wore without a tie, tasteful and age-appropriate. Not to mention coast- and season-appropriate. This was no Don Johnson, wearing a turquoise T-shirt and a white linen suit and Italian slip-on loafers without socks for a meeting in Manhattan in the middle of February, the way he had during the peak of his *Miami Vice* fame when Julia was still an assistant at Creative Talent. Whatever he may have lost over the years in terms of his career, David Cassidy still had his dignity.

And his dimples.

And his sparkly eyes.

Which were no less butterfly-producing and crush-inducing now than they were then.

Julia felt her face redden—she was sure her normally olive complexion was now the color of a groovy glowing lava lamp—while David Cassidy's music filled her head and her yellow-lined doodle pad:

♪ *I think I love you! So what I am so afraid of?*
C'mon, get happy! ♪

"Welcome to our makeshift conversation pit," Jack said, smiling as he referenced the seventies with obvious irony. Then he signaled her to join them.

Which she did.

But only after a slight delay:

Whatever happened to my Partridge Family lunchbox?

My Partridge Family thermos?

My Partridge Family poster and albums and eight-track tapes?

Did David and Susan Dey ever make out when they were on the show?

How come I never looked as good in crushed velvet hip-huggers as David did?

"This is my associate, Julia Einstein."

David Cassidy reached for her hand and shook it and when he did, time stopped and the earth moved. One of her earliest child-hood fantasies was coming true, and after all the years of working with celebrities, she finally understood what it felt like to be a drooling fan.

David Cassidy just touched me.

David Cassidy is polite and has good manners.

I ♥ David Cassidy.

"Hi," she said.

"Hi," he said.

She nodded without letting go of his hand. "I'm Julia."

"Yes. I know."

"Thank you."

"I know I speak for Julia, too," Jack interrupted, "when I say we've both very much been looking forward to this meeting."

Smiling and nodding vigorously, she glared at Jack. She wished he would just shut up for a minute so she could "process" the mo-ment: there she was, holding hands with David Cassidy on her first day of work! If his manager weren't sticking out his big furry paw for her to shake, Julia never would have let go of David's hand.

"I'm Brian Young."

She shook his hand without taking her eyes off David Cassidy. "Great. I'm . . . I'm . . ."

"You're Julia Einstein," David whispered, as if they were both actors and he was feeding her a line.

She almost collapsed with nervous laughter. "Thank you!" she said, reaching for his hand again. "Thank you so much!"

She was too busy making a complete fool of herself to notice that Jack had rolled his eyes and pointed to them to sit down. "Let's get started," he said as if he never got weak-kneed around has-beens even though she was certain he must have made a complete ass of himself in front of Kathie Lee Gifford, or Justine Bateman, or whatever other females lurked on the farthest reaches of his Wall of Shame.

"Getting started" in public relations meetings always seemed to mean "providing beverages," and so without bothering to ask any of them what they wanted to drink, Jack picked up the phone closest to the couch he was about to sit down on and called Vicky. Almost instantly she appeared with four individual bottles of chilled water on a wooden Zen-style tray and put it down on the table in front of them. Julia thought it was weird that Vicky didn't seem nervous at all with David Cassidy just inches from her beverage tray until she realized that Vicky probably had no idea who David Cassidy was because she was so young.

Jack handed the drinks out—a bottle of Evian for both David and Brian, a Pellegrino for himself, and a Poland Spring for Julia. Under different circumstances Julia definitely would have liked nothing more than to obsessively try to interpret what the distribution of water really meant—of course Jack took the Pellegrino because he was the most pretentious person in the room. But why had he given her an unimported Poland Spring instead of an imported Evian? Was it because she'd made googly-eyes at David Cassidy or simply because they'd run out of Evian?—but today there wasn't time to fully do the question justice.

"As I mentioned, we're all very excited here to have the opportunity to work with you, David," Jack said, sitting down next to Julia, who had finally collected herself and was acting her age. "Not only were you and your show a personal favorite of mine when I was growing up, but I know that John Glom was acquainted with your father and was a huge fan."

Shocked that he would reference David Cassidy's father in his opening salvo—and not even sure if John Glom was an actual person—Julia immediately shot a glance across to the other couch to gauge the reaction. It was a risky move on his part, she knew, one that would either endear Jack DeMarco to David or show him to be an opportunistic kiss-ass—Jack Cassidy was dead and there was, of course, no way to prove or disprove that John Glom, assuming he existed, had ever even met the man, let alone been a fan of his—and she held her breath until somebody said something.

David Cassidy smiled uncomfortably. "Thank you."

Brian Young, who hadn't yet said a word except his own name when he'd introduced himself but who had been staring at Julia's ample bosom with such unchecked lechery that she looked down to make sure she hadn't spilled coffee all over herself or that she wasn't inexplicably lactating, put his unopened bottle of water down on the table next to him and moved forward on the couch, causing the leather to squeak and squeal like a cheap whoopee cushion.

"I'm not sure if I made this clear to you when we first spoke," he said slowly, defensively, protectively, the way most managers and agents of has-beens generally did, "but David is speaking with several other agencies to see which one best suits his needs."

"Of course he is. Playing hard to get." Jack made a show of nodding magnanimously and closing his eyes like he was a big sport, and Julia couldn't tell if he'd known that fact all along or if he hadn't and was processing it now. Taking a swig from his little green bottle of Pellegrino, he leaned back on the couch, telegraphing the message that he enjoyed, even relished, exactly this sort of competition.

Brian leaned back and spread his arms out over the top of the couch, smug in the knowledge that he'd played his opening hand marvelously thus far, but his apparent victory didn't last long.

"The only problem with that strategy," Jack said, "is that there has to be interest in the client to begin with." He stared at both men on the couch and shrugged dismissively. "You can't play hard to get when no one wants the get."

Shocked and horrified, Julia stared down at her pad.

Not to put too fine a point on it.

"I think what Jack is trying to say here," Julia interrupted with an enormous and desperate smile on her face, "is that the business has become incredibly competitive. Which means that we have to become much more creative about achieving the goals of our clients."

Brian, clearly taking umbrage at the picture Jack had painted of his client as a loser and at his implied role in that loser status and completely disinterested in her bosom now, sat forward on the edge of the couch again.

"Let's just get one thing clear here," he said to Jack. "David Cassidy was, and still is, one of the highest-grossing, best-known, and best-loved recording artists in the world. His records have sold over twenty-five million copies, including four consecutive multi-platinum LPs. In fact, his newest album, *Touch of Blue,* was just released in the U.K. to fabulous reviews and very strong sales."

Jack smiled: Hyperbole and reference to Jerry Lewis syndrome (being famous anywhere else but here) = desperate has-been–speak.

Then he leaned forward and whispered:

"I'm well aware of the success of *Touch of Blue* outside the U.S. Which, if I'm not mistaken, is the *only* place it was released since the album still hasn't come out in America. Unless, of course, I missed it in *Billboard*." Jack had clearly done his homework and was now beating them all over the head with it. "I mean, no one releases an album in a foreign country without releasing it here because they want to. They do it because they have to. When their recording label passes on its option to release it here."

Brian shifted nervously in his seat and Julia almost felt sorry for him.

But she felt more sorry for David Cassidy, who was being forced to listen to Jack and Brian discuss his personal continuum of success and failure right in front of him as if he weren't even there. Despite the fact that this was standard operating procedure, Julia had always found these sorts of meetings difficult to sit through—the separating out from a potential client's life the wheat from the chaff—but this one was particularly brutal. Perhaps because she wasn't yet used to Jack DeMarco's "style": insulting, attacking, bullying, and shaming has-beens into agreeing to become clients.

Jack glanced over at Julia and, whether it was true or not, she could tell he thought he was home free—that he had sealed the deal, sunk the putt.

But then David and Brian asked her what she thought and all bets were off.

It occurred to her suddenly when they did, that Jack hadn't once asked her for her input, and in a flash she realized what should have been obvious from the beginning: that the reason he had asked her to stay for the meeting wasn't so he could see her perform in a client-acquisition situation, but so she could see him perform—so she would be impressed by his preparation, his delivery, and his ability to make people pay attention. He wanted to make sure that before Julia Einstein went home that day, she knew exactly who it was she was working for now:

Jack DeMarco, Jackass.

Motivated by an intense desire to beat Jack at his own game and by the freedom that came from knowing she had absolutely nothing to lose—she did, after all, as Jack had mentioned right before the meeting, already have this stupid job—Julia sat forward on the couch.

"I agree with Jack's ultimate goal, but I would focus instead on David Cassidy's many strengths, on all the things he's done right over the years," she began, speaking with euphemistic positivity the way she'd been trained to. "Because he has always been a musician, first and foremost—because he has never pretended to be anything he wasn't—the public knows that whatever ups and downs he may have had over the last three decades, David Cassidy is still David Cassidy, authentic in a way that most celebrities, past and present, are not."

She pushed her pad aside, tugged at her skirt in the hopes that it could be coaxed into just grazing her knees. But it wouldn't budge and for an instant she stared in horror at the impossible hugeness of her knees. "My main strategy would be to find a philanthropic or charitable organization that David is either already involved with or wants to get involved with and offer his services as a celebrity spokesperson. All celebrities need to have a cause, a platform. It maximizes their chances of interacting with the public and humanizes them."

David and Brian exchanged glances while Jack shifted uncomfortably on the couch.

"In the same way that Paul Newman's name has become synonymous with unprecedented business-driven philanthropy," she said. "In the same way that Elizabeth Taylor's name became synonymous with AIDS research, and that Jerry Lewis will forever be the face of muscular dystrophy, David could become associated with a prominent worthy cause. Using his celebrity in a way that is meaningful and that provides a service instead of using it to endorse a sneaker or a carbonated beverage would allow the public's first reconnection with him after all these years to be a completely positive one. All subsequent endeavors to reposition David in the entertainment industry would then have a far greater chance of succeeding, since the public would already be predisposed to being receptive."

Whether it was the content of what she'd said or merely the fact that the words had come out of her mouth and not Jack's mouth and were thus not insulting or offensive, both David and Brian responded immediately, David mentioning the charity he and his wife had started and Brian mentioning how he knew and could approach the executive directors of two different organizations: one for dyslexia and the other for attention deficit disorder.

Or autism.

He couldn't remember which.

"Not that it really matters," he added almost giddily.

It was when they wanted to go to Julia's office to discuss the matter further—*an office she hadn't even seen yet and wasn't sure existed*—that Jack stepped in to recoup his losses. Uninterested now in acquiring David Cassidy as a client since it was clear that both men had responded much more positively to Julia than they had to him, Jack stood up, walked over to the doorway, and poked his head out to ask Vicky if he had any messages. When he returned to the conversation pit empty-handed, he stuck his arm out.

"Gentlemen," he said, shaking hands and making it clear that the meeting was over. "Thank you for coming. We'll look forward to hearing from you."

Without walking them to the elevator or even asking Vicky to, Jack returned to his desk, picked up his phone, and started to dial, probably calling Information, Julia suspected, or the weather, or his home machine in order to save face. Since Julia hadn't seen her office yet and didn't even know where it was, she led them instead to the elevator, getting kissed on both cheeks in the faux-European way by Brian and almost fainting when David Cassidy took her hand in both of his to shake it.

When she returned to Jack's office, he looked up from his desk and smiled.

"You two should have gotten a room."

"Excuse me?"

"If I'd known you were so in love with Keith Partridge, I would have let you meet with him alone."

"I'm not in love with him."

"Yes, you are."

"I am not." She rolled her eyes and pulled her cardigan closed. "I was just a little shocked. I mean, you didn't give me any notice for the meeting and I was completely unprepared."

"That's life in the fast lane," he said, looking around his loser office without a trace of irony. "Anyway, now that that's out of the way, I'll show you around." He came out from behind his desk and bent down for the straps of her briefcase. "Don't forget your bag," he said, handing it to her from where she had left it on the floor. "*And* your pad." He turned around slowly and picked it up off his desk where she knew she hadn't left it and held it out. She grabbed it from his hands and shoved it into her briefcase.

"I'll show you your office first."

She looked at him warily, trying to gauge whether or not he'd flipped through her notes while she'd been escorting the Partridge Party to the elevator, then followed after him.

"Oh, and Julia? If you think of any questions later, just call me on my intercom."

She stopped dead in her tracks behind him and closed her eyes.

"But when you do, ask for 'Jack DeMarco, Jackass,'" he said. "That way I'll know it's you."

Later that morning, after the briefest of orientations—"Your office"—and introductions—"Jonathan Leibowitz, your assistant"—Jack called her back into his office.

"Mary Ford," Jack announced before getting up and walking around his desk with his hands tucked into the pockets of his pleated pants. He was wearing a cheap glen plaid suit with Top-Siders, and it occurred to her that Jack wouldn't be half as bad if he only dressed better. He was talking in bullets the way she remembered he had during her interview the week before—as if everything he said was to be written down immediately, it was that important—and Julia hurried to uncap her pen.

"Born: Marlene Fliegel," he continued.

Bullet.

"Claim to fame: Former star of screen—*All the While* and *What I Did for Love.*"

Bullet.

"And stage—*Kick Up Your Heels, Who's Afraid of Virginia Woolf?* And even some Shakespeare in London—*Macbeth, The Merchant of Venice.*"

Bullet.

"Current status: Former Hollywood legend desperate for a comeback."

Jack had looked at her over his glasses to make sure she wasn't missing anything, then added just in case she was:

"Hence the product name, 'Legend,' and the fact that she's retained our services."

Julia nodded, scribbled furiously.

Duh.

"Particulars and coordinates: Lifelong resident of the Ansonia apartment building on the Upper West Side. Frequent uninvited hanger-on in Hollywood, Miami, Paris, Cannes, Milan." Jack turned and headed back toward his desk. "Personal information: Lives alone. No husband. No male companion. No female companion. No dog. No cat. No hamster. No gerbil. No partner of any kind. All she has is an assistant. But every time she hires someone, they quit." He glanced briefly at his Palm Pilot, presumably to try to find Mary Ford's entry and the name of her most recent assistant, then thought better of it. "By the time you start working on this—like, tomorrow—there'll probably already be someone new, so let's skip this for now."

Assistants: full of hate.

"Twice married and twice divorced. First to former studio head and notorious drinker and womanizer Marvin Green: 1943 to

1957. Then to former studio head and notorious drinker and womanizer J. B. Heller: 1960 to 1967. Both splits were ugly and played out in the press." He glanced toward the towering white cabinets that lined the hallways just outside his office door. "Clips are in the files."

Ex-husbands: full of hate.

"Two children, one from each marriage: Lindsay Green and Bruce Heller. Lindsay Green, an actress slash writer slash activist-without-a-cause, lives in Los Angeles; Bruce Heller, a physician, lives here in New York. Anyway, neither one speaks to her. But at least the doctor keeps to himself. The daughter is a troublemaker, always trying to get attention."

Kids: full of hate.

Julia looked up. "That's sad."
Jack shrugged. "What's sad?"
She shrugged back. It seemed obvious.
"That she's alone and her children hate her?" Jack shook his head. "The only reason you're capable of compassion is because you haven't met her yet. Don't feel sorry for Mary Ford. She's a desperate client, paying for the right to suck the life out of us. You should know that by now."

Of course she knew that by now. She looked down at her pad and started to make a note, but the sharp sarcasm in Jack's voice interrupted her.

"And, umm, Julia?"
She looked up.
"Don't write that down." He sighed loudly and sat down behind

his desk, even more annoyed than before. "All I need is for one of your fucking notepads to be found and every word Jack DeMarco, Jackass, has ever said—off the record—to show up on 'Page Six.'"

She felt the back of her throat seize up and her face redden. She was either about to apologize or tell him what he could do with this stupid job, but something—thoughts of the mortgage? the car payments? The Scoob's upcoming preschool tuition bill?—stopped her.

"Positive personality traits," he continued, without even a hint of apology in his voice, half swiveling in his chair and stroking his left cheek with an open hand, as if trying to decide whether or not he needed a shave (he did): "None. Famous friends willing to do her professional favors before, during, and after the Legend launch: None. Hobbies: None." He paused and smirked. "Unless you consider torturing me a hobby. In which case I'd say she's an avidly devoted fanatic." He smirked again, clearly impressed by his own cleverness. "Hyperbolic redundancy intended."

Julia didn't blink.

"Client history: Mary Ford came to us two years ago," Jack continued. "At the time, she was doing voice-overs for Purina Cat Chow, Triscuit crackers, and Pontiac and wanted to break out of her non-status status via some sort of product line—makeup or skin-care products like Victoria Principal's or Tova Borgnine's. God forbid." He paused there and shivered with mock disgust: "Beware the has-been who wants creative control over her comeback."

Julia could tell that at this point Jack was expecting—dying for, in fact—a reaction on her part, but, still pissed about his earlier condescension and impatience, she gave up nothing: no smile, no nod, no eye roll.

"Failing that, she had suggested a diet-exercise-clothing-everything-but-the-kitchen-sink product line like Suzanne Somers.

But I had higher hopes for Mary Ford." He raised his chin and straightened his neck proudly, as if he truly cared about Mary Ford's destiny beyond where that destiny could possibly take him. "My idea of a comeback is not remaking someone into the next queen of QVC or late-night infomercials. I'm not interested in that sort of transformation: going from bad to worse."

He stood up then, came around his desk and leaned against the edge of it—his hands back in the pockets of his stupid pleated pants—right in front of Julia. "And so, after many heated arguments and much persuasion, I finally convinced her to go in a different direction."

Julia looked up at him, and when she did he leaned down and whispered practically into her ear:

"Nude mud wrestling."

Despite herself—and Jack, who didn't deserve it—she laughed. But only briefly.

Taken aback by how close he suddenly was to her—he had extremely blue eyes and he smelled nicer than she'd expected—at least his cologne was more expensive than his suits—and nervous that he would be able to read, upside down, what she'd written about him just moments before, she shifted in her chair and flipped to a fresh piece of paper on her yellow pad.

"Needless to say, I was kidding about the nude mud wrestling," he said, the not-so-subtle change in his voice a signal that he was about to revert to his previous level of professorial pomposity. "My vision for her comeback vehicle was, and still is, a fragrance. Something classic, elegant, timeless. Think Elizabeth Taylor's White Diamonds, one of the most successful perfume launches in retail history. When Mary finally signed off on my idea, our team here began planning the branding process: who would produce the fragrance; what the fragrance would cost and what level of retailer—

and thus what level of consumer—we were targeting; what message the packaging of the product and the advertising and marketing campaigns would convey."

He went back around to the other side of his desk and sat down, and from where she was sitting it appeared that his hands were finally out of his pockets.

"Which brings us to where we are today," he said. "Only a few weeks away from our launch of Legend. Much accomplished; much to be accomplished still."

Julia nodded, folded her arms across her chest. Despite his joke about the nude mud wrestling, she was getting rather bored and heavy-lidded just sitting there being talked at—especially since she had stopped making her notes. Her mind wandered to Leo, and she wondered what he was doing now, mid-morning, at school—Playing with trains? Playing with trucks? Playing with his peanut? She thought about what she would have been doing then, too: getting ready to pick him up, straightening the house, doing the laundry, wondering when Peter would get a job, if he would ever get a job, what would happen if he didn't get a job for a really long time. Maybe being at work would be a good thing after all.

When Jack took his glasses off and smiled sheepishly at her, she was a million miles away.

"Julia."

"Yes, Jack."

"I'm sorry for being such an asshole before. Especially on your first day."

"Thank you," Julia said.

He paused before putting his glasses back on. "Sometimes the stress of the job just gets to me."

"Sometimes it gets to me, too," she conceded.

"I'm glad you understand," he said, smiling a little too warmly. "My wife—well, she's never really understood."

Julia couldn't believe she was getting the my-wife-doesn't-understand-me business on her first day—so she did what she always did when an "unhappily married" man complained to her about his wife and which always stopped the conversation cold: Julia expressed interest in her.

"Does she work?"

"Yes, she works. She's Marketing Director for Clinique."

"Big job," Julia said, impressed.

"Yes, well, I guess when you're making life-and-death decisions about women's moisturizers all day long the way she does," Peter said, with bitterness that quickly burned off to sadness, "what we do here—career resuscitation—can seem pretty inconsequential."

After taking Julia to lunch at his favorite restaurant, Anthony's, the kind of old-time slightly shabby place with gigantic leather menus listing Shrimp Cocktail, Lobster Bisque, Oysters on the Half Shell, and Waldorf Salad on the left side and Pork Chops, Lamp Chops, and Steak Tartare on the right, Julia returned to her office, sat down in her chair, and felt the great grim yaw of the afternoon hours stretch out before her the way they never did in her previous work life.

Back then, the workday had always seemed too short, as if there was never enough time to do everything she needed to do. Now it seemed just the opposite: too many hours looming to fill up with stupid meaningless tasks that were going to deprive her of precious time with her Scooby-Doo.

Pushing her chair over to her grimy little piece of window with her feet, she finally had a minute to herself to set up her desk. She put the three framed photos of Leo she'd brought with her from home next to the phone and quickly downloaded a photo she'd e-mailed to herself the night before and installed it as wallpaper on her computer. That's when Jack appeared in her office.

He was carrying an armload of Legend files that he proceeded to drop on her desk, one by one, ceremoniously absolving himself of all responsibility for their contents:

Proofs from the previous month's photo shoot (Mary Ford in a chocolate brown sheared beaver coat on loan from Bergdorf Goodman which "she stole from the photographer's studio and which she still refuses to return despite repeated warnings from the store's legal department").

The various designs for the Legend packaging ("Bottle shape is critical—tall and thin—phallic—preferred by female and male purchasers alike two-to-one over short and fat—vaginal").

The prospective print ads for newspapers and magazines ("'Inside Every Woman Lives a Legend' and 'Every Woman is a Living Legend'—both of which Mary Ford insisted on and both of which I hate").

The list of retail outlets that would not stock the fragrance ("The elusive quartet: Bergdorf, Neiman's, Barneys, and Saks"); those that would ("The non-discriminating middle: Bloomingdale's, Nordstrom, Macy's, Hecht's, Filene's, Foley's, Bullock's, Lord & Taylor"); and those that were waiting in the wings ("The desperate masses: JCPenney, Sears, Kmart, Wal-Mart").

Once he'd emptied his hands and given her a rundown of what tasks she would need to tackle in the last crucial weeks—follow up with long-lead-time national magazines, trade publications, and top daily newspapers for feature stories; meet with the sales and marketing teams at Heaven Scent to finalize the proposed advertising campaign and merchandizing strategies; lock in and confirm details for media appearances, in-store appearances, and travel arrangements—he sat down in one of her two small folding vinyl guest chairs and looked around her still-bare office.

He sniffed, pushed his glasses up his nose. "So."

"So," she said back.

"So what do you think?"

"About the files?"

"About the job." He put his feet up on her desk.

Convinced there was only one right answer—a lie, always a lie—she obliged, though without her usual vigorous attempt to be sincere. Almost seven hours had passed since she'd been home, and she was feeling the cold-turkey withdrawal from Leo in her blood and bones. She missed him even more than she thought she would, and the idea of sitting behind this new desk hour after hour, day after day, week after week, and month after month until—and this is what she was so ashamed to admit and even to think—*until Peter found a job and she could quit and stay home again*—was unbearable. But she refused to give Jack DeMarco the satisfaction of watching her morph into a first-day-back-at-work crybaby puss-of-a-publicist mom.

"I like it," she said firmly enough to almost convince herself.

"Really?" He sniffed again, folded his hands behind his neck. "What do you like about it?"

"Well," she said, trying to contain her fatigue-induced Scooby-deprived sarcasm, "all I did was fill up my stapler, turn on my computer, and eat a salad. I'm sure if you ask me tomorrow, I'll be able to say unequivocally that I hate it."

He grinned. He seemed to like it, she noticed, when she was just a little bit mean to him.

Men.

"Oh, by the way," Jack said. "I heard from Brian Young. David

decided to go with PMK. But Brian said it was a very difficult decision. They were both very impressed with you."

And repelled by you.

Jack smiled, then tilted his head, assessing her.

"What?" She shifted uncomfortably in her chair. Her parents
had always looked at her the same way before she was married—
like she had a bird on her head—as if they were perpetually wondering where she had come from and what, if anything, would
become of her.

"Listen, I figured since we're going to be working so closely together, I should tell you, in the spirit of full disclosure, that I'm in
the process of getting divorced."

She looked down, then away. "I'm sorry."

He nodded, then stared at her again as if there were another bird
on her head.

"Go ahead," he said. "Ask me."

"Ask you what?" Looking across the room at him, she realized
suddenly that, at some point during the day, he had combed his
hair back off his forehead, just like David Cassidy.

"Ask me why I'm getting divorced."

Julia stared at him. "Are you kidding?"

"No, I'm not kidding."

"I'm not asking you that."

"Why not? Everybody always wants to know why people split
up—whose fault it was, what happened. Since we're going to be
working closely together, I figured we should just establish the facts
instead of you making incorrect assumptions."

"Look, Jack," Julia said, sitting up straight in her chair and
reaching for her briefcase to signal that she didn't want to continue
their conversation. It had been one fucking long first day—what
with the David Cassidy ambush and the lengthy Mary Ford de-

briefing and lunch at the poor man's Bull and Bear and the bestowing of the files—and she didn't think she could take any more. Especially a look through the dark cringe-inducing little peephole of Jack's troubled personal life. "I'm really sorry that your marriage fell apart. But I assure you that I have other things on my mind right now besides what happened with your wife and why."

"Soon-to-be ex-wife," Jack corrected.

She rolled her eyes. "*Soon-to-be ex*-wife."

"That's bullshit. You're dying to know who left whom, who failed whom." He paused briefly, set his jaw and pursed his lips. "It's human. People want there to be reasons why bad things happen. That's why random violence is such an unsettling concept: no apparent cause and effect, no apparent means of prevention."

Julia stared at him.

"It's the same with this job. Every time we pitch a has-been's comeback, the first thing the person on the other end of the phone wants to know is why: Why did the has-been fail in the first place? Why is the has-been worthy of a reversal of misfortune? Why is this comeback attempt different from all previous comeback attempts?" He leaned back in his chair, collected his thoughts. "I mean, I've wanted to ask you the same question," he continued, lightly biting the fingernail on the thumb of his left hand. "The question that I'm sure everyone has been asking you."

"And what question is that?" she said.

"Why you had to come back to work. Or what took you so long to come back to work."

Her mouth dropped open, and stayed open.

"It's hard, right?" he said, swinging his feet down off her desk and planting them firmly on the floor. "Either question makes your failure implicit. That is, are you a bad mother or just lazy? It puts you on the defensive, as if you owe the questioner an answer. Which you don't. People shouldn't have to explain their failures."

Before Julia could even address that last statement—before she could even begin to argue the position that she saw her past situation as a success and was trying to see her current situation not as a permanent failure but as a "temporary setback"—Peter would find another job and when he did, things could go back to the way they'd been before, whatever that meant—Jack stood up. Coming around the side of her desk closest to the window, he looked at her, then briefly at his own reflection in the glass.

"Which is why there's only one rule when you work for me: Never apologize for a client's downward trajectory. Failure is inevitable. Any magazine editor or TV producer or agent who doesn't understand that doesn't deserve a response. Much less, access to that client." He moved away from the window and rapped his knuckles three quick times on her desk as he passed it.

She looked up at him, and, because she was finally about to take the bait on the question of his divorce, she rolled her eyes.

"So whose fault was it?"

He stopped, then turned.

"Mine, of course," he said, his face overanimated and his voice full of false pride. "I fucked up."

They both nodded silently as he rapped his knuckles on her desk one last time before leaving her office for the day.

"Peaks and valleys, baby," he said, a sudden parody of a Hollywood hotshot. "Peaks and valleys. That's what life comes down to, in the end. Fucking geography."

— 8 —

It was well after six when Julia finally managed to leave the office that first night, and by the time she made it down in the extremely slow elevator and race-walked the four blocks up and two avenues over from Thirty-eighth and Madison to Grand Central, she had missed the 6:20 p.m. train back to Larchmont and knew she would have to wait for the 6:43.

Calling Peter as she raced through pedestrians and into the station—her big black shoulder bag heavy with the Mary Ford files and her feet hurting from yet another pair of shoes she hadn't worn in years—she wondered what he and The Scoob had done the rest of the day. But when Peter answered the phone in barely a whisper, she knew before he had to tell her that Leo was already asleep.

"I just carried him upstairs. He really wanted to stay up until you got home but he was so tired after his playdate with Batman that he just crashed after dinner."

It was a brief ride out of Manhattan to Westchester County—

thirty-two minutes—though now that the moment she'd been looking forward to the entire day wasn't going to happen—*seeing her baby*—she didn't care what time she got home. Watching the landscape of Upper Manhattan and the Bronx race past in the falling dusk through the window, she felt tears slip out of the corners of her eyes before closing them. But as she got closer and closer to home, she forced herself to concentrate on what she was going to tell Peter about her first big day—how she was going to spin it so he would believe that she liked being back at work.

She knew that the first thing he would ask her about when she walked in the door was her office—what it looked like (depressingly narrow; fluorescently lit); what was in it (an ugly metal desk with faux-walnut veneer on top, a cheap black-domed halogen floor lamp, one white function-room–style padded folding guest chair); where it was situated in relation to Jack (down the hall); the bathrooms (all the way on the other side of the floor); and "the action" (there was no action). She wished she'd just brought their digital camera to work and taken actual photographs of her new surroundings, but since she hadn't, Julia made a list in her head as the train made its way out of the city of things to tell Peter: about what a shitty old building it was and how it had one of those shitty old creaking elevators that people packed into with palpable desperation since they never knew when—or if—another car would come again; about how the John Glom Public Relations offices were, in a word, grim—with their unimpressive and inelegant lobby (a faux-teak desk, a giant, fake dusty potted palm tree, four Danish modern armchairs with avocado bouclé cushions, and a magazine holder filled with back issues of *Time, Newsweek, Us Weekly,* and, inexplicably, *Highlights*); and about her own office, which was half the size of her old office at CTM and which had a tiny slice of window through which, if she slid herself between her desk and the wall and craned her neck around the four-drawer gunmetal steel filing cabinet, a miserable view of an airshaft and a dark alley was possible.

But perhaps the grimmest feature of all and the one Julia had always felt separated great places to work from deeply depressing ones was the office-supply closet, which she asked her new assistant, Jonathan Leibowitz, to take her to right after she got back from her lunch with Jack. But instead of a closet, or a cabinet, or a storage unit resembling either or containing shelves of any kind, Jonathan Leibowitz led her to the small sink next to the coffeemaker in the office's tiny makeshift kitchen. There was a drawer right next to it and he opened it. Then he stepped aside.

She stared at him.

"What's this?" she said, unsure of what he was showing her.

"The supply drawer."

"The supply *drawer*?"

He nodded.

She laughed.

"What's a supply *drawer*?"

He didn't answer—couldn't answer—since outside of John Glom Public Relations—and her kitchen, come to think of it— such a ridiculous thing didn't exist, and had she not been used to the extensive and unlimited selection of office supplies barely contained in an entire office-sized room at CTM—the sea of pens (Rollerball, Sharpie, felt-tipped), pads (yellow and white; standard and legal), Post-it notes and Pendaflex hanging files in every imaginable color (primary, multicolor, pastel, neon, fluorescent), and every other office supply one could ever need (pencil cup holders; Post-it note dispensers; lamps and chairs), she probably would never have asked the question in the first place.

This was all there was, and all there would ever be here at *the loser firm where washed-up has-been publicists ended up.* She looked into the nearly empty drawer and registered its contents: a dusty half-filled box of blue Bic pens she thought they'd stopped making years ago, one shrink-wrapped pack of pink "While You Were Out" telephone message pads, and about a hundred little boxes of small paper clips. She grabbed as much as she could carry and went back to her office with Jonathan.

Jack hadn't told her much about Jonathan except that he had been there for a little over a year, but as she watched him slouching across from her and noticed the slight unevenness of his haircut which made her suspect he had cut it himself, she wondered whether he was tough enough and seasoned enough after so short a time to handle the task he was there to help her with: the Legend tour.

"So, Jonathan, have you had much to do with Mary Ford?" she asked gently. Julia always made the mistake of being too friendly with her assistants, treating them like friends and behaving more like an older sister than a boss, and she knew she was going to do it again now. But she couldn't help herself—so young and earnest and wide-eyed was Jonathan; so innocent and unassuming he was with his baggy concession-to-the-corporate-world khakis and his clean but faded and slightly misshapen John Lennon *New York City* T-shirt with the black collar and lettering and his choker of multicolored love beads; so unlike all the entitled Yale-educated, preternaturally polished, savvy and sharply dressed summer interns and assistants she had become so used to dealing with over the years at CTM.

"Yes, actually, I have. Not directly, of course, thank God, but in a support-staff capacity."

Julia shifted in her cheap armless swivel chair. How refreshing for once to hear an assistant not inflate his position!

"The person who worked here before you quit because she couldn't take it anymore. Mary Ford almost put her in a psychiatric hospital."

Unprepared for and shocked by his candor, Julia laughed loudly.

"Psychiatric hospital!"

"Really," Jonathan said, nodding emphatically as if he, too, had almost been put in a mental hospital. "It got pretty ugly."

"And by ugly you mean . . . ?"

"Abusive. I'd definitely say she was abusive."

"I see." Julia had stopped the laughing by then.

"Same thing with the person who worked here before that," he said, relaxing a bit and throwing his hands into the air with a Can-you-believe-it? look in his eyes. "Mary Ford was abusive to her, too."

"I see," Julia said again. She licked her lips and tried to figure out what to ask—or not to ask—now. Tempted to quit while she was ahead—Did she really need to know this on her first day?— she decided to try to extract the answer to her question as surgically as she could and move on.

"Now with Jack," she started slowly, shifting in her chair. "Has he had the same experience with Mary?"

Jonathan shook his head vigorously. "No. Absolutely not. His experience with Mary has actually been much much worse. If degrees of torture are quantifiable. Which I'm not sure they are. I've done a lot of reading on the subject, in fact, since I started working here—reading about American prisoners of war in Vietnam, for instance. Not to compare POWs with people who have unpleasant jobs, of course, since that would be incredibly disrespectful," he clarified. "But as a general rule, past a certain point with both physical and emotional abuse, I'm not sure you can make a distinction between varying degrees of pain and injury. Torture is torture, it seems. To say that someone was 'tortured a little' seems as inaccurate and absurd as saying that someone is 'a little bit pregnant.' "

Finding Jonathan's cogent analysis and philosophy and sensitivity not only impressive but immensely helpful, Julia sat forward in her chair, clasped her hands in front of her on her desk, and tried to appear calm. Yet inside she was starting to get nervous despite the fact that she had always had a remarkably high tolerance for the particular brand of suffering inflicted by the Mary Ford–level abuser. She hadn't lasted thirteen years at CTM and earned the nickname "the Celebrity Whisperer" for nothing.

"At first I thought that Mary Ford hated women, because of how she treated them," Jonathan continued. "Making fun of how they dressed, saying they weren't organized enough or smart enough or sharp enough to work with a star of her magnitude. But then whenever she deals with Jack it's like a bloodbath. It's like she gets some primal sense of pleasure and well-being from degrading him. I think she hates men more."

To follow Jonathan's previous train of thought, it was questionable whether hate, like torture, was quantifiable either. Hate was hate, wasn't it? Past a certain point—say, complete humiliation and psychic devastation?—it seemed pointless to attempt to create a graded continuum.

Julia couldn't help asking Jonathan where he had gone to school (City College), what he'd majored in (history), and what could account for his unusual fluency in psychodynamic language (both his parents were psychiatric social workers). She couldn't wait to tell Lisa about him—he was exactly the sort of person Lisa would want to hug and stare at in disbelief and wonderment as if he were a full-grown Smurf. But just as she was about to ask him twenty more questions, Jack had walked in and asked her for Patricia's contact information, which she'd reluctantly given him. And while she could have tried to continue their conversation after Jack had left her office, she chose not to. She didn't want to frighten Jonathan by chasing after him as he was leaving and smother him with questions on his way down in the elevator. And she also didn't want to let on to him that *she* was frightened. As any flight attendant could tell you, fear—undisguised and without containment—was contagious.

— 9 —

By the end of her first week Julia was still waiting for the okay from Jack to contact Mary Ford directly. But he wasn't budging.

"I just want you to focus on the actual work, on tying up the loose ends of the launch," he said when Julia asked him that Friday morning whether he thought she should at least call Mary and introduce herself as the new contact at the agency. "Besides, I think Mary might still be out of town."

"Where is she?"

Jack scratched his chin: a tic, his "tell"—a lie. "At Sundance."

"Sundance?" Julia could have sworn that she'd read about Sundance months and months ago in a back issue of *People* magazine. "Isn't Sundance in January?"

He scratched his chin again. "Then it was Telluride."

"Telluride is over Labor Day weekend." She knew this because Patricia had gone with a client the previous year.

More scratching. "Cannes?"

She had no idea when Cannes was and at this point it didn't

much matter. Jack was practically digging the skin off his face and was swiveling away from her in his chair as fast as he could.

Julia then remembered wanting to smell the perfume, so while his back was turned she glanced discreetly at his shelves and at his desk, hoping to locate the absurd conically shaped bottle of Legend that she had seen only a color Xerox of. But it was nowhere in sight.

Where would I hide if I were a giant glass phallus? she wondered briefly but intensely in the few short seconds before Jack swiveled back in his chair.

Julia was meeting with Heaven Scent at lunch, and when their two-person marketing team walked into Anthony's—which she had chosen because it was the one place she was sure she wouldn't run into anyone from her previous professional life—at twelve-thirty and came to the table, she thought they could have been sisters—even twins—with their long streaked blond hair and their nearly identical black pantsuits and strappy sling-back stiletto sandals. She figured they were in their very early thirties—Who was she kidding? The Mary Kate and Ashley Olsen look-alikes sitting across from her were obviously in their very early twenties—and while Julia grappled with the suddenly shocking fact that *she was probably old enough to be their mother,* she engaged them in small talk (the unseasonably muggy weather, the unusually slow state of the cosmetics business) and advised them to bypass looking through the unwieldy menu and just order the chopped salad, the house specialty.

She shifted in her seat, the backs of her legs sticking to the black pleather chair despite the air-conditioning in the restaurant and the dark tights she was wearing, then stared at the chalkboard above the bar where the daily specials were written. Except for her brief lunch with Jack earlier in the week, she couldn't remember the last time she'd been to a restaurant for a real lunch—a lunch without high chairs and sippy cups and Cheerios and accidental squirts of ketchup—and now that she was about to have one she felt suddenly confused, displaced—Where were the chicken fingers? The grilled cheese sandwiches? The bowls of yellow macaroni and cheese? Where were the paper placemats with the shapes and the animals to color in and the little boxes of cheap shitty crayons that were never as good as Crayolas? And why, come to think of it, were chicken fingers called chicken fingers?

She also felt sad. While it felt good to be out of the house, finally, after four years, wearing real clothes, she would have given anything to be sitting at Stanz with The Scoob, finishing his french fries for him and eating his crusts.

"After going through the files," Julia finally began after she and her companions ordered salads and iced teas, "I have a few questions."

Leeza and Alana nodded expectantly. Julia had already decided she liked them, despite their youth, spectacular figures, fabulous streaked hair, and the fact that she'd already forgotten who was who. If they hadn't each been wearing diamond-encrusted initial necklaces around their necks, she never would have been able to tell them apart.

"The first is about the scented blow-in cards. Which magazines are they going into and when are they starting?"

The two girls looked at each other, then at Julia.

"There are no scented blow-in cards," one of them said.

"No scented blow-in cards?" Julia blinked, incredulous. She'd never heard of such a thing! Scented blow-in cards were an absolute necessity in the launch and continued marketing of a new fragrance!

"Okay, then," Julia said, confused. "What about the peel-and-sniffs?"

They looked at each other again.

"No peel-and-sniffs," the other one said.

"No peel-and-sniffs either?" Julia said, then laughed nervously. "Now I bet you're going to tell me that there are no department store spritz-blitzes scheduled."

They shook their heads.

Julia sat back in her chair in disbelief while their lunch arrived.

"Something's wrong with the perfume," Julia said, putting the pieces together finally.

"It stinks," Leeza said.

"It really, really stinks," Alana added.

Julia quickly wondered whether stinkiness, like torture or hate, was quantifiable, but from the distressed looks on their faces she thought in this instance it actually could be. She stared down at her plate, at the multitude of squared cubes of ham, Swiss cheese, pepperoni, and at the big clumps of bacon and blue cheese, and she couldn't help thinking that it was a sea of fat broken up by almost no salad greens, just like the chart Peter had made at home of her color-coded absences. When Alana started to talk she looked up expectantly.

"Mary Ford wanted us to reproduce a fragrance that she had found years ago in Paris—a scent that a very prestigious perfumer had created just for her when she was very young and very, very beautiful," Alana began. "All she had when she came to us, of course, was the original empty flask, since all the perfume had evaporated years before, but one of our 'noses'—a highly trained scent expert responsible for creating perfumes, as they're known in the business—managed to identify the components by swab-

bing the inside of the bottle where faint traces of the fragrance remained.

"When the initial samples came in, she didn't like any of
them," Alana continued. "She made us go back and try again.
And again. And again. When the fifth batch of samples came in,
she found one that she loved. I remember watching her as she
smelled it. Her eyes closed for a few seconds and it looked like she
had been transported back to that time in Paris—her youth, her
beauty, the peak of her fame—which the scent clearly embodied
for her. It was quite moving. Here was this tough old bird—"

"Bitch," Leeza interrupted.

"Bitch," Alana conceded, "literally moved to tears over a fragrance. There are few things as powerful as a scent memory. So it
was clear from that moment on that Legend was very important
to her. Not just as a promotional vehicle, or a comeback vehicle,
but as a symbol. A symbol of loss—lost youth. Lost fame. Lost
love."

Julia stared down at her salad and pushed her plate away.

Lost appetite.

"But as the initial sell-in of Legend to department stores continued to be very disappointing, we were forced to cut corners in
the manufacturing process of the perfume."

"So Heaven Scent knew it had a failure on its hands and decided to try to cut its losses early," Julia clarified. She wanted to
be sure she understood the situation correctly.

They nodded. There was simply far less interest in the Mary
Ford name and image than they'd anticipated. Retailers were either passing altogether on carrying Legend or were unwilling to
give up enough of the coveted cosmetic-counter real estate space
such a fragrance launch required. And though they'd tried to get
out of the deal, the contract was airtight. Producing it and hav-

ing a dismal sell-in to stores and a virtually guaranteed dismal sale
to consumers, they learned, would actually be more cost-effective
than paying the prohibitive penalties for canceling the contract.

"Our hands were tied."

Back at the office, Julia paid Jack DeWack a little visit at his desk.

"So you can stop pretending that you can't find your one and
only sample bottle of Legend."

He looked up at her and she put her hands on her hips but
quickly took them off after becoming unnerved by the rolls of fat
she felt under her fingers.

"Jack. I know about it. That it sucks."

"Heaven Scent said that?"

"No. Actually, what they said was that it stinks. Or rather, that
it *really, really* stinks."

The voice from *How the Grinch Stole Christmas* came into her
head:

Stink.

Stank.

Stunk.

He shook his head dismissively. "Matters of taste are completely subjective."

"Subjective? Jack. Please. I might not have seen a movie in two
years, but I'm not stupid: if it's between the Olsen twins and you,
who do you think I'm going to believe?"

He stood up, readjusted his pants, and put his hands on his
hips in frustration. "Well, what the fuck am I supposed to do
about it? Manipulate time and space? Yes, Legend is not among
the finest fragrances of the modern world. I know that. But I also
know we're all contractually obligated to go through with our

ends of the deal—Heaven Scent produced it; now we have to promote it—so that's what we have to do."

Julia glared at him. "You should have told me."

He glared back. "Why? So you could turn down the job when I offered it to you? In case you couldn't tell, I was kind of *desperate*."

Unmoved, she shook her head in disgust at his dishonest behavior. Which was ridiculous, given the fact that he was a publicist and was therefore paid to lie.

"What does Mary Ford think about all this?"

Jack sat back in his chair. "She doesn't know."

"Mary Ford *doesn't know* that the perfume about to start shipping to stores is not the one she approved?"

He scratched his chin violently. "We need her to help promote the fragrance. Without her cooperation—without personal appearances in department stores that are carrying it—this would be a complete disaster. We'd be dead in the water."

While his reasoning made some sense, Julia still didn't understand why he wouldn't have wanted Mary Ford to know that it was the perfume company's fault for producing an inferior fragrance, not his. But there were bigger questions she needed answers to.

"As for informing her about the fact that the top tier of retailers passed on carrying the fragrance and the fact that we're not using most of the usual promotional tools in our marketing campaign," Jack began, "I plan on discussing those issues with her when the time is right."

Whenever that would be. Julia rolled her eyes, then sat down across the desk from him. "You should have told me that the legend behind Legend had driven both my predecessors to quit. And you should have told me that the perfume I was hired to promote was guaranteed to fail."

"You weren't hired to promote a perfume. You were hired to promote a person: Mary Ford."

"I thought that was the whole point here," Julia said. "That they're one and the same: Mary Ford and her fragrance. Connect the dots—make the sale. Make the sale—make the comeback."

Jack shook his head. "There's always a separation between the celebrity and their product. There has to be. You always have to factor in unforeseen circumstances like this. That way, if you have to, you can separate the two; distance the former from the latter."

Julia blinked rapidly, trying to ignore the visual that had just popped into her head—Mary Ford in full astronaut gear, orbiting the earth in her capsule of preserved fame that had separated itself from the original rocket ship that had delivered her into space—but in an instant it was gone and all there was in front of her was Jack, looking exhausted, and defeated, and very, very nervous. He stared at her for a few seconds and she could tell he was wondering whether she would say the two words she knew he'd heard so often before, the two words she knew he'd come to dread hearing most in the entire English language:

I quit.

But she didn't.

She couldn't. She hadn't even gotten her first check yet. It was up to her to keep her family afloat and she had no choice but to try to make the best of a bad situation.

"Listen, Jack. All I really want to do is smell the perfume already."

He swiveled for a few more seconds before reaching down into the credenza behind him, past a bottle of Maker's Mark bourbon and a framed photograph of him and his wife taken, Julia could tell from the comparative thinness of Jack's face and the fullness of his hair, years before in front of an unknown but spectacular body of water, and handed her the prototype of the phallic flask.

"Thank you," she said.

"You're welcome."

Back in her office with Jonathan, she closed the door and they smelled it.

He looked at her and she looked at him.

"Unlike torture and hate," she started.

"It seems stinkiness *is* quantifiable," he finished.

— *10* —

The following week Jack finally signed off on the big meeting.

"There's a photo shoot for *New York* magazine's 'The Return of a Legend' story tomorrow morning," he said, hands in the pockets of yet another pair of cheap pleated pants. "It's set for ten, which means eleven. Or twelve, depending on how long it takes Mary Ford's makeup people to plaster her face on. So get there at nine-thirty to be safe. Any questions?"

"No."

Not for him, anyway.

But of course she did have a question, a very important question: what the hell was she going to wear? On the train ride home through the darkness of the underground station and tunnels, Julia envisioned the quilted storage bag full of her old clothes that was in the back of the guest room closet—the clothes that she'd had cleaned and which she'd then carefully stored in the slow, quiet weeks before Leo was born.

She remembered those clothes now with a strange, unexpected

longing—*she loved those clothes.* Those expensively tailored suits and skirts and pants and collarless jackets under which during the day she used to wear simple white T-shirts, the sea of thin wool suits in black and navy and khaki that were the mainstay of her daily wardrobe in her past life at CTM. They used to hang in the closet of her old apartment separated by color so that she could, on any given day, for any given occasion—client meetings, client lunches, daytime client appearances and promotional events, nighttime film premieres—find something to wear in minutes.

Thinking back to the unencumbered ease of those days—the days before Leo when she would wake up and drink her coffee and read the three newspapers that were delivered to her apartment door every morning without interruption; when she would take a shower and dry her hair and put on makeup without interruption; when she would slip her clothes on over her hips and thighs and zip them, snap them, button them, and tuck them in without radical physical contortions or mental anguish—made her fully realize, maybe even for the first time, how much her life had really changed.

As the train slowed down for the Larchmont stop, Julia knew that it would be pointless to pull out that quilted storage bag since none of the clothes contained inside—all size 6—would clear her ankles and knees, let alone her front and back sides, so she forced herself to turn her attention to her current wardrobe, such as it was, which she knew would end up in a huge pile on the floor after dinner, each item tried on and rejected in a tear-filled haze of frustration.

She wished she'd been able to shop during lunch for something to wear, but because Jack had told her about the shoot so late in the day, there hadn't been time. And she also wished that there

had been time to watch some of Mary Ford's old movies before
meeting her, but as she walked home from the train station as fast
as she could, Julia forced herself to accept the fact that their all-
important first encounter would be far from ideal. But racing
across the lawn toward the house, she hardly cared anymore. She
was just dying to see her boys.

Julia let herself in through the front door and immediately saw
that the house looked neater than it had looked since she'd started
working. Leo had gotten out of preschool at one o'clock, and,
having been home with Peter ever since, they'd had plenty of time
to make a huge mess the way they usually did.

But unlike before, during the initial phase of their "transition,"
toys were not all over the living room and the big plastic red
Flintstones-like car that Leo loved to drive himself around in all
over the house, using his feet to move and steer and stop, was not
parked in the middle of the foyer.

Instead, the living room was shockingly neat and straightened,
with toys and videos and trains stored in places she'd never known
existed and organized in ways she'd never thought possible.

Speechless, she took off her jacket and turned to hang it and
her shoulder bag up on the hook in the vestibule.

But the hooks were gone.

So was the small table on which they normally unloaded keys,
change, wallets, cell phones, and mail, and their accumulation
of crap—trains, Matchbox cars, half-eaten sandwiches, par-
tially sucked lollypops—upon walking in the door. Still holding her jacket and her bag, she walked slowly across the hallway
toward the kitchen the way she always did so she wouldn't trip
over Legos and Lincoln Logs. But tonight the foyer was a completely clear expanse of floor, which, by the way, had even been
vacuumed.

And tonight there was an unusual smell coming from the kitchen: Dinner.

Leo, who had been sitting at the kitchen table eating Pirate's Booty from a bowl instead of straight out of the bag, slid off his chair and ran to her. Hugging her thigh, he wiped all the powdered white cheddar cheese puff residue onto her skirt, leaving a thick yellowish smear. Had she not missed him so much and had she not already known that the skirt was not in the running for tomorrow's wardrobe competition, she might have panicked, but instead she lifted him up and held him as tightly as she could, registering again the weird fact that Pirate's Booty, unlike Cheetos, always smelled vaguely like vomit.

Peter greeted her with a kiss and a glass of Diet Coke with ice. She looked at it, and then at him, in shock. Gone were his khakis and button-down shirt—instead, he was wearing jeans and a gray T-shirt over which he wore the apron that said *L'Chaim!* which her parents had given him the previous Hanukkah when they'd come over with a plate of her mother's inedible potato latkes—and he seemed to be vibrating with energy and excitement. As he slow-poured himself a glass of Diet Coke over ice, too—the glass tilted, the speed of the pouring controlled in order to preserve as much of the carbonation as possible (he had worked as a bartender during his final year of business school and had been fanatical ever since about the correct way to pour carbonated drinks)—she noticed he hadn't shaved. It was the first time since his unemployment that she'd felt a pang of concern about his mental state, but when he pointed to the oven with a huge smile on his stubble-covered face, she forgot all about him.

"Chicken potpie," he said. "Your favorite. I found a recipe."

"You made chicken potpie from scratch? For me?" Her mouth dropped open.

"I wanted to do something special. It's been a stressful time for you, going back to work."

She was surprised to find herself suddenly blinking back tears.

He led her to her chair at the kitchen table and sat her down in it before returning to the oven. Sipping her drink and watching Peter check the Martha Stewart cookbook he'd slipped into a Lucite holder that someone had given them but that they'd never used, she reached out for Leo and pulled him onto her lap. She closed her eyes and buried her nose in his still-damp hair, wondering how Peter had managed to give Leo a bath *and* make dinner.

"You smell so good," she said.

"Daddy washed my hair."

"He did?"

"With watermelon shampoo."

"Where did Daddy get watermelon shampoo?"

"At the big store."

"What big store?"

"The big store where we get the big snacks." Leo pointed to a box on the floor by the pantry that contained a thirty-six count of little individual Cheez-It packages.

"So you went to Costco," Julia said, putting it together.

"With Bubbe and Papa."

"With Bubbe and Papa?"

Leo nodded. "And we had lunch there, too. Pizza."

Julia tried to smile but she couldn't help feeling insanely jealous. *While she was at work all day, dealing with idiotic Jack De-Marco, they all got to go to Costco!* It didn't seem fair. But then, nothing did when it came to their current situation. If she hadn't been so distracted by the smells coming from the oven, she might have said so.

"What happened to the coat hooks?" she said instead over Leo's head and over the din of Peter setting out plates, tossing the salad, and opening and closing the oven. "And the entry table?"

Peter beamed. "I moved them."

Julia sucked on an ice cube and slid her hands up Leo's shirt and ran them over his soft, chubby stomach and hips. "Why?"

"I'm trying to reconfigure the flow of the house so that things move more smoothly." He motioned for her to follow him to the back door area. "By shifting the point of entry from the front door to the back—moving the coat hooks, moving the table, and, in essence, creating a mudroom here instead of there—we're able to free up the space in the vestibule and move everything now to the rear of the house. Backpacks, lunchboxes, shoes, boots, sneakers, raincoats, umbrellas."

"Why?" she asked again, like a three-year-old.

"Because that way, like I said, you improve *flow.*" He began moving his arms in a synchronized swirling motion as if to explain, illustrate, and clarify.

"I hadn't realized we were having a problem with flow before."

He nodded, as if it were something that had been on his mind and troubling him for quite some time. "We had a big problem with flow," he said, without a trace of irony. "A big, *big* problem."

"Then why did you, a professional—and pathological— organizer, wait so long to get us organized?"

He shrugged. "When I was working I didn't have the time."

She nodded. She'd meant *after* he'd stopped working, but she didn't want to ruin *the flow* of their conversation.

"I also reconfigured the laundry sorting system."

Her eyes immediately went toward the ceiling to the second floor, where the washer and dryer were.

"What laundry sorting system?"

"No more individual hampers in Leo's room and in our room. Now there's one centralized sorting center in the laundry room itself. This eliminates a step—the transporting of unsorted laundry to the laundry room from the hampers themselves—and allows the laundry to simply be sorted at the same time you deposit it in the three wicker baskets I've put in there and labeled. Again," he said, his arms in a synchronized reverse swirling motion, "flow is improved."

Peter stopped talking about flow and took his potpie out of the oven, brought it over to the table, and set it down between them. Then he took the oven mitts off his hands, sat down, and unfolded his napkin onto his lap.

They both stared at the perfect Jiffy Pop–like poof of the potpie, shiny with brush strokes of a professional-looking egg wash, without speaking.

"It smells incredible," she whispered, knowing the crust alone probably contained at least one stick of butter ("Actually, it contains two sticks of butter," Peter informed her when she asked), and then added reverentially, "It's so beautiful I wish we didn't have to ruin it by eating it."

"I know. I kind of want to take a picture of it."

"We should."

Peter laughed. "No. That's ridiculous."

"No, it's not." Julia slid Leo off her lap, walked him to the train table in the living room, and came back with the digital camera. She took two pictures—one of the potpie with Peter grinning in the background and one close-up of the potpie alone in all its perfectly formed poofed glory—then sat back down. Peter blushed with pride, and relief (she knew he was glad she'd taken the pictures), then picked up the knife and served them each a large wedge.

For a minute neither of them spoke—so delicious was the rosemary-flecked crust, the thick jagged pieces of roasted chicken, the cubes of Yukon Gold potatoes with the skin still on, and the savory gravy. She knew they were thinking the same thing—*When was the last time they'd cooked a decent dinner, midweek, just for themselves? Had they ever cooked a decent dinner, midweek, just for themselves? No wonder people cooked with so much butter: it made everything taste good*—and when they both finally looked up from their plates, their eyes met. Julia reached out across the table for Peter's hand and squeezed it tenderly in wordless gratitude (her mouth was full) before retracting it so she could serve them each seconds.

After giving Peter a quick overview of her day and telling him about the Big Event tomorrow, she asked him about his day.

"When I dropped Leo off at school, there was a sign-up sheet looking for volunteers."

"Volunteers for what?" She'd only just left and already she felt completely out of the preschool loop.

"For a Halloween party, a holiday bake sale, and a potluck dinner."

Having cleaned her plate twice, she still couldn't help ogling what was left of the potpie. She was tempted to pick a chunk of crust off the pie but restrained herself when she remembered that it was going to be hard enough trying to look presentable the next morning without gaining another two pounds of butter weight overnight.

"So I signed up."

"For what?"

"For everything."

Confused and overwhelmed—Costume making? Cookie and casserole baking?—Julia shook her head. "Why did you sign me up for everything? You know I don't have time to do things like that now."

Peter put his glass down and lowered his eyes. "I didn't sign you up. I signed myself up."

Julia nodded and forced a smile. "Oh."

"I want to get involved," he said. "I want to throw myself into it. I figured while I've still got the time I could do something useful."

She continued nodding and smiling as the back of her throat tightened.

"They're very disorganized, you know," Peter said, clearly feeling a need to explain. "There's no centralized planning committee, and nobody's really in charge." He moved his arms around again in a synchronized swirling motion. "There's no flow."

He reached for her hand this time and when he did she thought of little sinks and toilets and smocks and cubbies and snacks. This was Leo's first year at preschool—a preschool she had picked out after visiting seven preschools, a preschool she had planned on being involved with and had been involved with for Leo's first two weeks there—packing his first lunch, making sure he was toilet trained (or that he at least knew what being toilet trained meant). It was the new beginning she had been looking forward to feeling a part of after the previous year's miserable experience, when they'd sent Leo to the highly regarded and difficult-to-get-into "educational playgroup" at the home of Gerte Hallstrom, whom she and Peter had almost instantly referred to as "the Dour Swede" since she never had anything good to say at pick-up. ("Leo wouldn't wear his mittens." "Leo didn't want to sing during circle time." "Leo didn't want to eat the big, huge glutinous hunk of flavorless wheat bread we baked this morning.")

Part of her was glad that Peter was getting so involved in Leo's life and enjoying his new role as full-time father, yet another part of her was struggling. Except for the housework, staying home was the guiltiest pleasure in the world: watching cartoons, eating snacks, taking naps, not having to get dressed and schlep into an office to spend hours away from your child. She knew a lot of women would disagree with her and she knew she wasn't supposed to think this, but there wasn't anything on her desk that was half as interesting to Julia as Leo was.

All she could think about was how she was missing out on this next phase of Leo's development; how the mothers she'd gotten to know would forget about her and the ones she hadn't gotten to know would judge her for not spending enough time with her child. But in the end it wasn't the other mothers she cared about. It was The Scoob she cared about. It was all the little milestones and firsts—and lasts—she was afraid of missing: Life was short; time was precious; children didn't stay young forever.

And so, after helping Peter with the dishes, she decided to forgo the two-hour fight with her clothes she knew she would lose. Instead, after stepping in and out of her closet with surgical precision—removing two hangers: one pair of black pants and one simple long black jacket—she climbed into bed with Leo and read him five of his favorite books: *If You Give a Mouse a Cookie, If You Take a Mouse to School, If You Take a Mouse to the Movies, If You Give a Moose a Muffin, If You Give a Pig a Pancake.* As she drifted off to sleep along with him, she couldn't help wishing for just one more book in the series:

If You Take a Has-Been to a Photo Shoot . . .

When the industrial elevator clanged to a stop, Julia got out and headed down a dark concrete hallway. Predictably, Frank Sinatra—classic has-been comeback music—was booming through the walls, and as she got closer to the photographer's studio the music practically knocked her over.

"I'll make a brand new start of it—
In old New York."

Once inside the tall metal doors marked JAMES PERRY PHOTOGRAPHY, the ultimate in has-been comeback music—Billy Joel's "New York State of Mind"—was next on the mix tape.

She shut the door behind her and leaned against it. She'd been to countless celebrity photo shoots during her earlier career, and this didn't seem any different from any other—there was all the usual technical equipment (draped muslin backdrops, bright lights on stands, white umbrellas tilted at various angles to catch light or deflect it), the obligatory scene-setting "props" (a café chair, a bar stool, a claret-colored velvet divan, an enormous white slipcovered wing-back armchair). As she continued to look around the vast space, the hubbub continued around her—lights were being adjusted, a long table with stainless steel coffee urns and platters of muffins and scones and doughnuts and fruit salad was being set up, and at least fifteen to twenty assistants who worked for both the photographer and for *New York* magazine were running around, trying to make sure everything would be ready the moment the principals—Mary Ford and James Perry—were ready.

At first Julia didn't see Jack, but then she noticed him—kneeling down in front of the gray muslin backdrop and a set of lights and making one of those ridiculously pretentious "shot framing" gestures with his hands. He was wearing a gray wool suit with a black turtleneck sweater underneath—clearly an attempt to look the part of arty-and-cool-publicist (as if such a thing existed)—but the intended effect was unsuccessful. It wasn't that Jack was completely unappealing, it was just that he was a dork: a dork in a giant black probably fake cashmere turtleneck sweater that practically swallowed him up whole.

A look of grave concern crossed his face, and then, after turning his body slightly and adjusting his "frame," a look of relief replaced it. He had, it seemed, after much intense concentration, finally found the perfect shot. Crossing the room, Julia was careful not to get in anyone's way—so busy and important were all the photographer's assistants running to and fro, hither and yon!—and made her way over to Jack. He seemed happy to see her, and though she couldn't say she was exactly happy to see him, she was certainly relieved to see a familiar face.

"Micromanaging as usual," Julia said lightly, wishing she could reach down and pull the turtleneck down to uncover some chin.

"I just want to be sure they shoot her from the waist up," he said, loud enough for two assistants with light meters and Polaroids hanging from straps around their necks to overhear. "That's the most flattering angle for her. Otherwise, you get into the leg area and the thigh area and the hips." He shuddered, made a face, then finally came out of his crouch and put his hands away. "With a woman her age, it could get ugly."

He winked at the two assistants—one female and one male who looked at him like he was a perv—and then nudged her toward the table of food. But she wasn't interested: she never ate while she was on duty.

She scanned the room once more before turning back to Jack. "So where's Mary?"

He pointed to the far end of the loft. "Behind that partition. Having hair and makeup. Once she's finished there, she'll change into various outfits on loan to *New York* magazine for this shoot from the Donna Karan showroom."

Julia moved slowly toward the partition but stopped when she got to it. Despite all her jadedness and all she had learned over the years about fame and celebrity—that it was an illusion, a myth, a cruel trick played on the American public in order to sell magazines or books or movie tickets or record albums or perfume—Julia couldn't help feeling excited. Sure, Mary Ford was a has-been. Sure, she'd done cat food ads and car commercials and had virtually no acting career left to speak of. But she was still a legend! And for the first time since she'd taken the job, she allowed herself a moment of unchecked exhilaration as she peeked around the partition.

Sitting in a black ultramodern Herman Miller swivel Aeron chair with a white sheet draped over her to protect her clothing was Mary Ford, looking every bit the movie star. She was an exceedingly handsome woman, with a strong square jaw, deep green eyes, and an overwhelming allure that belied her seventy-four years, and though she must have had some cosmetic surgery done at some point (who in Hollywood hadn't?), her face bore none of the telltale signs of radical and repetitive plastic surgery—the too-tight eyes and mouth; cheeks and brows and chin immobilized and unable to convey emotion from too much Botox; lips too full of collagen to look natural. Her yellow-blond shoulder-length hair had clearly already been styled, and a tall man with bright orange braids was putting the finishing touches on her makeup while a moving force field of stylists and beauty specialists buzzed and swirled around her.

For the first time, Julia heard Mary Ford's trademark voice— low, rich, with its learned and well-practiced patrician inflections (in almost every interview Mary had given over the decades, she had always spoken openly and proudly about the hours of speech and vocal coaching she had endured during the early days of her career in order to erase the Brooklyn accent she had grown up with)—and even though she had said something completely mundane and unremarkable—"Don't overdo it with the hair spray, Pippi Longstocking"—the words sent a shiver through Julia and reminded her of the inexplicable phenomenon of spending time with celebrities: how average moments like this one were simultaneously fascinating and incredibly banal.

Pippi Longstocking stood back and sprayed three short bursts of hair spray into the air just above and to the sides of Mary Ford's head—then waited for the tiny beads suspended in space to float down and land on Mary's hair—and she watched him like a hawk through the mist. When it cleared and settled on her hair, she glared at him and rolled her eyes.

"I said *don't overdo it* with the hair spray. I didn't say *spray it into the air like it's Chanel No. 5.*" She snapped her fingers and motioned for the can. "Give it to me," she said, and then redid it to her own satisfaction.

"Ray Milland and I were shooting *The Bridge to Nowhere* and I found him tremendously sexy," Mary Ford said with a little swivel of the chair and her arm holding the can of hair spray straight out in front of her until one of Pippi Longstocking's assistants dove to retrieve it like a ball boy at Wimbledon. "It was about a year after *Dial M for Murder* had been released and one day—I was quite young and confident in those days, you know, not like I am now, beaten down by life and trying to scratch and claw my way back to the middle . . ." She paused briefly so the group of stylists could register her self-deprecation and laugh at it as if what she had just said couldn't be further from the truth, before continuing. "I slipped a note under his dressing room door with my phone number that said *Dial M for Mary.*"

Mary caught Julia's eye in the mirror and winked. Julia, like a rube, turned around to see if there was someone standing behind her for whom the wink was actually intended, but there was no one else there.

Mary Ford just winked at me.

I ♥ Mary Ford.

"And did the great Mr. Milland ever call?" Pippi said as he stood behind her, his hands hovering just above the airy confection of her hair in an attempt to assess his work.

"Yes. He did," Mary said, the tone of her voice the perfect cocktail of dry wit, annoyance, and actual disappointment, which charmed the group of stylists even more than they were already charmed. "But after our first and last dinner together he asked me why it was that my hair always looked like it could withstand the winds of a Class Four hurricane." She winked at Julia again but this time Julia restrained herself from turning around. "Since then I've told every single stylist who's ever worked on my hair the same thing."

"Don't overdo it with the hair spray!" Pippi repeated dutifully, and when he did, Julia knew he would never forget that nugget of infinite wisdom as long as he lived.

The banter between Mary and Pippi and the rest of the crowd of stylists continued while Julia remained on the fringes, until Mary suddenly half-swiveled toward her and said: "Who are you?"

Julia was so absorbed by the conversation that had now predictably moved on to other celebrity-friendly topics such as Botox and Chinese herbs and natural laxatives that it took her a second or two to realize that Mary Ford was staring at her expectantly.

Mary repeated her question. "Hello? Who are you?" When she snapped her fingers at her, Julia came out of her trance.

"I work with Jack DeMarco at John Glom Public Relations," Julia finally said, with more nervousness than she would have liked and with far less charm than she would have wanted. Hoping to distract Mary Ford from her inexplicable omission—the fact that she'd left out a crucial piece of information, her own name!—she stepped forward and reached out her hand. But Mary Ford's hand was underneath the protective sheet and several awkward seconds passed until she was finally able to get it out from beneath the layers of cloth. When they finally did shake hands, Julia noticed the impressive stack of yellow-gold rings with brightly colored stones in them and the vintage men's Cartier watch with a well-worn chocolate brown crocodile strap on her wrist. Mary Ford was one of the few celebrities she'd ever met who actually had good taste in jewelry and she couldn't help feeling tongue-tied with awe and excitement.

"For a minute I thought you were Jack's replacement," Mary said, rolling her eyes. "But no such luck."

Julia laughed nervously.

"And I was going to say: *Mutatis mutandis.*"

But when it became clear that Julia didn't get the Latin reference, Mary rolled her eyes again. "'That having been changed which needed to be changed,' or, if you want the Latin for Dummies translation, 'Finally they got rid of that idiot.'"

Julia felt her cheeks go hot with shame.

"Where did you go to college?" Mary said, noisily sucking something out of her teeth. "Vassar?"

Stunned, Julia nodded.

"I could tell. They stopped teaching the classics there years ago. Or at least making the core classics mandatory." And just as Julia was wondering how Mary could possibly have been so familiar with the academic curriculum and requirements of her alma mater, Mary added: "My daughter went there. Against my wishes. I wanted her to go to a real college like Wellesley. Where no boys would have been around to distract her or convince her that dancing in a local Poughkeepsie strip club might earn her course credits."

"Is that where you went?" Julia asked.

"That's where I would have gone if my family had had the money to send me to college. But they didn't. So the only education I got was at the School of Hard Knocks."

Mary Ford shifted in her Aeron chair and sucked at her teeth again. "So how did you get stuck working for Jack DeMarco? In case I haven't made myself clear, I'm not a fan."

Julia laughed, and Mary continued without giving her a chance to answer.

"The man has a bigger ego than I do. If I learned nothing else in Hollywood when I was coming up in the business, it was to always be aware of who the real star in the room was and never to eclipse them. But every time I see him he can't get out of his own way. I told him early on, I said, 'Jack, I have news for you. When we walk into a room it's me they're looking at. Not you.'" She rolled her eyes yet again. "He still doesn't get it."

Julia could feel herself grinning from ear to ear—Mary Ford couldn't stand Jack either!—and she was completely surprised and shocked that no one had bothered to mention to her how funny Mary Ford was! And how sharp and perceptive she was! And despite the fact that she'd forgotten to tell Mary her name and that she'd barely done anything besides laugh like a giddy photo-shoot hanger-on, she was suddenly glad that she'd come—and even gladder that she'd taken the job.

"So are you coming with me on my tour or do I still have to go with him?" Mary said, looking at herself in the mirror and making subtle yet expert adjustments to her hair.

"I'm not sure," Julia said slowly, explaining to Mary what Jack had told her—that while he was still planning on doing most of the traveling for the Legend tour, he would probably need Julia to cover a few of those cities.

"Thank God," Mary said, then stared at Julia in the mirror. She could feel Mary's eyes on her—up and down, from her hair (dark brown and shoulder length and brushed back into a neat ponytail), to her minimal but well-applied makeup (foundation and tinted lip gloss with a touch of mascara), to her outfit (a plain black suit)—and she instinctively sucked in her stomach the way she always did when she was around anyone other than Leo. She couldn't tell what Mary was thinking but it couldn't have been all bad: after all, the woman just asked Julia to travel with her.

"I'll talk to Jack and tell him that I want you to come with me instead," Mary said, unfazed, as if not getting what she asked for wasn't an option. "Which he'll agree to, of course, since he's afraid of me. Then when he tells you about the change in plans, he'll pretend it was all his idea." She winked again and looked across the loft for Jack. "Hey, Jack Be Nimble!" she hollered, summoning him over with her index finger. "I want to talk to you."

Jack, who had just bitten into a giant mushroom cap of a muffin, turned and ran past Julia to Mary's side. Taking her cue, Julia backed away a few steps and watched Mary talk at Jack and Jack nod his head up and down like a bobble-head toy. As the crowd of stylists closed in on Mary again and helped her out of the makeup chair and over to the large walk-in closet that contained a long wardrobe rack, Julia couldn't help but feel that despite the fact that she hadn't performed anywhere close to her previous level of ability, she was at least doing better than Jack, who looked like he was getting the shit kicked out of him. That tiny measure of success and even tinier morsel of Schadenfreude propelled Julia to follow the group across the room to the clothes and watch as Mary slid the squeaking hangers down the long metal bar in search of something to wear. Jack stayed behind.

"Well, *this* is fabulous," Mary said, holding out an espresso-colored matte-leather long jacket with a Nehru-style collar. "I might just have to take this home with me."

The group surrounding Mary laughed, all except for a small nail-biting young man with a shaved head and an impossible number of tiny gold hoops running along the entire edge of his right ear standing right next to Julia. He elbowed her lightly and she bent down as he whispered in her ear:

"You don't think she was serious about taking the jacket home with her, do you?"

Julia shook her head. Though she'd met Mary Ford only five minutes ago and didn't know what she was serious about, she couldn't imagine that she was serious about taking a six-thousand-dollar Donna Karan leather jacket home with her.

But then again, there was that small matter of the still-missing sheared beaver coat from Bergdorf Goodman. Not to mention Jack's comment that first day about how Mary's daughter had given interviews about her mother's kleptomania.

"Because these clothes are only on loan to the magazine," he— Romaine was his name—continued, biting into his almost non-existent thumbnail with such force that Julia was afraid he might actually draw blood or gnaw off the tip of his finger. "I'm personally responsible for making sure everything's returned to the showroom directly after the shoot."

Julia tried to reassure him but when Mary Ford finally walked past Julia and out toward the lights and the latest musical selection—the insufferable Celine Dion—and James Perry's tripod, she was wearing the leather jacket, Julia noticed with alarm, *as if she owned it.* Over the next two hours, though, Mary went through so many different wardrobe changes that Julia figured she'd forget all about the jacket by the time it was time to leave.

But when the shoot was finished and when Mary Ford went back into the wardrobe area to change and came out again—her bags packed, her coat on—Julia could see with horror that the rack of clothing was all but empty. The leather coat was gone, as were all of the bodysuits. All that was left were five or six naked hangers still swinging from the pilfered rack.

Romaine grabbed Julia and dug his fingers into her upper arm. His lips were moving but no words were coming out. Which didn't matter since Julia knew what he was trying to communicate. For several seconds she stood there next to him watching Mary come toward them as if she weren't about to abscond with well over ten thousand dollars' worth of merchandise stuffed into her well-worn Louis Vuitton garment bag.

Romaine approached Mary and started to cry, explaining in between desperate sobs that he was personally responsible for the safe return of the clothing to the designer's showroom. Mary nodded and put her arm around him condescendingly and walked him toward the door of the loft.

"What's your name, little man?" Mary asked.

"Romaine."

"Romaine? Like the lettuce?"

He shrugged defensively. "It means 'Roman' in French."

Mary rolled her eyes toward Julia for support. "Yes, I know that. Why do you think they use it to make Caesar salads?"

Momentarily distracted, Romaine's expression changed and he looked up at Mary, completely intrigued. "That's so interesting. I've never heard that before. Is it true?"

She rolled her eyes again. "No, it's not true." She shifted the strap of the obviously heavy garment bag from one shoulder to the other and turned again to Julia. "Who does he work for, this one? Jack or the photographer?"

"The magazine."

Mary nodded as if to process the whole triangulation of the event, but Julia suspected it was really so she could buy herself some time to figure out how she was going to get through the door with the stolen clothes.

"Now listen to me, Little Caesar," Mary started slowly. "Donna Karan and I are close personal friends. As soon as I go home I'm going to call her and settle up with her directly."

Removing her large arm from around his narrow shoulders, she waved goodbye to the crowd of assistants that was now dismantling the shoot and that seemed to have no idea—and couldn't have cared less—that a grand larceny had just taken place. When the huge metal door slammed behind her, Romaine turned to Julia in a panic.

"I thought you said she wasn't going to steal the clothes!" he cried, in a high-pitched wail. Then he flipped open his cell phone and speed-dialed his office. "*Now* what am I going to do?"

When Julia got back to the office sometime after two without Jack—he'd left the shoot before her even though she hadn't seen him sneak out—she couldn't help feeling foolish. She'd been slimed—charmed, sucked in, seduced—by Mary Ford, who was as cunning and sly as a compulsive shoplifter, and as she left Jack's office and walked back to her own, all the excitement and exhilaration she'd felt earlier in the day completely left her body.

Julia Einstein: starstruck sucker.

It was a bush-league mistake, one she couldn't believe with all of her years of experience she'd made, and one she was too embarrassed to tell anyone about.

Anyone except Jonathan Leibowitz.

Sitting in her office with the door closed behind him, he listened attentively as she recounted the events of the morning—how, before the theft of the clothes, Mary Ford had actually been quite friendly to Julia; about how she had made fun of Jack and said she couldn't stand him; and how she had specifically said she wanted Julia to travel with her instead of Jack.

Jonathan nodded his head knowingly. "She was splitting."

Julia stared at him, bewildered.

"'Splitting' is what people like Mary Ford—who are usually diagnosed with borderline personality disorder, by the way—do to manipulate and control others."

Julia's eyes widened. Advanced Abnormal Psychology, like Latin, had not been a required course of study at Vassar either.

"In other words, they divide and conquer."

Jonathan sat forward on the edge of his chair and blinked quickly as if he couldn't believe that everything he'd been forced to listen to his parents talk about at the dinner table his whole life—pathological narcissism, personality disorders, idealization, transference and countertransference—was actually coming in handy.

"First, Mary finds someone who seems sympathetic and responsive to her needs, someone eager to please."

Julia nodded slowly.

Me.

"Then, she charms the person by temporarily making it seem like they are uniquely competent and especially likable. Especially compared to the other incompetent and unlikable person."

Me and Jack.

"Naturally, it's hard to resist the temptation to believe such praise. Even if it's true," he added quickly, then fingered his love beads.

Julia tried to smile.

"As a result, tensions that already exist are magnified by the intensification or manipulation of those who are 'good' and those who are 'bad.'"

Me and Jack.

"The 'good' person eventually betrays Mary's idealization by some evidence of human frailty." He shifted in his chair, then sat cross-legged, as if the story was finally about to get really good. "Overcome by the intense sense of rage and betrayal this evokes, Mary then turns on the person like a deadly enemy and attacks. She then goes off in search of someone else to idealize and use as protection, but the person she seduced and left behind feels demeaned and humiliated."

Julia put her head in her hands. "I feel like a boob," she whispered.

Jonathan nodded sympathetically. "Don't."

"I can't help it. I should have known she was just manipulating me."

"Look, if it makes you feel any better, Mary did the same thing to both your predecessors before she turned on them. And I'm sure when she first met Jack she did it to him, too, probably telling him that John Glom was past his prime and she wanted someone young and hungry like him to orchestrate her comeback."

Julia's mouth fell open. "So John Glom *is* an actual person."

Jonathan laughed. "You didn't know that?"

She shook her head. "Have you ever seen him?"

"No," Jonathan said.

"Has Jack?"

"I don't know. I don't think so. He lives in L.A. and he's really old. I don't think he's had anything to do with the business for a long time."

She felt better, but she still felt vulnerable. She had been so caught up in her own excitement at being back in the game and her desire to prove to herself that she could still manage an impossible situation and succeed where so many others had failed that she was completely blindsided by the fact that Mary Ford would use her the same way she used everybody.

Julia Einstein: clearly desperate for a comeback, too.

— *12* —

Five days before the Legend tour was to begin, Jack called Julia into his office. As Mary predicted, he told her that he'd decided that she would be the one to go on the road with Mary Ford. He said the words slowly and, she would think later when she told Peter the story, with the relief of a drowning man—a selfish, desperate, cowardly drowning man who sits on the head of his drowning companion in order to save himself—about to be pulled from the water.

"You think you can handle it?"

"Of course I can handle it."

Jack DeWack: scaredy-cat.

Saturday she would take Mary to her first in-store event, at the Bloomingdale's on Long Island (the flagship store in Manhattan had passed on arranging an appearance); Monday they'd leave for Washington and Atlanta; and the week after that it would be Boston, Chicago, Detroit, and Miami.

Because of the change in travel plans, she and Jonathan had a lot to do in very little time—switching all the flights and hotel reservations and contact information for all the limousine companies, department store events directors, and hair and makeup people from Jack's name and phone numbers to her name and phone numbers. And since she was eager to dig into the re-arrangements without delay, she ordered in what had already become their "usual"—tuna sandwiches on whole grain bread, a Diet Coke for Julia, and a can of grape soda for Jonathan.

When the call came that the food delivery had arrived, Julia handed Jonathan a twenty and he picked it up at the reception desk and walked it back to Julia's office and then they spread everything out on the desk—the food, the napkins and plastic forks, and the bags of Fritos Julia couldn't help ordering because she knew he liked them. She also couldn't help smiling when, after Jonathan cracked open his can of grape soda and took a long drink from it, little purple grape-soda marks appeared at both corners of his mouth, making him look like a benevolent teenage version of The Joker.

"I love tunafish," Jonathan said, unfolding the white waxed deli paper of his sandwich.

"Me too," Julia said back. But what she loved even more was the fact that he called it "tunafish" instead of just "tuna"—the only other person in the world who still did that was her mother.

Just as she was remembering how she used to take soggy tuna-fish sandwiches to school in brown paper lunch bags, her mother called. It was the first time since Julia had started working that her mother had called her—usually Julia called her mother—because she didn't want to disturb her at work.

"I hope I'm not bothering you," her mother said.

"Of course you're not bothering me." She signaled to Jonathan to start eating without her. "We're just having lunch."

"Who's we?"

"My assistant and me."

"The boy with the beads?"

Julia laughed. "Yes, the boy with the beads."

Jonathan looked up from his sandwich and smiled.

"What are you eating?"

"Tunafish sandwiches," Julia said happily, wishing she could start eating hers already. "So is everything okay?"

"Everything's fine."

"What's Leo doing?" Julia and her mother had virtually the same conversation every time Julia called from work on the days her parents babysat Leo, and there was something about the repetitive *Groundhog Day* nature of them that she found incredibly comforting.

"He just ate his lunch."

"What did he have?"

"Macaroni." Her mother was of the generation of people who still used "macaroni" as the generic word for pasta. "And a chicken finger. And two matzoh balls."

"You made soup?" Julia asked, hoping she wasn't going to come home to a plastic container of flavorless, fat-free, salt-free chicken broth in her refrigerator.

"No, Peter did. He came over and showed me a new fancy recipe of his." Her mother paused and Julia could tell she was making a face. "It's a little too *ongepatchket* for me—too many ingredients."

Julia laughed. Peter loved that word, *ongepatchket*—which meant overly complicated or detailed—even though it was one of the few Yiddish words he had trouble pronouncing.

"That's because it's so *ongepatchit*," he'd say.

"*On-ge-PATCH-ket*," her mother would correct him.

"*On-ge-PATCH-kit*," he would try again.

"*On-ge-PATCH-KET*," her father would correct again.

"Anyway," Julia said, remembering her mother was still on the phone. "What's Leo doing now?"

"He's playing with his Papa," she said, her voice brightening. "The game where he pretends to keep falling asleep in the middle of a sentence. Leo loves it. Just like you did."

Julia smiled. She had loved it.

"Leo loves his Papa," her mother said, sighing.

"Leo loves you, too."

"Oh, I know," her mother said, but she could tell, her mother was glad she'd said it.

There was an awkward pause and Julia shifted in her seat. "Was there something you called to tell me?"

"Yes."

Julia thought she heard a catch in her mother's voice and it sounded like she was trying to collect herself. "What? What's wrong?"

"Nothing's wrong. I just called to thank you."

"To thank me for what?"

Her mother blew her nose and Julia could tell she was smiling. "For Leo."

Julia hung up and blew her nose, too, then forced herself to focus on the piece of paper Jonathan had just handed her—the quantities of Legend each of the department stores had taken in the cities she and Mary were traveling to. Grateful and impressed by his thoroughness (he'd even included the exact location of each of the cosmetics departments so she would look hyper-prepared), she nodded and he nodded back. Though they'd worked together for only a few weeks, she and Jonathan had already developed their own boss-assistant routine and now behaved with the intimate understanding of an old married couple. Jonathan had quickly learned to anticipate Julia's needs (a Starbucks Venti half-caf with half-and-half to get her through the first part of the day and a grande mocha to get her through the second part) and weaknesses (the fact that she was technology-challenged by small electronics: cell phones, Palm Pilots, laptops, iPods, and was un-schooled in the official academic language of human behavior). She had just as quickly learned to understand him (that for free food he would do almost anything for her, that he was too nice to ever become a major player in the business of entertainment public relations, which only made her adore him more).

In addition to the travel rearrangements they had to make, the other important task they faced was to confirm Mary Ford's instructions and demands regarding her appearances and her hotel accommodations. As they ate their sandwiches, they both read through the seven-page document of demands that specified "folding chairs and tables not be used for any of Miss Ford's appearances. Such furnishings are not only physically uncomfortable but also offensive to Miss Ford's aesthetic sensibility" and that "all product-signing tables should be draped in high-quality white linen and adorned with a vase of fresh cut flowers comprised of only white flowers, exclusive of lilies."

Jonathan took another long drink of grape soda, wiped his mouth with the back of his hand, and told Julia to turn to page 2 of the list.

"'Mary Ford requires constant hydration and the following beverages must be available to her at all times: (1) Fresca (chilled) in cans (not two-liter bottles) and (2) Volvic brand bottled water or Smart Water brand bottled water (room temperature). No other brands of bottled water—and no water in "sports-tops" bottles—are acceptable.'"

He flipped ahead several pages and read aloud again:

"'As Miss Ford is extremely sensitive to smell, no strong odors should be present in her presence.'"

He put the list down and stared at Julia. "She's going to be promoting a *perfume*. In *perfume sections* of department stores. How do you prevent the presence of *perfume* in *perfume sections*?"

Julia shook her head. She'd seen—and had to enforce—dozens of these ridiculous lists of demands, and Mary Ford's, though obviously annoying, was not, to Jonathan's disbelief, among the worst in circulation. Everybody in the business knew about Mariah Carey insisting that her tea be made only with Poland Springs water and that "bendy straws" be provided for champagne sipping; about Cher requiring a separate room backstage just for her wigs; and Jennifer Lopez—perhaps the most notorious diva to emerge in recent years—demanding that expensive tuberose-scented Diptyque brand French candles be lit not only in backstage areas *but throughout all passageways that lead to those backstage areas,* that her bodyguards refer to her at all times as "Number One," and that all personnel in hotels and concert hall venues be instructed not to look her directly in the eye unless spoken to first.

"Celebrities," Julia said. "They're just giant babies who want attention and instant gratification all the time."

Jonathan swallowed the last bite of his sandwich and sat back in his chair, holding his almost-empty can of grape soda in his left hand, exposing a little rope bracelet on his wrist just under his shirt cuff. She had never noticed the bracelet before and wondered if some gentle-souled but pierced and tattooed vegetarian girlfriend had given it to him. She was dying to ask him—dying to find out what he did when he went home after work, what television shows he liked, and what his favorite movies were—but she knew they couldn't afford to kill an hour.

"It's actually something called 'Acquired Situational Narcissism,'" he said, sitting up now in his chair. "My parents were telling me about this professor of psychiatry at Cornell who treats celebrities and was the first person to give the condition a name."

"Classic narcissism," he explained, was a personality disorder with symptoms that included lack of empathy, grandiose fantasies, excessive need for approval, rage, social isolation, and depression, and it was caused by a problematic transition between infancy, when all humans are natural narcissists, and age four, when a more realistic view of the world should develop.

"People who aspire to stardom tend to be more narcissistic than others," he added, pushing the bag of Fritos toward her so they could share, "but they don't develop a true narcissistic personality disorder until they begin to achieve success."

"Or failure," Julia countered. "Has-beens are usually more demanding than non–has-beens."

"Has-beens are more full of rage. And more desperate to hang on to what they feel they're entitled to: fame, fortune, servitude."

While Julia cleared away the lunch, she told Jonathan about Joan Crawford's list of requirements during promotional appearances for the Pepsi-Cola Corporation and for movies—how the chauffeurs of her "air-conditioned Cadillac limousines" were told never to exceed forty miles per hour while she was in the car; how she traveled with a minimum of fifteen pieces of luggage and how a separate luggage van and luggage handler were to be dispatched to meet every flight and accompany her bags back to the hotel; and how it was actually stated in the list of requirements that "Miss Crawford is a star in every sense of the word and everyone knows she is a star." At least a line like that wasn't included in Mary's list of demands.

Just as they were about to finally get down to work, Jack's assistant, Vicky, darted into her office.

"Meredith Baxter-Birney's agent is on hold and he's really upset," she said.

"Who's Meredith Baxter-Birney?" Jonathan whispered.

Julia was about to explain—*Bridget Loves Bernie; Family Ties; The Betty Broderick Story*—but she could tell Vicky was panicking.

"Where's Jack?"

"At lunch. Not answering his cell phone."

"Shit."

Julia remembered that Jack had mentioned to her in passing the previous week that Meredith Baxter-Birney was going to be shooting an infomercial in New Jersey for a line of skin-care products she had agreed to endorse, and she suddenly wondered if a flight had been canceled or a connection missed en route from Los Angeles. But when she picked up the call, she gathered, from what she could make out from the bad cell phone connection (the agent was, of course, in his car on the freeway), that the situation was far worse than that.

"The limousine that had been sent to pick up Ms. Baxter-Birney at Newark Airport is white."

Julia waited to hear whatever was to follow: that this white limousine's engine had failed, or that this white limousine's air-conditioning didn't work, or that this white limousine's driver was dead. But all that followed was this: "White limousines are unacceptable because they are vulgar and cheap-looking. This requirement of travel was made clear to Mr. DeMarco in writing early on in the star's business association with John Glom Public Relations."

Julia was momentarily stumped. White limousines, though ubiquitous in Hollywood, were almost nonexistent in Manhattan. In fact, she couldn't remember whether she'd ever even seen one in the city. Not that it mattered. What did matter was that a celebrity—a client—*a has-been*—was in crisis and it was her job to remedy the situation as quickly as possible.

The first thing she did was try to figure out what would cause a Manhattan-based car service to use a white limousine instead of a black one—and she quickly realized since she now read the paper every morning on the train that it must be because it was Fashion Week in New York. "Fashion Week" drew thousands of models and celebrities into the city in such volume that most limousine companies would undoubtedly have depleted their fleets of vehicles and outsourced to other car services in the tri-state area—like New Jersey—where there were tons of proms and probably few people who had an emotional and aesthetic aversion to white limousines.

The second thing she did was call Patricia. When they'd worked down the hall from each other, she always called Patricia with important questions she couldn't immediately answer. Even though every time she called Patricia with an important question she couldn't immediately answer, she had to endure Patricia's excruciatingly annoying know-it-all tone. But at this particular moment, as at others throughout her career when she was under the gun to perform, Julia couldn't afford to think about her own ego.

Putting Meredith Baxter-Birney's agent back on hold, she dialed Patricia's various numbers on the other line until she finally reached her on her cell phone. Patricia was having a simultaneous manicure-pedicure around the corner from her office, and because all extremities were being worked on, one of the young girls employed by the nail salon had to fish Patricia's phone out of her bag when it started ringing and hold it up to her ear so she could answer it.

Julia rolled her eyes. "Is she still holding the phone?"

Patricia laughed. "Wait. She has to take my earring off. Otherwise I can't hear you."

"I feel kind of weird talking to you while some service person is holding your cell phone against your head."

Patricia laughed again. "Time is money."

"I wouldn't know about that right now," Julia said. Sitting in her depressing little office with a lifetime supply of Post-it notes but without a decent pen or lamp, she realized that in a matter of days, she would once again be performing such unspeakably servile tasks for Mary Ford as the young girl in the nail salon was performing for Patricia.

But back to the life-and-death matter at hand.

"Do you know of a driver currently in possession of a black limousine in the vicinity of Newark Airport?"

"Well, there's my driver."

"Your driver?" Julia swallowed. "You have a driver?"

Patricia cleared her throat. "Yes."

Julia felt suddenly very small, as if the chasm of professional success and advancement had grown extremely wide during the years she was home with Leo, not paying attention to the world she'd left behind. She had more in common now with Jonathan Leibowitz than with Patricia. It was the only moment she could ever remember feeling the sting of regret or doubt about the decision she'd made four years ago to quit her job, but it passed quickly.

"It's just a sedan, though. Not a stretch," Patricia clarified.

Like it mattered.

"What's her flight number? I'll call Mario and have him high-tail it out there right now."

Julia gave her the information, then sat down in her chair. Feeling both grateful for the favor and guilty for questioning Patricia's motives when she always, in the end, came through for her, Julia thanked her.

"Anytime."

"I owe you one."

"You owe me, like, a hundred."

Julia laughed, finally, too. "As soon as I get my first paycheck, I'll buy you lunch."

"Let me have Leo for a sleepover and we'll call it even," Patricia said before her cell phone cut out.

13

In the limousine on the way to pick up Mary for her Long Island Bloomingdale's appearance the following morning, just blocks away from her apartment building on Seventy-second and Broadway, Julia's cell phone rang.

Jack.

He was probably calling to remind her about Mary Ford's brunch—mini bagels with smoked salmon and cream cheese from Marche on Madison and Sixty-ninth Street which Julia had called ahead for and picked up twenty minutes before. Or to make sure she'd found Mary's Specified Beverage—Fresca—the grapefruit-flavored diet drink oddly popular in the sixties which was now almost impossible to find—which she and Radu, her favorite driver from Manhattan Transport who still remembered her from when she worked at CTM, had frantically spent over an hour scouring the supermarkets for on the Upper East Side and then on the Upper West Side before finding two dusty six-packs in a D'Agostino's on the corner of Broadway and Sixty-sixth.

"I just wanted to give you a heads-up on something," Jack said.

"On what?"

"I came clean with Mary."

Julia tried desperately not to slide off the long smooth car seat and into the middle of the limousine as it came to a stop. They had just pulled up in front of the Ansonia, and Radu had already jumped out and approached the doorman to ring Mary's apartment to let her know that they were ready and waiting.

"What does that mean, Jack?"

"It means I told her."

"You told her what, exactly?"

"Everything."

"You told her that her perfume sucks and that it's destined for failure?"

Jack was quiet. "Not in so many words, but yes, that was the message."

Julia felt all the blood start to drain out of her extremities. She looked out the window again and saw the doorman stepping onto the sidewalk as Mary strode out of the building toward the line of long black cars that were waiting at the curb. It was all happening in slow motion—Mary lumbering forward like some prehistoric beast from *Jurassic Park* and the ground shaking with every step; Julia trapped in the car behind the tinted windows with her mouth open and no way to escape.

"Are you crazy?" she yelled into the phone. "I'm about to be stuck in a car and at an event with her *for six or seven hours* and *this* is the time you pick to finally 'come clean'?"

"Julia, I kept it from her as long as I could. Better she finds out from me now than from some cosmetics counter clerk next week when you're all alone with her." He paused and sighed loudly.

"She's not going to be mad at you. You have nothing to do with any of this—you just started. It's me she's going to blame."

Mary was just feet away from the car now as Julia considered the extremely high bullshit quotient of Jack's response—which was certainly a clever way to spin his unspeakably bad timing and which, given Mary's propensity for "splitting," might end up being entirely true. But when it suddenly registered that Jack was using the future tense to refer to Mary's reaction to the bad news, she asked Jack what Mary had said when he told her.

He paused, then lowered his voice. "I didn't actually talk to her. I e-mailed her."

"When?"

"This morning."

"Did she write back?"

"I don't know. I haven't checked."

Julia stared at the phone, then folded it back up without even saying goodbye. Mary had now reached the limousine and Radu was opening the car door for her. Seeing the expression on Mary's face and knowing what she'd be in for, stuck in the car all the way out to Long Island, Julia had a cartoon fantasy of sliding down the long backseat and jumping out the left door as Mary was coming in through the right door. But before she could imagine what would come next—running down the center strip of Broadway, then over through the park and down to Grand Central to go home—Julia felt a massive shift in the atmospheric pressure and gravitational force of the earth:

Mary Ford was in the car.

"Where's that idiot Jack?" Mary said as she maneuvered the substantial bulk of her body with a surprising lack of agility into the backseat and practically onto Julia's lap. Mary was huge—five feet eleven inches—and her once reed-thin figure had thickened considerably over the years since the peak of her fame. Which was why the exquisite stolen matte-leather Donna Karan jacket she was wearing that camouflaged her girth so brilliantly came in so handy.

When Julia didn't answer—couldn't answer—was unable, despite all of her experience in situations just as miserably uncomfortable as this one, to speak any words at all—Mary snapped her fingers in her face and added:

"Hey, genius. I asked you a question. Where's that idiot Jack? He sent me an e-mail this morning and I have a good mind to cancel this whole tour."

Shocked by the radical change in Mary's behavior, she panicked at the question: should she acknowledge the fact that she, too, considered Jack to be an idiot? Or should she sidestep the whole question of idiocy altogether and simply answer the question of where Jack was? And while she did, her mouth had opened and closed once, twice, three times, gasping for air.

"You look like a blowfish," Mary Ford barked, poking Julia in the tender flesh of her upper arm before mimicking her opening and closing her mouth with unabashed cruelty, "Blowfish blowfish blowfish."

Julia's mouth opened and closed again—she knew that it did because she could actually feel the thin film of saliva on her lower lip drying from the breeze her blowfish motions had created— while she tried desperately to come up with a response to Mary's question and to process the fact that compared to the first time they'd met, *Mary was behaving like a madwoman.* And as the limousine pulled away from the curb and squeezed its way into traffic, Julia couldn't help thinking, yet again, how ironic it was that so many people were obsessed with the ethical treatment of and prevention of cruelty to animals when publicists—*actual people*—were being verbally abused and tortured every day of the week.

"Come on, One Fish, Two Fish, Red Fish, Blow Fish. Spit it out," Mary barked again, poking and snapping.

Julia rubbed the spot on her arm where Mary had been jabbing at it and wondered briefly whether, underneath the thin wool of her suit jacket and cashmere sweater, an ugly purple bruise was already beginning to form there.

"I think, after your conversation, Jack assumed he wasn't traveling with you," she finally managed.

Mary stared at her coolly. "Going to Long Island isn't 'traveling.'"

Julia was confused: she thought Mary didn't even want Jack to come!

"I think he thought it was," she said, as softly as she could.

"Well, that's rich," Mary said, tossing her head back until it hit the leather headrest with a dull thump. "Jack DeMarco parsing out sentences." She laughed bitterly, tucked a section of her shoulder-length yellow-blond hair behind her right ear, and came at Julia again before she could move away:

"What is he now?"

Poke.

"A fucking—"

Poke.

"Linguist?"

Poke.

Julia winced and tried to ignore her painful flesh wound and her mounting anxiety.

"Well . . ."

"That was a rhetorical question, you idiot." Mary pursed her lips in disgust. Then she addressed the row of backward-facing seats inside the limousine as if an audience had suddenly appeared there:

"She's an idiot and her boss is a pussy."

Julia's face froze into a tense smile—the default expression publicists often resorted to when they didn't know what to say or do—and a small, hard knot began to form between her shoulder blades and radiate down to her lower back.

"Jack Be Nimble drops a bomb on me this morning about how my perfume is a disaster and then he disappears." She pulled at the leather jacket and readjusted the collar of the silk blouse—also stolen—then turned to Julia.

"An appearance somewhere on Long Island instead of in Manhattan. I should have stayed home and watched *Meet the Press* with that disloyal little sellout, Georgie Porgie Stephanopoulos," Mary continued, picking at some nonexistent lint on her charcoal gray pants before looking absently out the window. "I met him once, actually. At the Kennedy Center. We were both being honored for our commitment to the Democratic Party. He's quite short, you know."

Again, Julia tried to figure out how she should respond to Mary's comment. Should she say that no, she didn't know firsthand that George Stephanopoulos was quite short since she'd never actually met him in person although of course she'd always heard that he was and he certainly appeared to be every time she had seen him on television? Had Mary purposely mistaken the show he was on—it was *This Week with George Stephanopoulos*, not *Meet the Press*—in order to test Julia's knowledge of the media (which was, admittedly, not as good as it used to be) or had she really made a mistake, in which case it would be unwise for Julia to correct her?—but before she could decide what to do, Mary had already returned to the subject of Jack.

"Jack be nimble, Jack be quick. I'll beat him with his candle-stick."

Distracted by the third instance of Mary's nursery-rhyming that day—Wasn't nursery-rhyming an early indication of psychosis? Or schizophrenia? And, if so, why did nursery rhymes even exist? And why were we supposed to read them to our children?—Julia started to explain—to lie, actually—about how badly Jack had felt because he couldn't make it and how he would have come today if he could have (he hadn't exactly asked her to cover for him but she assumed he expected her to say something other than the truth: that he'd "had enough of that hag for the week, thank you very much"), but Mary poked her one last time.

Radu, who had such a severe crew cut and sad eyes Julia had always suspected he'd probably survived an internment camp or some other kind of extreme deprivation at one point in his life, appeared silently concerned. Though his face betrayed no emotion all day, she saw him looking at them in the rearview mirror as they made their approach to the Midtown Tunnel:

"I hope Jack remembered to tell you to bring me my Fresca."

Poke.

"And my little bagels."

Poke.

"Otherwise I might have to eat you. And I wouldn't even have to fatten you up first."

Poke.

And that's when they entered the tunnel.

And everything went black.

When Radu finally stopped in front of Julia's house just after three o'clock on that clear blue Saturday afternoon in October, he jumped out from behind the wheel and opened the door for her, practically bowing as he held her hand and pulled her from the black hole of the backseat.

"Never," he whispered with discreet astonishment, "never in all my years driving have I seen anyone as mean as Miss Ford."

Were it not for her need to get as far away from the car—and the day—as quickly as possible, Julia wouldn't have rushed through her teary goodbye with Radu. After all, he was the only living witness to the full extent of the torture she'd endured that day—the torture that had occurred during the four-hour round trip in the car, that is, not the torture that had occurred during the two-hour promotional appearance itself. And for that she would be eternally grateful.

Julia walked quickly across the lawn which Peter had mowed and edged and raked with obvious care and precision, and nodded perfunctorily at Bobby Barth, their next-door neighbor who always seemed to be around when she was. Keys in hand and adhering to the "new flow" dynamic, she headed for the back door and let herself into the house—the now expertly organized well-oiled-machine of a house—the house they might have to give up—*sell, unload, ditch*—if Julia could not find a way to renegotiate the terms of her recent reemployment with Jack.

I'll understand if you have to fire me, but I'm afraid I won't be able to travel with Mary Ford.

Putting her keys into the little wicker basket Peter had marked *Keys* and dumping her shoulder bag into the large basket on the floor Peter had marked *Bags,* she headed for the living room, carefully sidestepping two fire trucks, three dump trucks, and what appeared to be an entire school of cheddar Goldfish carefully arranged in a nearly straight line nose-to-tailfin from the hallway to the kitchen—clues to how Leo had spent his day which she

was grateful that Peter had not yet had a chance to clean up. Feeling numb from the familiar sort of exhaustion the overproduc-
tion of adrenaline had always left her with and which now, at
thirty-six, she felt she might truly be too old to handle without
the risk of permanent cardiac damage, she had neither the energy
nor the will to change out of the clothes she'd sweated in all day
like a pig and into her favorite soft mental-hospital-style white
cotton flowing yoga pants she never actually used for yoga and
matching oversized T-shirt that she'd bought late one night on
QVC while she was pregnant and couldn't sleep.

Safe now on the giant slate-gray velvet sofa that she and Peter
had splurged on before he lost his job and that was, she realized
as she felt a sharp pain under her left buttock, apparently the new
rail yard for a seditious group of those creepy little Thomas trains,
she closed her eyes and rehearsed the line she would tell Jack De-
Marco when she reached him, the line she'd come up with in the
limousine on the ride home from the Upper West Side where
Mary had been dropped off less than an hour before.

*I'll understand if you have to fire me, but I'm afraid I won't be
able to travel with Mary Ford.*

There was an elegant simplicity to that sentence, a haiku-like
quality to it, and she was certain if she hadn't been perfecting it
and repeating it over and over in her head like a Zen mantra all
the way up the FDR Drive, across the Triborough Bridge, and
onto 95, she probably would have had to make the car pull over
so she could vomit somewhere on the side of the road.

Knowing that Peter and Leo were out for the afternoon—at
the playground, or the mall, or at that horrible Gymboree place
where there didn't seem to be a single square inch of rug or
padded mat that some child hadn't sneezed, coughed, or peed
on—Julia collapsed on the couch, suit and sweater and black

three-inch-heeled boots still on, and tried to focus. Behind her head on the side table was the phone recharging itself in its cradle. She removed it and started trying to get Jack on the phone.

But he wasn't answering.

Of course he wasn't answering.

Why would he want to hear her raging into the receiver—*She screamed at me! She yelled at me! I thought she was going to hit me!*—when it was "his idea" for her to travel with Mary Ford in the first place?

I'll understand if you have to fire me, but I'm afraid I won't be able to travel with Mary Ford.

Not that it would be easy, of course, since the only things she'd ever quit in her life were smoking and her old job right before Leo was born, and she wasn't used to taking the easy way out of anything. But this time the easy way looked like the only way and now all that mattered was escape.

It was sometime after four when Jack finally answered the phone, and when he did Julia was shocked; she'd been dialing and redialing for so long that she'd half expected him never to answer at all.

For a second or two after they'd said hello, there was an awkward silence, one that Julia interpreted as coming from a deep well of guilt and empathy on his behalf regarding her suffering. So sudden and unexpectedly touching did she find this moment of silence that she took it as a sign—a sign that, though they had argued almost incessantly since she'd started working for him, he was, indeed, a human being after all.

For an instant she considered not saying what she had called him up to say, but when he began cross-questioning her about the events of the day—*How many people were there? How many units of Legend were sold? Did the media we begged to cover the event (the loser at the Associated Press whose pieces never seem to run and the other loser at* CBS This Morning *whose segments never seem to air but who both have official legitimate press passes and thus make it look like we've done our jobs) actually show up?*—it all came back to her, the parade of indignities and humiliations waving and smiling and making its way down the center of her brain like a noisy high school marching band.

Here were the two hundred people lined up outside the store and the three hundred people lined up inside the store that Julia had to push Mary through:

"You should have gone ahead of me into the crowd, not behind me, you idiot."

There were all the little yellow Post-it notes with names the customers had written on them that Julia removed from the boxes of Legend before handing the boxes back to Mary:

"Slow down." "Hurry up." "Stop being such a spastic blowfish."

And telling her what name to sign on the box with her big, thick black Sharpie pen so each one could be personalized for the purchaser:

"Speak up. I can't hear a goddamn word you're saying." "Shut up. I can't hear a goddamn word this customer is saying."

And how to spell it:

"Is that 'Catherine' with a 'C' or 'Katherine' with a 'K'?" "'Mirranda' with two 'r's? What moron spells 'Mirranda' with two 'r's?"

And the can of Fresca—which Julia had to constantly check for temperature and fullness:

"It's too warm." "It's too flat." "Get me a fresh can now."

And last but not least, the first thing Mary had said to Julia as they both crawled back into the limousine:

"You'd better get with it, kid, or you won't last a full day with me."

She knew that this was her moment to speak and to be heard,

to tell Jack what she'd rehearsed over and over again all afternoon in the car, but her mind suddenly went blank. The elegantly simple haiku had disappeared and in its place had come new words.

"Go ahead and fire me," she yelled, as the front door opened and Peter walked in with Leo draped over his shoulder, asleep. "But there's no way I'm ever going anywhere with that fucking animal again."

14

Of course Jack didn't fire her.

And of course Julia would go back on the road with Mary.

Julia needed the job and Jack needed her and neither of them had any leverage to negotiate.

But Julia also needed clothes for the trip, so she used part of her precious Saturday to shop—an endeavor that was depressing under even the best of circumstances (finding clothes to wear around the house), but so extremely depressing under these circumstances (finding clothes to wear to work) that she would rather have had her gums scraped than schlep around the White Plains Mall and Loehmann's wasting money on cheap "career separates." The other part of the day she used to finally look through her Container Store Travel Package. She hadn't touched the bag since she'd picked it up from the store, because it reminded her of her dinner with Patricia and of what a geek she'd felt like for being so excited about winning it.

As she was refolding and rerolling and reconsolidating her

things for her first work trip in years, she couldn't help wishing that the Container Store had included a "child-storage case" (she imagined something about twice the size of a cat transporter, made out of black nylon and equipped with air holes and a sturdy shoulder strap with lots of inside pockets for small toys and snacks) so that she could have taken Leo with her. But since they hadn't, she had to spend what little time there was left on Sunday staring at him and taking digital pictures of him which Peter loaded onto her laptop so she could look at them from her hotel rooms while she was away.

Later that afternoon, she squeezed in a playdate for Leo with Adam at Lisa's house—a ruse, really, for Julia to kill three birds with one stone: spend time with Leo; let Leo have some time with Batman; and most importantly, catch up on what she'd missed all those weeks she'd been out of the preschool loop: Juice.

"There is no Juice," Lisa said, shaking her hair emphatically. "When will you believe me when I say that nothing ever happens out here?"

Julia rolled her eyes. "We live in Larchmont. Not on the moon. I must have missed *some*thing."

Lisa rolled her eyes back—*It might just as well be the moon,* Julia knew she was thinking but not saying—and pretended to think really really hard. "Except of course for the fact that we're all in love with your husband."

Julia laughed, then waved her away. "Shut *up.*"

Lisa reached across her kitchen table and grabbed Julia's arm. "No. I'm serious. It's like he's one of us. Only better. Because he's organized. He's teaching us all how to be more like him. For the past few Wednesdays after drop-off he's taken us all to the Container Store and helped us pick out things like magnetic bulletin boards and filing systems and supplies to make our own *Family Binder.*"

"What's a family binder?"

Lisa tightened her grip on Julia's arm, too thrilled to let go. "It's a three-ring notebook that you 'customize' by filling it up with plastic inserts and colored tab dividers and business card holders and pocket folders so that with a simple three-hole punch you can organize everything from medical insurance forms to summer camp brochures to take-out menus. Then he's going to help each of us make a *Home Flow-Chart.* He wants us to start thinking in color-coded blocks of time so we can learn to see the Big Picture."

Julia extracted her arm from Lisa's grip so that she could drink her coffee, then watched the boys playing just beyond the kitchen in the hallway outside Lisa's living room. Maybe she was crazy but she could have sworn that Leo looked taller, older, different. If that was the big picture—that she was missing out on Leo growing up—then she didn't want to look at it. She wanted to see only the small picture—the little tiny snapshot she always kept in her head of him and that she always saw when she closed her eyes at her desk—the image of him in those plaid pajamas, his tattered blanket in one hand and a train tucked into the other, staring up at her as if he loved her more than anything else in the world.

That night, after she'd looked in on Leo sleeping, his face serene and peaceful and pristine against the fire engine pillowcase and sheet and duvet cover set from Pottery Barn Kids that Patricia had brought him when they'd moved him out of the crib and into a bed the year before, Julia couldn't believe that she would actually be leaving without him early the next morning. She'd never spent one night away from him since he'd been born, and she didn't know how she was going to be able to stand it.

"You'll be okay," Peter said, when she joined him on the couch.

"No, I won't."

"You will. You'll get busy and the days will fly by and before you know it you'll be back home."

She knew he was right, and though she appreciated his reassurance, she couldn't help wanting to beat him. It was easy for him to say since he wasn't going away from Leo for days to be tortured and abused like an animal by an animal. She also couldn't help feeling annoyed by the implications of what he wasn't saying: that Leo would be fine without her.

"So Lisa told me all about your playgroup," she said, as if she'd caught him in a lie.

"What playgroup?"

"The Container Store Playgroup. The one where you take her and Pinar and Monika and Hilary shopping to get them organized. Sounds like you're not just tagging along, but leading the pack."

He nodded. "It's been fun."

"Who knew that being a stay-at-home mom could be so much fun?" she said sharply.

Either he didn't get her tone or was choosing to ignore it. "Did she tell you about our plan?"

"What plan?"

"The plan to all march together in costume in the Ragamuffin Parade?" That was Larchmont's annual event on Halloween night.

"Yes, she told me," Julia lied.

"It'll be fun."

Again with the fun.

"What are you going to dress up as, a color-coded Family Binder?"

Julia laughed and Peter did, too. "Something like that."

The more he talked and laughed, the more annoyed she got. While she was getting pummeled by Mary Ford, Peter was home yukking it up with the Preschool Moms.

"Do I get a vote?"

"Sure," Peter said, as if the thought had never occurred to him. "What do you think we should dress up as?"

Julia shrugged. "Let me sleep on it."

"While you're away," he continued, "I'm going to make the gingerbread house and bring it into school for their Halloween party."

Julia's mouth dropped open. "*You're* going to make the gingerbread house? I thought *I* was going to make it!"

Peter looked stunned by her reaction. "I know. But I assumed you wouldn't have time. You're away all this week and next week."

She threw her hands in the air. "Fine. Fuck it," she said, getting up off the couch and heading for the stairs. She could feel the weeks of guilt and jealousy about not being home anymore surfacing and all the rage she didn't want to admit to having about being the sole breadwinner while Peter stayed home and baked and organized surging right behind it.

She tried to shake the feeling of infantile unfairness but it was gripping her by the neck and she could barely breathe. It was, after all, *her* idea to buy the kit from the Martha Stewart Catalog the year before, and *she* was the one who made it the first time. But Leo was only two when she'd done it—too young to care how much effort she'd put into trying to impress him. And she was so lost in her fantasy of creating the kind of home and childhood for Leo that she didn't have—one that was fun—where the mother spent thirty-three hours over six days and over two hundred dollars making a fabulous Edward Gorey–esque mansard Victorian with a mock-slate roof (imported licorice discs), bats hanging from the eaves (slips of black royal icing), a warm glow emanating from amber glass windows (interior battery-operated light source behind hard candy "panes"), where the smell of gingerbread and the sound of pans being thrown in frustration and the F-word being screamed countless times filled the house— that she was too distracted to care that he didn't care. He was too young; she'd try it next year when he was older. Which is why over the summer before she'd gone back to work she'd vowed to make it again in the fall when Leo would be three and when Peter would have a job again.

When she went upstairs to their room and shut the door, Leo's T-Rex pajamas were under her pillow and she could see the traces of him all over the room—trains and Matchbox racecars and socks and board books on the nightstand and on the floor. She could just imagine what the afternoons and early evenings were like when she wasn't home—Leo and Peter eating dinner downstairs, coming up for bath time and then spending the hour or so before going to sleep reading books and playing in the big bed. Peter might as well be taking a stake and driving it straight into her heart—that's how much it hurt knowing that he was taking over her role so seamlessly and effectively.

Holding Leo's pajamas in her hands, she tried to figure out why she felt so shitty. She should feel lucky to have a husband who, suddenly thrust into the role of stay-at-home parent, was doing such a great job. She should feel lucky to be able to leave in the morning for work and not give the care and feeding of her child a second thought. She should feel lucky to be able to take a break from being stuck at home for three long years and have a chance to reclaim her career and spend some time back out in the "real" world.

Shouldn't she?

Peter came in and sat down on the edge of the bed.

"I'm sorry," he said.

"For what?"

"I should have known the gingerbread house would upset you. It was your thing—your special thing with Leo—and I shouldn't have taken it away from you."

"Don't be sorry. I was just being a baby. I think it's great that you're going to make it."

He nodded. "I know things are hard for you, being back at work," Peter said. "But it's not easy for me either—being home; pretending I have a purpose in life, that I'm not a loser. I mean, Jesus, *I'm fucking unemployed.* I've been unemployed for over *six months.* Who knows when I'll get a job."

She took his right hand in hers and squeezed it. "You're not a loser. And you do have a purpose in life. You're Leo's father. And you're really really good at it."

"So what?"

"What do you mean, so what?"

"Nobody cares. I'm just Unemployed Guy. Stay-at-Home Guy. Pathologically-Organized-Guy-Who-Takes-All-the-Moms-to-the-Container-Store Guy."

Julia laughed at the last one. "Who called you that?"

"Lisa."

She nodded. "She's just jealous."

"Jealous of what?"

"Jealous that you're Amazingly Helpful Guy."

"She is?"

Julia nodded. "She is. Her husband's never home."

He shrugged as if he didn't care, but she could tell he did and that he was feeling ever so slightly better.

"And you're going to get a job, Peter. We just don't know when. So we have to be patient. It's going to work out." She took his left hand in hers and kissed it. His wedding band was cold against her lips and his fingers smelled like soap. Soon his hands would smell like cloves and allspice and gingerbread dough, and his fingernails would get stained with black food coloring. The more she pictured Peter swearing in frustration and realizing, after the first batch of gingerbread dough wouldn't roll out flat enough or big enough to trace the giant front façade template, that he was in way over his head with this particular project, she could feel her crankiness subside and the calm finally set in.

"So, when are you going to start baking?" she asked, pulling him over to the pillows and under the covers with her.

He dropped his head, shook it slowly. Despite his Acquired Situational Judaism, he was still such a good Catholic, so susceptible to guilt and shame.

"Please," she said, poking a finger into his ribs. "I want to see you suffer."

He laughed.

"Which is what's going to happen when you try to melt a pan full of sugar and water so that it liquefies and turns amber so that you can pour it into the window spaces and it doesn't melt—but just dries out and crystallizes again and you have to throw it away and do it four more times before it works."

"Listen, maybe I should just buy one of those kits from Linens 'n Things. The kind with the walls and the roof already made that you just glue together."

"No way," Julia said. She hadn't had this much fun in weeks—imagining him tormented by what he had blithely referred to when she'd made it the previous Halloween as that "neat holiday craft project."

He squirmed under her poking finger and wrestled himself on top of her.

"But when you build it and put it together," she said, giggling into his neck, "don't forget to *improve the flow!*"

Still laughing, he kissed her on the forehead and rolled off her and over to his side of the bed. Then he closed his eyes, yawned, and shook his head. They lay there for a few moments in blissful silence, until Peter sighed loudly and with great exaggeration.

"God, I'm exhausted," he said.

"Me too."

He turned to her. "Oh, good."

She turned to him. "What's that supposed to mean?"

He smiled wanly, his eyes still closed. "Just that I'm too exhausted to, you know, *do* anything."

She leaned up on one elbow. "Who said I wanted to do anything?"

"I thought you were trying to, you know, get me in the mood." He slid over to her before she could thwart his efforts to cuddle. "I mean, we haven't even done it once since you started working again."

"You thought *I* was trying to get *you* in the mood? I thought *you* were trying to get *me* in the mood. I mean, who was on top of whom?" She winced at the formality of her sentence construction, but she couldn't help feeling just a little ridiculous—not because she'd actually been in the mood and Peter had rebuffed her

advances but because she hadn't been and he'd rebuffed her anyway.

Not that it mattered, since in seconds they were both fast
asleep, snoring and drooling and snuggling like there was no tomorrow. Which was one of the recent wonders of married life: the
cure-all of sleep.

—*15*—

Julia felt like a dead man walking early the next morning at La-Guardia as she made her way down the ramp to the US Air shuttle to Washington.

She and Mary were the first to board the aircraft, and once Mary informed the lead flight attendant that they were switching seats—she wanted the front row, directly opposite the entrance to the aircraft and right next to an emergency exit—she moved toward the window, still crouching beneath the overhead compartment, and turned to Julia.

"You know, I don't even know what your last name is."

Julia smiled. It was only on the top of every single page of the itinerary she had handed Mary in the limousine on the way back from Long Island, though she wasn't about to point that out.

"You do have one, don't you? Or are you one of those idiots who only goes by their first name?"

"It's Einstein."

Mary raised an eyebrow in disbelief. "*Einstein*? As in Albert?"

Julia smiled again. She'd been the butt of this joke ever since she could remember, and she wondered, yet again, why she didn't just pronounce it differently—the wrong way—*Einsteen*—to avoid all the inevitable annoying comments.

"Why the shuttles don't have first-class sections I'll never understand," Mary said, loudly enough to be heard by both flight attendants squished into the nearby galley-kitchen. "With senators and congressmen and reporters and journalists and movie stars flying up and down the Northeast corridor, you'd think they could separate us from the riffraff and give us some decent accommodations."

A vision of her fantasy accommodations for Mary Ford appeared in Julia's head and floated inside it like a little gas bubble—a padded cell with a soundproof door, a gigantic padlock, round-the-clock security and administration of meds—and as she rushed to take off her new black suit jacket and shove it and her stowable piece of wheelable luggage above her head and slide her briefcase underneath the seat in front of her, Mary started handing her things to put away: her quilted Barbour coat ("The Queen of England wears the same coat, so you better find a proper wood hanger for it"), her yellow Louis Vuitton makeup case ("This always goes under my seat, with the strap facing forward in case I need to get at it during the flight"), a small black nylon Prada zippered pouch bag ("Here, hold this until I tell you I need it") which Julia referred to in private as the Claus Von Bülow bag and which later she would come to find out contained a variety of dental hygiene implements (including a travel-size toothbrush and toothpaste; dental floss and dental pick) that Mary Ford used after each and every joyless meal they were forced to share ("The gums are the final frontier, the last vestige of youth. And when they go, it's all over").

Once Julia had followed Mary's instructions to the best of her abilities (which is to say, to Mary's complete dissatisfaction), Mary told Julia to get out the schedule, the airline tickets, a copy of the ad which was supposed to have run in that morning's *Washington Post* in order to promote her evening appearance at Nordstrom, and any other materials she might have in her possession which related in any way to the tour.

"I don't like surprises. If you have a stick of gum in that bag of yours, I want to know when you plan on chewing it." Mary glared at Julia and settled into her seat, trying to increase the slack on her too-tight belt. "I don't like being underprepared or underinformed. I want to know everything there is to know about the store I'm appearing in before I step into it, and I want to know everything about an interviewer who's interviewing me before I sit down with them. I don't want to get blindsided again the way I was by Jack Be Nimble. I don't want to walk into a reporter's trap."

Poke.

"Traps are for bears."

Poke.

"Stupid bears."

Poke.

"Papa bears, mama bears, and baby bears with shit for brains."

Poke. Poke. Poke.

Julia tried to nod as calmly as she could, but Mary's latest psychotic-sounding string of nursery rhymes was making her uncharacteristically flustered. Desperately trying to remember the story of "Goldilocks and the Three Bears" but confusing it with "The Three Little Pigs" and "The Three Blind Mice" (Julia suddenly wasn't sure which story was which and whether or not it even mattered), she pulled the files out of her briefcase and— despite all her Container Store packing and organizing accessories—paper clips popped off and became entangled with rubber bands and manila envelope clasps; her cell phone and the Palm Pilot Peter had lent her and tried to show her how to use and her hairbrush fell onto the floor of the plane and rolled into the aisle before she could catch and retrieve them.

As Mary grilled her, Julia found it possible to answer only half of her questions correctly—she knew which three female celebrities Barbara Starr, the *Washington Post* Style writer who was scheduled to talk to Mary that afternoon, had most recently profiled (Diane Keaton, Gwyneth Paltrow, the Duchess of York); she knew how many daily newspapers were part of the Gannett group (101) and what their combined paid circulation was (7.6 million; 2.2 million for *USA Today* alone) and how many Fox television affiliates there were (39); and she knew which, if any, of the competing celebrity fragrances Nordstrom carried in its beauty department (Britney Spears' and Sarah Jessica Parker's).

Mary shifted in her chair and stared at the long line of distracted, oblivious passengers filing onto the plane. Taking her sunglasses off, she sat forward in her chair, talking a little more loudly than she usually did.

Julia had initially wondered why Mary would have wanted to sit in the very first row of seats—risking being recognized and bothered by curious celebrity seekers throughout the flight. But as Mary's eyes continued to sparkle and her instantly recognizable voice got louder and louder, Julia realized that she'd chosen the first row precisely *because* she wanted to be recognized. Only the flight was already half full and not one person had stopped, stared, whispered, blushed, or pointed.

"Talk about ironic. I spent so many years trying to disguise myself so I could walk down the goddamn street without being mobbed that now no one recognizes me anymore." Mary forced an even broader smile, then laughed and readjusted herself in her seat until finally someone—one of the flight attendants—a sweet, young, bottom-heavy blonde with cornflower blue eyes and bright pink lipstick—approached.

"Excuse me," the woman said, with the exact proportion of nervous excitement, servitude, and caution most people displayed when addressing celebrities.

Mary Ford smiled, deeply satisfied. Finally, she had been "spotted." And since all it took was one person to make a has-been's day—*just one!*—Julia was practically giddy with relief.

The flight attendant blushed slightly and lowered her voice, and when she did, Mary looked at Julia: she couldn't wait for the unsuspecting young woman to make a complete fool of herself.

"You know," the flight attendant began politely, "this is an emergency row. And we usually ask that people who sit here be capable of opening the door in case of—"

Mary's smile quickly faded—instantly she understood that the flight attendant had not recognized her but had approached her only in order to ask them to change their seats. And Julia knew Mary well enough to know that her embarrassment would quickly turn to humiliation and then to rage.

"In case of what?" Mary barked, her face a protective mask covering the raw embarrassment and disappointment underneath.

The flight attendant's smile faded. "In case of—"

"What are you telling me? That I'm too old to be sitting here?"

Mary squinted at the pin just above the young woman's left breast—a pair of fake gold wings with black lettering—while the flight attendant blanched, horrified that Mary's loud voice had carried to the rows immediately behind them and to the steady stream of passengers still filing in.

"What does your name tag say?"

"Jill."

"Jill," Mary repeated. *"Jill the Pill went up the hill to annoy and insult the passengers,"* she singsonged.

The young woman, visibly confused and frightened, looked at Julia for help, but Julia, confused and frightened herself—this was, after all, the first time she had really been out in the world with Mary Ford, not just trapped in a private torture chamber in the back of a speeding limousine with her—could only shrug helplessly and empathetically.

"You don't know who I am, do you, Jill?" Mary continued without bothering to wait for a response. "Well, you should. You should know who I am. Go call your parents from one of these stupid airphones that never work and tell them that you met Mary Ford today and she refused to move her seat because even though she's seventy-four she's fully capable of opening an emergency exit door on an aircraft."

Jill backed away, and as she did, Mary turned to Julia.

"You call US Air as soon as we land and complain about this Jill," she stage-whispered. "Then you call Jack or whatever idiot booked our travel arrangements and tell them to switch our flights. I'm not flying US Air for the rest of the trip. Then get a bottle of water from Jill. I don't want to be dehydrated when we land."

For the next ten minutes Julia was so busy following orders like that, that she didn't have time to remember to get scared the way she usually did every time she got on a plane ever since Leo had been born. But the instant the aircraft started to back out of the gate and taxi toward the runway, Julia put her pad between her legs, closed her eyes, and sat on her hands so Mary wouldn't see them shake.

She could feel Mary staring at her as the plane sped down the runway and then lifted into the air—those twenty or thirty seconds during every flight when Julia would always stop breathing because, convinced she was about to die and seeing her whole life flash inside her head, she would become full of deep regret and longing for all the things she had never done and would never do: volunteer in a soup kitchen, learn to cook simple everyday meals for her family, live to see Leo grow up. As the plane began to finally level off out of its steep incline, Julia opened her eyes.

"Well, this is all I need," Mary said, throwing her hands up in the air melodramatically and seeming to defy the g-forces that were still pushing them back in their seats. "A publicist who's afraid to fly. Don't tell me you get airsick, too, because I'm not going to sit here with one of those vomit bags under your chin for the whole flight. I did that for my daughter every time we flew somewhere together, and all the thanks I got was having her complain to *People* magazine years later that my forcing her onto airplanes constituted severe physical and emotional abuse."

Julia tried to dismiss the airsickness accusation by shaking her head vehemently, but she was afraid Mary would interpret her emphatic denial as a de facto admission of guilt so she forced herself to stop. Her untarnished flying record was something she'd always been exceedingly proud of, as a matter of fact, especially given all the times she could easily have gotten sick due to extreme turbulence, weather, or mental anguish: the connecting flight from Denver to Aspen with Michael Caine, the flight from New York to Chicago with Ted Danson, the flight from Dallas to New York with Shirley MacLaine. Despite being plagued by motion sickness when she was a child, she hadn't had a relapse during her entire professional career.

Mary looked around the cabin for Jill, then motioned for her to come over.

"Albert Einstein here needs a drink," she said, rolling her eyes, then paused to consider the available options. "Get her a vodka tonic with a lot of ice." She smiled now at Jill as if they were best buddies, coconspirators in cahoots to get Julia, a complete incompetent, minimally functional.

More splitting.

"She looks like the Bloody Mary type, but the last thing I need is for us to hit an air pocket and all that tomato juice to come back up and go all over this suit. Then I'd have nothing to wear to my appearance at the Pentagon City Mall tonight."

Julia wasn't the Bloody Mary type, actually—in fact, she hated tomato juice almost as much as she hated vodka, not to mention that she wasn't about to drink something with the word "Mary" in it—but she didn't argue with Mary, especially after Mary had ostensibly done her a good deed: seen to her during her moment of need. Instead, she sat back and tried to ignore the puffy clouds out the window as the plane gained altitude.

When Jill returned with the vodka tonic, Julia felt obligated to drink it—or, at least, to make it look like she was drinking it—but on her empty stomach she could feel a hot finger of heartburn starting up her chest and radiating to her throat. Mary's mood had shifted again and before she knew it she heard Mary telling Jill all about Legend and Jill listening intently as if nothing had ever happened.

"Do you have a boyfriend?" Mary said, eyeing Julia's vodka tonic.

Jill nodded sweetly.

"And what about you, Einstein?" Mary said. She checked Julia's left hand for a wedding ring until she spotted the platinum band and modest emerald-cut engagement ring. "What's your husband's name?"

"Peter."

"Peter Peter Pumpkin Eater."

Poke.

"Had a wife and couldn't keep her."

Poke.

"He put her in a pumpkin shell."

Poke.

"And there he kept her very well."

As Jill moved away, Julia decided once and for all: she hated nursery rhymes and would rid Leo's shelves of them the minute she got home.

"Of course that little Jill has a boyfriend," Mary continued, nudging Julia with her elbow and engaging in still more splitting. "She's young and she has a nonthreatening career." She reached for Julia's drink as if it was hers to share and drained the cup. "Unlike me, who can't find a man because all the men I go out with say I intimidate them."

Julia herself would have used different language—*frighten, terrify, traumatize*—to describe what Mary Ford would do to a man sitting across the table during a dinner date. It was, in fact, much the same language Julia would use to describe what Mary Ford did to her in a limousine, or at a table in the cosmetics section of a department store, or on an airplane—and she made a conscious effort to remember to tell Peter about Mary's comment. She would, in fact, have reached for her pad again to make a note— *Mary Ford finds the fact that she scares the shit out of men a complete mystery*—but the pilot announced that they had just begun their initial descent to Reagan National.

The plane banked left, then right, then left and right again. All that motion plus the vodka in her system would have been more than enough, on a good day, to easily unsettle Julia's stomach and destroy her equilibrium. But this, of course, was not a good day. It was a terrible day. The stress of being trapped on a flight with Mary Ford and knowing she was stuck with her for the next two days in Washington and Atlanta made the liquid in her stomach suddenly lurch upwards and before she knew what was happening she was pawing frantically at the empty space in front of her for an airsickness bag. But, being in the first row, there were no seats in front of her, and since there were no seats in front of her there were no seatbacks, no seatback pockets, no in-flight magazines, and, most importantly, no airsickness bags. Just an unread complimentary copy of *USA Today* on the armrest between them.

She called Peter from her room at the Hay-Adams Hotel, where she was lying with a cold facecloth on her forehead and a can of ginger ale on the bedside table, and told him what had happened next: how she had gotten sick into the newspaper right there next to Mary the moment the plane had landed, and how Mary was so outraged that she threatened to call John Glom himself to have both Julia and Jack fired. And the fact that it was Julia, not herself, who was surrounded by flight attendants and given a wheelchair escort off the plane and through the airport to where the limousine was waiting, didn't help. When they got to the car, Mary insisted that Julia sit up front with the driver instead of in the backseat next to her.

"How are you feeling now?" he asked once she'd stopped talking.

She closed her eyes, pressed the damp facecloth to her cheeks,

and saw the morning's events flash on the black screen behind her
eyes.

She wished she were dead. "A little better."

"Do you think you can handle the rest of the day?"

She turned to the night table and moved the bottle of ginger
ale and the glass of ice. Then she picked up the schedule and read
through it.

There was the three o'clock *Washington Post* Style section interview in Mary's suite across the hall, the *Live at Five* in-studio
news segment, and, of course, there was the main event: the six
o'clock Legend signing just over the bridge in Virginia. Julia
couldn't imagine how she was going to get through it—not only
how she was going to handle the first full day of press interviews
and another hellacious public appearance, but how she was going
to face Mary after the disastrous flight.

"You'll get through it. You always do."

She groaned.

"Just pretend it didn't happen."

"Peter. I threw up on her."

"You didn't throw up *on* her. You threw up *near* her. Into a
newspaper. There's a difference. And whatever you do, don't apologize. I mean, fuck it. She deserved it. There's no excuse for her
to give you such *tsuris*."

Julia laughed finally, and then she heard Leo's soft voice on the
other end of the phone. Her heart constricted: it was the first
time they'd ever talked on the phone.

"Mommy?"

"How are you, my Scoob?"

"Good."

"How was school?"

"Good."

"Are you having fun with Daddy?"

"Yes."

"What did you do after school?"

"We went to the store."

"The big store with the big snacks?"

"No. The store with the red cars."

Food Emporium. Leo loved the carts with the red plastic cars attached to the front that he could climb into and pretend to drive.

"Daddy bought me dinosaur chicken. And mac and cheese. And a present."

"What kind of present?"

"A train."

"Which one?"

"Mavis. It's black and white."

"I can't wait to see it."

"Hey, Mommy?"

"Yes, my sweet?"

"When are you coming home?"

"Soon. I'll be home soon."

"But I want you to be home now."

"I will be home."

"Will you be home tomorrow?"

"Not tomorrow. The day after tomorrow."

She could hear Leo breathing through the phone but he wasn't saying anything.

"Hey, Scooby?" She closed her eyes and felt tears slide out from under her lashes while she waited for him to answer.

"Say yes to Mommy, she can't see you," she heard Peter say in the background.

"Yes?" Leo said.

"I miss you."

"Mommy?"

"What, my sweet?"

"Are you still working on the railroad?"

"Yes, I'm still working on the railroad." She wiped her eyes with her palm and then her nose with the back of her hand. She couldn't believe how ridiculous this was. Four hours and already she was falling apart. And before she could tell Leo she loved him, Peter was back on the phone.

"So I saw the gang at pick-up," he said.

"Did anyone ask about me?" Julia said lightly, hoping he wouldn't be able to tell she'd gotten all sloppy. "Or have they forgotten about me?"

"Yes, they asked about you. I told them that you'd left this morning and they seemed very impressed."

"And now you can impress them tomorrow, too—'Oooooo! Julia's in Washington, D.C., with a has-been, recovering from a stress-induced vomiting episode!'" She shook her head. "So what are you going to do for dinner?"

"Your mother came by this morning with more chicken."

Julia closed her eyes and reached for her glass of ginger ale. "I'm sorry."

"It's all right. She means well. I'll throw it out and take Leo to Stanz instead."

She nodded and looked out the window through the thin white sheers beneath the heavy chintz drapery. The room she was in had an amazing view of Lafayette Park and the White House, and if she hadn't been so miserable she would have been struck by the view; by the trees which were still green and full here in the South in mid-October; and cheered by the idea of ordering room service—something like a B.L.T., or a cheeseburger and fries—

and watching cable while having complete control of the remote. But she was lonely. And sad. Letting the sheers fall from her fingers, she turned away from the window and back to the phone.

Julia sighed. "I hate this. I want to go home."

"I know. It sucks."

Her eyes started to fill again with tears and she indulged in a fleeting fantasy of Peter picking Leo up early from school and racing over to the Westchester airport to catch a flight to Washington to be with her—there was plenty of time before the interviews and the Nordstrom event were to begin, and the junior suite she'd been upgraded to because she was with someone famous who was complaining loudly was certainly big enough for the three of them.

Then she blew her nose and wiped her eyes for the last time. The sound of Peter's and Leo's voices had lifted her spirits and she could feel herself finally start to rally.

Getting up and showering; changing her clothes and staring at the files she had brought with her—the files Mary had found so pathetic and incomplete—Julia steeled herself for the rest of the day. Walking across the hall to Mary's suite at three o'clock and sitting through the interview with Barbara Starr and the brief shoot with the *Post* photographer she'd brought along; calling for the limousine at four-thirty and walking Mary through the hotel and getting her into the car in time for her five o'clock news segment; getting back into the car and racing across the Potomac to the east entrance of the Pentagon City Mall, where two uniformed security guards met them and escorted them to the Nordstrom cosmetics department, where a respectable though not unmanageable crowd of almost three hundred people were waiting along with an extremely excited store manager and three extremely excited sales professionals—Julia felt like she was getting her sea legs back again.

Sitting next to Mary at the table and handing her box after box of Legend, she felt herself play her part of this staple of public relations performance art—*The Celebrity Product Signing*—with absolute perfection: performing the exquisitely precise choreography of movements (the readying of the pen, the removal of the Post-it note, the simultaneous sliding of the box and leaning over to stage-whisper and repeat the spelling of the customer's name, the simultaneous handing of the signed box back to the customer and removing of the next Post-it note, etc. etc) without error and all while knowing precisely when to replace the Sharpies and the cans of Fresca. Keeping the flow of this ballet, this pas de deux, during a signing at a pace that was neither too hurried nor too slow was as much an art as it was a science, and after Mary had put her signature on every box in the store and after they were back in the limousine and riding up in the elevator of the hotel, Julia felt an enormous wave of relief: the event had been free of disaster. At nine-thirty p.m., the day, finally, was over.

At least, she thought it was.

"Where do you think you're going?" Mary said as Julia put the key in her hotel room door—the door that was directly across from Mary's which was now open and through which she had just walked expecting Julia to follow.

"We haven't had dinner yet and I'm starving," Mary said, over her shoulder. "You call room service while I change out of these clothes."

Mary peeled off her jacket, her silk blouse, and her scarf and walked through the suite from the bedroom to the bathroom and back again wearing nothing on top but a giant white bra while

Julia, exhausted and crestfallen and more than a little mortified by Mary's partial nudity, trailed slowly after her.

"Order me a Cobb salad and two vodka martinis extra dry. And get yourself something substantial—you need to get your strength back after this morning," she said, unzipping her pants with one hand and reaching into the closet for a giant white terry-cloth robe with the other. "I want to go over tomorrow's schedule and see what guest that idiot Charlie Rose who never shuts up has on tonight."

— 16 —

It was well after midnight when Mary Ford finally finished with Julia for the day: finished eating her room service dinner next to her on the chintz sofa while watching Donald Trump ("A vulgarian who I'm actually quite fond of") being interviewed by Charlie Rose ("Again with the interrupting and the talking over the guest. Why does he invite them on if he's not going to let them talk?"); finished unzipping her Claus Von Bülow bag and poking and sucking at her gums with the various implements contained therein; finished going over the next day's schedule, which left Julia with more questions both logistical ("Will there be an airline escort person—someone wearing a red blazer, holding a walkie-talkie, and with access to a golf-cart vehicle—waiting for me at National Airport and another waiting on the ground in Atlanta to escort me on and off the planes?") and practical ("How is my Fresca supply holding up?").

Placing the breakfast room-service order form on the outside doorknob (a basket of croissants, tea with milk and lemon, and a "medium ripe medium size" banana) as she left Mary's room and stepping across the hall, Julia could hardly believe when she slipped the plastic key into the slot of her door and heard it click that she was finally alone. But her relief was short-lived when she realized that after only a few short hours of sleep—assuming she'd even be able to sleep—she was going to have to wake up and start all over again.

After changing into her big white pajamas and brushing her teeth, she sat down on the bed, stared at the clock, and then at the phone. It was now almost twelve-thirty—far too late to call home and talk to Peter and find out what the rest of his and Scooby's day had been like: what specific ideas he'd come up with to reconfigure the flow of the preschool; what else he'd done around the house to make it practically buzz with efficiency; what he and Leo had eaten at Stanz after disposing of her mother's chicken; whether or not he'd started on the gingerbread house project.

She glanced across the room and saw her laptop, still in its case on the desk where she'd left it when she'd checked in hours before, and though she was dying to see if Peter or her mother had e-mailed her any digital pictures of Leo, caught in various moments throughout his busy little day—at the kitchen table eating a mixture of Life cereal and Honey Nut Cheerios for breakfast; heading out the door with his Thomas the Tank Engine backpack that was almost as big as he was and his Scooby-Doo "Mystery Van" lunchbox that took up the equivalent parking space in his cubby of a giant SUV; napping on their bed in the afternoon with his blanket and surrounded by his favorite stuffed animals—two kittens she and Peter had bought for him when he was still a baby from FAO Schwarz before the unthinkable happened and it had closed down briefly and an elephant with ears the size of Dumbo's—she could barely move.

Neither did she have the energy to e-mail Jack—to tell him how many people had shown up at Nordstrom (fifty fewer than had shown up at the Long Island event) and how many units of Legend were sold (314)—disappointing numbers all around. But bad news could always wait, and it wasn't even like Jack was expecting to hear anything different.

She lay back on the bed and then reached into her suit pocket for her cell phone. At several points during the event she'd felt it vibrate and now she flipped it open until the little polka song played. Scanning the Caller ID list, she saw that Peter had called twice and Jonathan had called once from home in Brooklyn.

She listened to their voicemails—Peter's two drowsily affectionate messages and Jonathan's concerned and apologetic one, delivering the bad news that the *Atlanta Journal-Constitution* had canceled its interview with Mary for the next day—then folded up the phone and closed her eyes. She knew she would take the brunt of Mary's annoyance about the newspaper's cancellation the next day, but Julia couldn't think about that now. All she could think about was how good it felt to finally be alone in her hotel room in her big white pajamas, with nothing else to do but remain prone on the 400-thread-count sheets and the down feather bed.

As her mind drifted on its way to what she assumed would be a deep and instant sleep, she remembered back to all the times when she was younger that she had traveled for days on end like this with clients—lying beached on huge hotel beds after twenty-hour days, ordering room service, wishing there had been enough time to use the deep bathtub and the miniature bath products before checkout, and watching too many reruns of *Dallas* or *Mary*

Tyler Moore in the dark before her mind finally switched off and she was able to fall asleep.

Sometimes, right before she fell asleep in those hotel rooms, with their plush carpeting and their heavy drapes and the Chinese vase bedside lamps with the soft light coming through their pleated silk shades, she used to get a strange and vaguely pleasant sensation that she was floating, half awake and half asleep, through days and hours and cities and airports. She loved hotels—good hotels—loved their hushed anonymity, their amenities, their creature comforts; loved how they provided her with a brief otherworldly interlude from her cramped, comparatively Spartan Manhattan apartment, from the bills that were waiting to be paid, the dry-cleaning that was waiting to be dropped off, the pile of work she always brought home with her from the office to finish at night or over the weekend. She'd loved the clear-cut challenges of those client-escorting trips—the military precision required to set up and complete each mission, the challenge of solving or coping with unexpected problems (traffic tie-ups, severe weather, canceled interviews, underattended events), the pride she took at her ability to keep her cool (or, at least, to make it look like she was keeping her cool) in even the most tense and pressure-filled situations.

And even though she knew there was more to life than feeling a deep sense of satisfaction at knowing the phone numbers and e-mail addresses of fifty newspapers and magazines without ever having to look them up or knowing the beverage preferences and food restrictions of every single one of her clients without having to write them down on the inside of her hand in tiny letters, and even though she often felt disillusioned by the spectacular rudeness of her clients and by their shocking lack of gratitude during those long trips, she had always enjoyed the challenge.

Until she met Peter. That's when the trips got harder and harder to make: because suddenly there was someone to miss, someone who missed her, someone she couldn't wait to come home to.

Falling into a deep sleep now, on top of the covers, cell phone still in hand and all the lights on, Julia had no idea how long she'd been asleep before the relentless, ear-piercing buzzing woke her. Sitting up in the bed, looking at the unfamiliar furnishings and surroundings—nightstands and lamps and floral drapes and bed-spreads—she had, for an instant or two, no idea where she was or what was going on. And then she remembered:

I'm in a hotel.

In Washington, D.C.

With Mary Ford.

And the noise I'm hearing is the hotel fire alarm going off.

She jumped off the bed and raced to the door. Opening it the way she knew she shouldn't (in case of fire, she'd once read in *Reader's Digest* during an excruciatingly long layover in Denver, one should not only drop to the ground since smoke rises, but also feel the door for heat), she peeked out into the hallway.

It was empty.

No frantic panicked guests, no firemen with big boots and rubber coats, no axes and hoses.

Julia closed the door behind her and ran to the phone next to her bed and called the front desk. But the line was busy, proba-bly because everybody else in the hotel was doing exactly the same thing.

She ran back to the door and peeked out again. This time she saw a small group of middle-aged men gathered in the hallway, milling around in robes and slippers and trying to smooth down their messy hair. As Julia watched them a few took the fire stairs

down to the lobby, while the rest—clearly well-heeled businessmen who were used to having enough information to make informed decisions—were still waiting to hear whether this was
actually a fire in the building or whether it was a false alarm.

Standing in the hallway, she stared across the carpeting to
Mary's door, trying to will herself to act:

Knock on it!

Pound on it!

*Alert her to the fact that there's a possibility the hotel might soon
go up in smoke!*

But she couldn't.

Not just because she knew that knocking or pounding
wouldn't do much good since Mary obviously hadn't heard the
incredibly loud fire alarm (in addition to her two martinis, she'd
had an after-dinner brandy from the minibar), but because she
knew that more drastic action would have to be taken: she would
have to let herself into Mary's suite with the extra key Mary made
everyone who traveled with her keep in case she lost hers and
walk into her room and physically shake her, wake her in her bed.

*I'd rather have all my finger- and toenails pulled from my body
than go back into that room and touch her.*

She closed her eyes and tried to think what Jack would do
here—he'd probably be halfway to the lobby right now with his
cell phone in one hand and his Palm Pilot in the other in case
there really was a fire and he had to switch hotels in the middle
of the night—but because she'd spent seventeen straight hours
with Mary and had been awoken so suddenly out of a dreamless,
druglike sleep, all she could see was this: Jack dressed in pleated
knickers and a vest, jumping nimbly and quickly over a candle-
stick on his desk.

Julia ran back into her room and called the one person in the world who would not only know what to do in a situation like this, but who would also still be awake this late at night.

"There's only one right answer," Patricia said, her voice full of absolute clarity and certainty. Patricia loved nothing more than being the picture of calm and the voice of reason when everyone else was frantic. And she also loved nothing more than saving Julia from imminent failure.

"Which is?"

"Make damn sure there's a fire first before you wake the beast."

"You're sure?"

"Of course I'm sure."

"Why?"

"Because chances are it's just a false alarm."

"But what if it's not a false alarm? What if it's a real fire and I get out and she doesn't?"

Julia could just see the headlines: LEGENDARY FILM ACTRESS MARY FORD DIES IN HOTEL FIRE, PUBLICIST SAVES SELF.

"You're panicking," Patricia said with annoying calmness. "Why are you panicking?"

"It's been a long day."

"A bad day?"

"An unbelievably shitty day."

"What happened?"

Julia knew if she stayed on the phone Patricia would get it out of her that she'd thrown up on the plane, and Julia just couldn't bear to share that right now. Besides, she could barely hear herself think with the incessant noise of the fire alarm. So instead of answering she told Patricia only that she was going down to the lobby and that she would call her from there.

Closing her door behind her, Julia—in her exceedingly comfortable but extremely unflattering white pajamas, with their

drawstring waist and wide legs and flood-level cropped length—
raced down the hallway and into the stairwell along with all the
be-robed and be-slippered businessmen to find out from the
front desk whether or not the hotel was on fire.

Which, of course, it wasn't.

News that Patricia couldn't help responding to when Julia
called her from the lobby with her usual: "I told you so."

Patricia called Julia several times the next day while Julia and
Mary were in Atlanta to check up on her and see how things were
going, but Julia didn't have the time or the psychic energy to describe her daily horrors. Instead, when she landed at LaGuardia
the following morning, she called Peter from the back of the limousine.

"Nu?" he said. "Where are you?"

"I just dropped Mary Ford off at the Ansonia and now I'm on
my way back to the office to debrief Jack DeWack and pick up a
bunch of shit that Jonathan's been working on while I've been
away."

"Did you get the photo?"

Though she was feeling slightly carsick from the limousine
ride, she smiled. She still didn't understand how those picture
phones worked and she didn't care. All she knew is that she'd
barely be surviving without it.

"He's cute, isn't he?" Peter asked, and the image of Leo on the
toilet with a big grin and a thumbs-up popped into her head.

"Please," she said. "He's too much."

"So how was Atlanta?"

Before she could tell him about Atlanta, she had to tell him
about the fire alarm going off in Washington and how Mary had

greeted Julia in the morning with an eye-roll and finger-wagging for not waking her ("So, Einstein, were you just going to let me burn?"), having found out about the incident from the room service waiter who'd served her breakfast; how angry Mary was when there was no escort waiting for them curbside at National Airport despite Julia's repeated frantic calls to American Airlines all morning ("You tell Jack to change our flights. I'm not flying American for the rest of this trip"), but how quickly she recovered when she saw that there was a proper first-class section ("Finally, a little service") and when both male flight attendants instantly recognized her ("The gays have always loved me, don't ask me why") and asked for autographs ("Hold off on that call to Jack. American is quickly redeeming itself"), becoming so expansive and almost human that she actually took Julia's hand during takeoff and held it until the plane had leveled off somewhere over West Virginia; and how, by the grace of God, there was a uniformed security person waiting for them when they landed in Atlanta who drove them on a giant golf cart–like vehicle through the airport to baggage claim and then to the limousine.

Then she told Peter how, upon checking into the hotel, Mary was pleased to see that it was the "good Ritz-Carlton" (as if there ever could be such a thing as a bad Ritz-Carlton) in the Buckhead section of Atlanta, the one that was close to all the good shopping and which contained the only five-star restaurant in the entire city (if not in the entire state of Georgia), and how despite the newspaper's cancellation, the five o'clock news television interview for the local NBC affiliate had gone so well (the producer on duty that afternoon had been well into her fifties, which meant, unlike most of the teenagers working at television and radio stations these days, she knew who Mary was) that Mary had barely registered, or at least not mentioned, the fact that there were at least fifty fewer people at that evening's Macy's signing (not even two hundred and fifty) than there had been the night before at the suburban Washington Nordstrom.

But what Julia didn't have time to tell him about until she got home was her late-night dinner with Mary Ford at the Ritz-Carlton's restaurant. On the way, Mary had once again taken Julia's hand and held it as they walked through the hotel lobby and into the dining room until they were shown to a black leather corner booth in the middle of the restaurant.

An immediate flurry of giddy activity ensued—six waiters, all of them male, approached the table, delivering enormous leather menus with gold tassels hanging from their spines, taking their drink orders and racing back to the table with Mary's vodka martini and Julia's club soda with lime. Mary leaned back in the booth and let out a contented sigh.

"Finally a civilized moment," she said, clearly pleased by the waiters' attention, the muffled whispers of several tables of late-night diners, and the instant effects of the vodka and vermouth.

"You must be exhausted," Julia said. She was exhausted, and she was thirty-five years younger than Mary.

Mary brought her drink to her mouth, her lips pursed with such movie-star poise that it looked as if she were about to kiss the glass.

"I am exhausted. But I like feeling exhausted. Feeling exhausted means I'm busy, and being busy means I'm still alive. The minute you stop in this business, they think you're dead. And I may be old but I'm not dead—yet."

Julia smiled politely and Mary sighed again, slightly annoyed. Mary divided people into two categories—chatterboxes and clams—and Julia knew she'd pegged her as a clam the minute they met.

"So, Einstein. Tell me about yourself."

Julia took a long, slow sip of her club soda to buy herself time. It was always unwise for publicists to talk about themselves, even when invited to do so.

Mary rolled her eyes. "You're just like my daughter, Lindsay. She never tells me anything. I bet your mother says the same thing about you, too. Am I right?"

"That's the least of what she says about me."

Julia grinned and thought about her mother then, and her father, wondered what Leo had done with them that day after school; if they'd done puzzles or watched videos, and what her mother had made him to eat—fish sticks or macaroni and cheese or pasta with butter. Leo didn't know enough to question her cooking—to him it was just Bubbe's food, prepared and served between kisses and hugs, and whatever it may have lacked in taste or eye appeal was made up for with love and caring. His blissful ignorance and her parents' unconditional helpfulness during this transition made her feel like a shitty little ingrate for all the times she'd looked her mother's gift chickens in the mouth and refused to eat them. She swore when the trip was over and she got home she'd stop complaining about the food and eat it and make a big deal about pretending to like it.

Mary looked as if she had suddenly been transported back to the trenches of motherhood. "From the time she was a little girl I couldn't get anything out of her. 'What did you do today, Lindsay?' I would ask. 'Nothing,' she would say. 'Where are you going?' 'Nowhere.' 'Who are you going out with?' 'Nobody.'" She picked the olive out of her glass and held it between her fingers for a second or two before popping it into her mouth.

"Daughters are impossible," she said, still chewing. "I should know, since I was an impossible one myself. Which is why I'm lucky I also have a son. Bruce. Boys are much more forgiving of their mothers than girls."

Julia remembered what Jack had told her that first day in his office about how neither of Mary Ford's children spoke to her, and she wondered now if he'd been misinformed—at least about Mary's son.

"At least he doesn't give interviews on *Inside Edition* and *Access Hollywood* about what a terrible mother I was. Or pose nude for *Playboy*." She shook her head. "A *vilda chaya*, my daughter."

Julia smiled.

"You know what that means?" Mary said, her eyebrow raised.

"An animal."

"A wild animal," she corrected.

Mary leaned back in the booth, fingered the enormous but exquisitely simple diamond studs in her ears, and nodded at Julia with her chin. Despite the fact that she clearly got a charge out of Julia's understanding her Yiddish reference, Julia could tell that talking about her daughter was upsetting.

"Tell me about your husband, Einstein."

"Well," Julia said slowly. "He's unemployed."

Mary raised her eyebrow again. "I ask you to tell me what your husband is like and you tell me he's unemployed? Sounds like a very happy marriage."

Julia felt her cheeks go hot with shock and embarrassment. "I don't know why I said that," she whispered to herself, shaking her head.

"Yes, you do."

Julia stared at Mary.

"Because you're angry."

"No, I'm not."

"Of course you are. Peter Peter Pumpkin Eater was supposed to support you and now he's not. I don't care what anyone says these days about how it doesn't matter who earns the money. It does matter. It always has and it always will." She picked her drink up and took another long sip. "That's why my first marriage ended. Because I was making more money."

Julia shook her head. Mary was getting it all wrong: Peter had been laid off! He'd been looking and looking for another job but he hadn't been able to find one! Not to mention the fact that he was taking care of The Scoob and the house while she was gone, which, she knew from personal experience, really *was* work! But Mary didn't seem interested in her explanations.

"How old is your little boy?"

"Three and a half." Julia smiled. She was just about to add that three and a half was such a great age—the talking, the independence, the blossoming of an actual person with likes (white food) and dislikes (fruits and vegetables), hopes (toys and presents) and dreams (trains, trains, and more trains). But she realized she'd thought that about every stage of Leo's life—when he was a newborn, throughout his infancy, from formula to milk and from bottles with plastic nipples to sippy cups, from a crib to a bed, and from diapers to Pull-Ups to Bob the Builder underwear— and she was afraid that Mary would say something to quash her innocent joy the way most parents of grown children often did.

"What's his name?"

"Leo."

"Leo the Lion," Mary said. "An August baby."

"Actually, he was born in April."

"Then why Leo?"

Julia was momentarily surprised by the question and didn't

quite know what to say. No one who didn't know her or her family well had ever asked her that question before so she'd never had to come up with an answer.

"I had a brother." Julia paused, unsure of how to continue. "I mean, I would have had a brother. He died when I was four. His name was Leo."

Julia barely remembered her brother—he'd died when he was seven from a blood disease that no one had ever heard of and that she could barely pronounce—but she'd felt his presence all her life in the form of his absence from her parents' lives. It was as if a big black hole was blown out of them, a big black hole that was wide and deep and endless and that could never be filled, no matter what she did or how hard she tried to make them happy. There were just their whispered questions once a year, but every year, on his birthday—*He would have been ten now; what would he have looked like? He would have been twenty; who would he have become?* It wasn't her black hole of loss and grief but she'd lived in it nonetheless, growing up inside the lonely rooms of their quiet house with an aching desire to please—which was probably why she loved being a mother so much and why she'd ended up doing what she was doing for work: trying to satisfy people who could never be satisfied.

"From the look on your face it's clear that Leo is the light of your life."

Julia smiled even wider.

"So show me a picture already."

Julia fished through her big black bag and pulled out her picture phone. Scrolling through the pictures, she finally found one of her favorites: Leo in red plaid pajamas from The Gap, sitting at his little table in the kitchen with his fork raised and his cheeks full of pancakes.

She thought of the morning Peter had taken the picture. It was the Sunday before she'd left on her trip, and her parents had come over for brunch. This was the only way Julia felt she had ever even come close to giving her parents some semblance of true joy—having Leo and moving back to Larchmont after he was born—and she knew from what her mother had tried to express on the phone the previous week and the way they showered Leo with the kind of unconditional unchecked love and affection that they'd never been able to show her that whatever had died in both of them all those years ago had come back.

Mary took her smart-looking rectangular black half-glasses out of her purse and put them on. She looked at the photograph of Leo and then at Julia.

"That's some nose on him," she said, her eyes lingering on Julia's nose for several uncomfortable seconds before she finally reached for one of the huge leather menus on the side of the table.

Julia snatched the phone back and threw it into her bag.

No wonder Mary's children didn't talk to her.

She was a *chaya*. A *vilda chaya*.

Mary, who had disappeared behind the gigantic Ritz-Carlton menu, finally came out from behind it and took her glasses off.

"I wonder if they have a veal chop."

Julia, still enraged by the remark about Leo's nose, couldn't have cared less. But out of a sense of professional duty she glanced quickly down the list of "Steaks and Chops" on her own menu. She didn't see one listed. Not that it mattered, of course. Ordering off the menu—a mainstay of entitled-celebrity behavior— was just one of the many things publicists were required to endure.

Mary jutted out her chin to signal to the all-male waitstaff that she was ready to order, and when two of them—both in their mid-fifties and neither of them French—arrived at the table, pens and pads poised, Mary's eyes sparkled. She loved nothing more than being waited on. Literally.

"You've got two ravenous women here," Mary said with charm and just a touch of sass, "one of whom needs an answer to a very important question."

Hunched slightly, pens and pads at the ready, they nodded eagerly in unison at her inquiry about the availability of a veal chop.

"Yes, I'm sure we can accommodate you, Miss Ford," the first said.

To which the other added: "We will check for you."

Mary thanked them, then asked for a wine recommendation, then ordered a glass of the California merlot the first waiter had suggested. Sipping her wine while waiting for an answer to her question, Mary turned the conversation back to the topic she and Julia had most in common.

"Jack Be Nimble called me this morning. He wanted to know how things were going."

Grateful to be distracted from the still-painful wound of Mary's comment about Leo's nose, Julia was instantly annoyed at the fact that Jack had gone around her and was calling Mary directly.

"I told him it was going as well as could be expected. Given the circumstances. That he's an idiot."

And that Mary was a Borderline Personality.

"When I signed on with John Glom Public Relations, I thought I was getting Glom himself," Mary continued. "Glom and I go way back. He knew my first husband. That's how old Glom is. But then Glom fobbed me off on Jack. Who advised me to go on QVC and sell a line of face cream like Victoria Principal or Tova Borgnine, God forbid. Or a line of exercise and diet products like that idiot Suzanne Somers."

Not knowing which one of them to believe—Jack had blamed the whole QVC idea on Mary and now she was blaming it on him!—Julia thought it safest to say nothing and just allow Mary to continue.

"I was the one who came up with the idea of a perfume. I was the one who said we should model it on Elizabeth Taylor's perfume." She took a sip of wine and shook her head with obvious disapproval. "Liz Taylor. Who still thinks she's Cleopatra on a hot tin roof. But what she's doing up there with that crazy Michael Jackson I'll never know."

Julia folded the red straw from her drink in half. She was starting to get nervous that the waiters weren't returning fast enough for Mary with a verdict about the veal chop. But just as she turned her head to see where they were, they reappeared.

"Yes, Miss Ford," the first waiter said, beaming with pride and bowing slightly. "I have just talked to the chef and he tells me that there is a veal chop in the house."

Mary smiled and gave him something Julia knew he would never forget—a that's-my-boy wink—then threw her head back. "Fabulous," she purred.

"Yes," the second waiter added. "We are in luck."

"*In luck*?" Mary's smile faded and she looked at him dubiously. Julia could tell something about the flippancy of the word *luck* in relation to food quality had unnerved her.

"Yes," he repeated, again beaming with pride. "We have a veal chop for you."

She made a face. "Is it fresh?"

The waiter beamed. "Of course it is fresh."

"How fresh?"

He bowed his head again, closing his eyes briefly, as if the topic of the freshness of food was sacrosanct. "*Very* fresh."

Mary seemed unconvinced. She looked at the second waiter. "What do you think?"

"We will check again for you."

Mary rolled her eyes as the two raced back toward the swinging kitchen doors like the obedient terrorized flying monkeys from *The Wizard of Oz*. Only this time they returned almost instantly.

"The chef tells me the veal chop is very fresh," the first waiter said.

The second waiter paused, hesitating slightly. "He says it is fresh."

Mary Ford turned herself in the booth to face the waiters head-on. "Well, which is it?" She looked from one waiter to the other. "Frick here," she said, pointing at the first waiter with her thumb, "says it's very fresh. And then Frack here," she pointed with her other thumb, "tells me it's just fresh."

"The chef told me the veal chop was just delivered this morning," Frick said, sticking to his story.

Frack again looked at Mary and hesitated slightly. Clearly he was going to stick to his, too. "The chef told me it's possible the veal chop was delivered a day, maybe two days, ago. Which would still make it quite fresh."

"Fresh. Very fresh. Quite fresh." Mary rolled her eyes at Julia and then up at them. "You two should get your stories straight since obviously one of you is lying."

Julia cringed with discomfort as the two waiters, having been duly shamed, flew back to the kitchen for the third time while several tables of diners stared. But this time when they returned—with the chef—carrying the raw veal chop in question on a platter for Mary's approval, Julia wished she could have crawled under the table and out of the restaurant.

Mary put her glasses on as Frick and Frack lowered the platter in front of her, but seeing it only seemed to annoy her more.

"Well, I don't know what I'm looking at. I'm not a goddamned butcher." She took her glasses off, sighed loudly, and looked up at the chef with his white jacket and toque. "If you say it's fresh, I guess I'll have to take your word for it. What choice do I have?"

The chef clasped his hands in front of him.

"You could select something else from our very full menu of options," he said in a heavy accent.

Knowing she had annoyed and offended him and knowing it was time to make a decision already, she told him finally, as if she were doing him a great favor, that she'd take the veal chop after all.

"Make sure it's well done," she said, and as the three left, she stage-whispered to Julia:

"French men. Such big egos."

When they finally finished their dinner—Mary cleaning her plate and ordering a slice of key lime pie and coffee for dessert, then taking out her Claus Von Bülow bag and poking between her teeth; Julia barely making a dent in the green salad and— what else?—grilled salmon, which on any other night she would have devoured in minutes but which now, on her third full day of travel, she barely had an appetite for, given all the adrenaline coursing through her body from all the stress she was dealing with—Julia signed the check to her room and the two of them slid out of the black leather booth. As they got off the elevator and walked slowly down the long carpeted hallway toward their rooms, Mary slowed down.

"The fragrance Legend was supposed to have faithfully reproduced was given to me by my father, you know. He took me to Paris when I was nineteen to show me where he'd been born, and while we were there he brought me to an old friend of his family's, a very famous perfumer."

They continued toward their rooms, but Mary's pace slowed even more, either from fatigue or by design: Julia could tell she wanted to have time to finish her story.

"My father was terribly attractive. A real ladies' man. He made my mother's life miserable but I adored him." She paused a moment to suck at her teeth. "You know what he did for a living?"

Julia shook her head.

"He sold hairbrushes. Door to door."

A few seconds passed in silence before Mary turned to Julia.

"What about your parents?"

After what Mary had said about Leo's nose, Julia didn't want to answer any more personal questions, but it was late and they were all alone and there seemed to be no getting around it.

"They're retired now," she said protectively, "but my father was an accountant and my mother taught elementary school."

"So you're like me. From humble beginnings. But ambitious."

Julia was surprised that Mary thought of her as ambitious. She'd never thought of herself that way, but maybe she had been, once, a long time ago, before she'd quit her job.

Mary slowed down on the final approach to their rooms.

"Coco Chanel said that a woman should wear perfume whenever she expects to be kissed," Mary said. "And Heinrich Heine wrote that perfumes are the feelings of flowers. I may never be kissed again but I still wear perfume. And I still have feelings."

They stopped in front of Mary's door and she put her hand on Julia's arm and tugged lightly on her suit jacket.

"Come in with me for a few minutes, Einstein," she said, slipping her plastic key into the slot and opening her door. "You can help me decide what to have for breakfast and we can see if that idiot lets whatever idiot he has on get a word in edgewise this time."

—*17*—

Back at work the next morning, Julia found Jack talking on the phone. When he looked up at her in his doorway and didn't say anything or motion for her to come in, Julia felt the urge to give him the finger, but instead she continued down the hall toward Jonathan, who waved from his cubicle and followed her to her desk. The two of them barely fit in her tiny office.

"Welcome back!" He put a giant Starbucks cup down on her desk. "I thought you'd need this."

Julia stared at the coffee and then at Jonathan. "I could kiss you."

Jonathan took a step back, laughed, then mimed drawing a line: *"Boundaries!"*

She laughed, too, and when she did she realized it was the first time she'd cracked a smile in days. "You're very thoughtful."

He shrugged. "It's no big deal."

"Yes, it is. It's a very big deal. And not just because this stupid cup of coffee is about a quarter of your weekly salary." She reached into her briefcase to give Jonathan the souvenirs she had brought back for him. "Here," she said, handing him a snow globe with the U.S. Capitol inside that she'd picked up for him in the gift shop of the Hay-Adams when she was buying matching Washington Wizards basketball shirts for Peter and Leo. And then, because she still couldn't get over his thoughtfulness, she gave him the assortment of soaps and shampoos and shower caps that she'd swiped from both hotels and that she'd planned on keeping for herself. "I thought you'd get a kick out of these." She'd slip a ten-dollar bill into his big black messenger bag later.

His face, already full of delight at the kitschy retro coolness of the snow globe, now registered shock at the sight of all the free miniature sample-size toiletries.

"Wow," he whispered, with unironic reverence. "These are so cool. And I really need shampoo."

Julia remembered suddenly what it was like trying to make ends meet on an assistant's salary; what relief she used to feel when she didn't have to pay for lunch because someone older with their own office was putting it on their expense account; how getting free tickets to a movie screening felt like winning the lottery.

Just as Jonathan sat down and she started to tell him about the trip, Jack intercommed her. She rolled her eyes at Jonathan, picked up her coffee and dragged herself down the hall.

"We have a situation," Jack said when she got to his office.

Julia sat down in one of his guest chairs. "Now what did I do?"

"You didn't do anything."

"Because it's not my fault Legend isn't moving."

Jack shook his head. "It's Mary's daughter, Lindsay. The one in L.A. The actress slash writer slash activist-without-a-cause."

"What about her?"

"Well, she found a cause. Or a cause found her. Animal rights. PETA."

"So? What does that have to do with Legend?"

"It has everything to do with Legend. PETA is preparing to release a statement that names Heaven Scent Cosmetics as one of the top five violators of the Animal Welfare Act (AWA), the federal law that governs the humane care, handling, treatment, and transportation of animals used in laboratories. And Lindsay Green, Mary Ford's daughter, is spearheading this effort, using her mother's new fragrance as the main focus of the campaign."

"Shit." Julia sat back in her chair. A montage of news clips played in her head of rabid animal activists attacking women wearing fur coats with cans of red spray paint and tofu pies. The last thing she needed was for Leo and Peter and her parents to see her and Mary covered in whipped cream or covering their heads like convicts on *Entertainment Tonight* or in *People* magazine, escaping some disastrous in-store signing.

"By tonight the broadcast media will have the story—*Entertainment Tonight, Access Hollywood, Inside Edition.* By tomorrow the print media and the morning shows will have it. Perfect timing."

"Shit." All she wanted was to get home early and start the weekend; now she felt like she'd never get there. She uncapped her pen and flipped to a clean page on her pad, then took a long sip of coffee.

"So Heaven Scent still does product testing on animals?" she asked.

"Apparently."

"But most of the big cosmetics companies have stopped testing on animals exactly because of this sort of public relations pressure and fear of being 'outed.'"

"So?"

"So—I suppose we should have known that," she said.

"I suppose we should have," Jack said sharply, hating, Julia knew, to be blindsided this way. "And I remember telling both of your predecessors to look into that very question when we first embarked on this project. But they were never very good at follow-through."

Julia thought it was strange that Jack wouldn't have known about Heaven Scent before signing on with them—judging from how prepared he had been for the David Cassidy meeting, she couldn't imagine that he wouldn't have found out everything there was to know about them before helping to approve a deal on Mary's behalf—but there was no time to waste wondering why. Jack was standing up at his desk and flipping pages and opening up file folders, and she could tell by the way he pulled up his pants by the belt and readjusted himself (which he did all the time and which she hated) that a list of bulleted orders was about to come out of his mouth.

The first thing Jack told her to do was find Mary Ford's son, Bruce—a pediatrician with a practice in Manhattan and a clinic in the Bronx. Handing her the phone numbers for both offices, he told her to try to convince him to talk to the press, preferably on camera, to defend his mother and counteract the negative publicity this loose cannon of a half sister of his was generating.

But when she finally did locate him at his Manhattan office and managed to get him to call her back, he politely declined to involve himself in what he called "the unseemly public battle of wills my mother and sister have always insisted on engaging in."

Without being able to offer up Mary Ford's son to the media, Julia knew she had to try to talk PETA out of whatever public protests and publicity stunts they were planning. This was, she knew, an incredible and ridiculous long shot, given the fact that the PETA people were known to be zealots, but she thought she had to at least try. But after two hours of talking with the public affairs office of PETA and with the Olsen twins and Heaven Scent's in-house counsel, Julia was shocked to go back to Jack's office having negotiated what appeared to be a temporary truce:

"If Mary agrees to film a public service announcement for PETA decrying the use of animals in cosmetics testing and if we agree to pull the print ad of Mary wearing the sheared beaver coat, PETA will scale back their attempts to completely disrupt her public appearances and allow the promotional efforts and store appearances for Legend to continue."

Jack's mouth fell open.

"You did what?"

Julia repeated herself even though she knew he had heard her the first time. "Of course, there's nothing we can do about the initial wave of negative publicity this will generate—like you said, all the entertainment shows already have the story and are planning on running it—complete with sit-down interviews with Lindsay and B-roll footage of Mary Ford from her old films—over the next few days. But we're heading into a weekend, which is good, since that'll slow down the news cycle and take the wind out of the story by next week."

"Whose idea was the PSA?"

"Mine."

"Whose idea was it to scale back the protests?"

Wasn't it obvious?

"Uhm, mine."

"I wish you'd checked with me on that first."

Now her mouth fell open. "Why?"

"Because just like the United States, I don't believe in negoti-ating with terrorists."

Julia couldn't help but laugh out loud.

"Jack. I just convinced the fiercest and most fanatical animal protection group in the world to put the pin back in their grenade and you wish I'd checked with you first? Why? To make sure they spelled your name right on the press release?"

"You don't understand."

"No. I guess I don't." She shrugged dramatically—her arms going up into the air and then noisily falling back down to her sides.

"Look, Julia. This is the deal. The Legend campaign is—and was always going to be—a complete disaster. Which is why in order to fulfill the contractual obligation of our original mis-sion—to create a successful comeback for Mary Ford—we needed to figure out a way to use Legend as a point of depar-ture—as a means, not an end."

She finally got it. "You knew about Heaven Scent. That they still did animal testing."

He nodded.

"And you leaked it to PETA."

Jack shrugged with false modesty.

"And to Mary's daughter," she finished. She blinked while she tried to fit the pieces together and comprehend the big picture. " 'Separate the celebrity from the product.' That's what you said."

He smiled, deeply gratified. Clearly there were few greater pleasures for Jack DeWack than having his own words quoted back to him.

"So that's where it was going to end?" Julia asked, even though she didn't have to. "That was your solution to the Mary Ford problem? To have negative publicity around Heaven Scent serve as the engine for her comeback?"

Jack smirked. "I don't think there was much more of a comeback in the cards for her. It was clear from the dismal sell-in of the perfume that her fan base was limited at best. That's why I brought PETA and Mary's daughter together—the publicity generated by the protests would have deflected attention away from the shitty perfume we couldn't get out of producing and marketing while simultaneously directing attention toward Mary herself."

"But the attention directed toward Mary would be negative attention. Negative attention of the worst kind. A has-been in favor of animal cruelty. A daughter publicly attacking a mother and sabotaging her. How could that possibly have a positive outcome?"

Jack shrugged. "There's always the sympathy factor. The public loves an underdog. The politics of the issue would have evaporated quickly and then people would have felt sorry for Mary, getting blindsided by her daughter, whose sole purpose for embarrassing her mother was to get attention for herself."

Julia couldn't help but see—and even admire—the clever logic of his plan, but she had trouble accepting the abject cynicism of it.

"What about Mary? When are we going to tell her and *what* are we going to tell her?"

"I'll call her before I leave the office tonight and tell her what's coming. But I'm not going to tell her that I orchestrated it." Julia could swear she sensed just the faintest twinge of disappointment in Jack that the bones of what she was sure he considered to be one of his most brilliantly manipulative scams ever would be buried in the client-relations graveyard.

"What if she finds out? Wouldn't it be better if she found out from you than from her daughter or some *Entertainment Tonight* producer?"

"Lindsay's not going to tell her."

"How can you be so sure?"

"Because that was part of the deal. She'd get exposure—and the opportunity to attach herself to a politically-correct cause—in exchange for doing us this little favor."

Julia couldn't help but bristle at the sound of her complicity in the matter.

"It's like I told you when you first interviewed for the job," Jack said, reaching for the phone, which was her cue, she knew, to leave. "There are times when a has-been isn't meant to come back. And this is one of those times."

But it wasn't one of those times for Julia.

The minute she got home for the weekend, she ran up the walk, into the house, and hunted down The Scoob, hugging him for as long as he would let her, which was longer than she expected but not as long as she wanted. Changing into her favorite pants, which felt a little looser, sitting down to dinner (Greek salads with grilled chicken on top from the take-out place around the corner), and then finally, at the end of the night, sleeping in her own bed next to Peter and The Scoob (she knew she wasn't supposed to let him sleep in their bed but after four nights away from him she didn't give a shit what all the books said), she knew how good a comeback could feel.

— 18 —

Patricia was coming over for dinner on Saturday night, and whenever Patricia came out to Larchmont on a weekend night she slept over. In her mind, Larchmont was "the country," and because it was "the country" she thought it didn't make sense to travel that far for anything less than an overnight.

"Sorry I'm late," she said when Julia picked her up at the train just after six. "But a Thermage appointment opened up at the last minute and I figured I'd squeeze it in."

"What's Thermage?" Julia asked, reaching for one of Patricia's three overnight bags.

"It's the latest advance in nonsurgical wrinkle management and prevention."

"You sound like a press release."

"I am a press release. Thermage is a client."

Julia put Patricia's luggage and a shopping bag full of presents for Leo into the trunk of the Volvo. "What do you need with wrinkle management and prevention? You don't have any wrinkles."

"But I will."

"But you don't yet."

"But I would if I didn't do things like this."

"But you're only thirty-six."

"So are you."

"I know."

"So what's your point?" Patricia said with her low-slung tight jeans, her expertly highlighted blond hair, and her trademark firm ass that seemed to be defying science by becoming firmer as Patricia got older.

"That you're too young for wrinkles."

Patricia laughed and slid into the car. "The only one who's too young for wrinkles is my Scoob. Now take me to him."

They left the parking lot and made a quick stop at the supermarket to pick up a few last-minute items Peter needed for dinner. He was preparing an incredibly complicated sounding four-cheese vegetable lasagna (having deviated from his original intention of making an incredibly complicated sounding three-meat lasagna after remembering that Patricia didn't eat meat) from *Cook's Illustrated*—a magazine so infinitely detailed and complex and with so many directions and ingredients and diagrams it was the perfect match for Peter's obsessive-compulsive love of order and perfection. Then they stopped at the local Blockbuster Video to get a movie to watch after dinner.

Julia and Patricia traced the outer perimeter of the store, looking from floor to ceiling at all the new releases—most of which, at almost seven p.m. on a Saturday night, had already been taken out. But after coming to the end of the line and being unable to agree on a single thing to rent—Patricia had seen everything, Julia had seen nothing—Patricia suggested they rent some of Mary Ford's old movies.

"Do we have to?" Julia said. She wanted to forget about Mary Ford, not host a Mary Ford Film Retrospective in her living room.

"Yes."

"Why?"

"Because that's what you do when you're a big-time publicist. You show off your client to anyone who will listen."

By the time they got home, the house was filled with the smells of Peter's dinner. Leo was in his favorite pajamas—the ones with the moons and planets from The Gap that were way too small for him with rips in both knees that neither Peter nor Julia had been able to talk him out of—and when he saw Patricia and she saw him, both their faces instantly lit up. Watching Patricia lift him into her arms, Julia couldn't help registering her taut biceps and triceps and her shocking lack of underarm flab and wondered what, if anything, Thermage could do for other parts of the body besides one's face.

After a long hug, Patricia finally gave Leo the bag of presents she'd brought for him: a faux-leather bomber jacket from a French children's clothing store on Madison, two Bob the Builder videos, and the Thomas the Tank Engine battery-operated Carousel and Zoo Animals set. Overwhelmed and overjoyed, he disappeared into the living room, where he remained amazingly quiet and distracted for the next hour during the last part of Peter's dinner preparations.

"I thought you always said he couldn't cook," Patricia said, clearly impressed, when Peter at long last brought the picture-perfect lasagna and salad and basket of garlic bread to the table before disappearing again into the kitchen.

"He didn't. Until I went back to work. At first he seemed to be doing it out of necessity but now he's really into it. It's like Martha Stewart moved in. Not that I'm complaining, of course."

Patricia's eyebrow went up. "Yes, you are."

"No, I'm not."

"Yes, you are. You're thinking he should get a job already—a *real* job."

"This *is* a *real job*. Being home, taking care of a child. I mean, I should know. I did it for almost four years." Julia rolled her eyes and laughed a little too loud.

"Hey, I don't blame you," Patricia said. "I'd probably be thinking the same thing if I were married and my husband was starting to like being home a little too much. Although I must say—" she paused long enough to look around at the neat and well-organized room and smell the food, "I think I could get used to this."

Julia nodded. So could she.

"Then what's the problem?" Patricia pressed.

"There is no problem."

"But?"

"But yes," Julia finally conceded. "I'm thinking he should get a real job already."

"Any leads?"

She shrugged. "I don't know."

"You don't talk about it?"

"Not anymore."

Julia had assumed Peter stopped talking about his visits to the executive placement office because things had been so hectic with her travel schedule, but now she wondered if he was losing interest in his hunt for gainful employment. He certainly had his hands full with Leo and Batman and coffee after drop-off with the preschool moms. Not to mention all the cooking and shopping and household chores, which, now that she thought about it, she didn't miss at all, and which he was far better at than she ever was.

Case in point: the architectural-baking project that was now well under way. The house had reeked of gingerbread when she'd come home on Friday, and when she'd opened the refrigerator there were all the pieces baked and carefully wrapped and waiting to be assembled. All the obscure black licorice candies had been located and purchased and even the family schedule flow-chart had been updated to include his scheduled timetable of progress, with turquoise squares labeled *Gingerbread* in heavy concentration all week. By Saturday morning the house was glued together, and by the time she'd done her errands in the afternoon and come back from the train station and video selection process with Patricia, the roof was covered with rows of black licorice discs and the shutters cut from grape Fruit Roll-Ups were hung.

Not exactly the project-from-hell she'd experienced.

She wanted to explain to Patricia that there was a difference between not missing the housework and all the labor involved with being home with The Scoob and missing being home with The Scoob himself, but it was too hard.

Or maybe she just couldn't explain it to herself.

Peter had a cold bottle of white wine in one hand and the digital camera in the other when he came back to the dining room. Patricia, thinking he was going to take a snapshot of her and Julia, leaned across the table and posed, smiling.

He looked confused. "Oh. Okay," he said finally, as if suddenly understanding the misunderstanding. "Let me just get a few shots of the food and then I'll take one of the two of you."

If the food hadn't looked and smelled so spectacularly good, Patricia probably would have made merciless fun of Peter for taking pictures of the food, but once she tasted the lasagna and the salad and the bread, she was silenced. By the time dessert arrived—in the form of a chocolate layer cake with mocha butter cream frosting that Peter had made using another incredibly complicated recipe from *Cook's Illustrated*—Patricia herself picked up the camera and took the pictures. Already impressed by Peter's startling range of domestic abilities (his cooking, his reorganization and reconfiguration and creation of "new and improved household flow" he'd described during dinner, and the chart with all the colored blocks of time she had seen in the kitchen), Patricia was about to be even more impressed when Julia, who had gotten up from the table sometime after nine to put Leo to bed, returned to the dining room, Scoob-less.

"He wants you," she said to Peter, forcing a smile. Then she turned to Patricia and continued to smile as if her life depended on it—which, given her fragile working-mother's ego right now, it kind of did. "He usually wants me to put him to bed. But I guess since I've been away, he's gotten attached to Peter."

Peter tried to contain himself but he couldn't help grinning. "We've started doing this new thing," he said. "It's called 'Making a Sandwich.'" He stood up at the table, wiped his mouth, and took one last bite of cake and swig of coffee. "After I read to him, we get the long body pillow from our room and I roll him up in it."

"Since when does he know what a *wrap* is?" Julia said, incredulous, as if he couldn't possibly have changed that much to have learned about wrap sandwiches in the short time she'd been working.

"He doesn't know what a wrap sandwich is," he said, putting

his arm around Julia and kissing her in an attempt to be reassuring. "He just calls it a sandwich because he's inside the pillow."

Peter told them to leave the dishes and start the movie without him since it might be a while, so Julia went into the living room with the Blockbuster bag and got very busy with the videotape boxes in an attempt to hide her devastation from Patricia. But it didn't work.

"I don't get it. Aren't you relieved?" Patricia said, settling onto the couch with her wine and helping Julia with one of the video boxes. "I mean, it gives you a break, a little time to relax."

Julia glanced up at the ceiling above the living room and tried to ignore the peals of laughter coming from Leo's bedroom.

"Especially after the week you had with the whole white limousine debacle and the hotel fire alarm."

And she didn't even know the half of it. Within minutes Julia filled her in on everything except that first fateful plane ride— the veal chop incident, the PETA situation, and the solution she'd come up with which Jack had told her only made matters worse for the already doomed Legend product launch.

"This Lindsay Green sounds like a real piece of work," Patricia said.

"Like mother, like daughter. Do you know anything about her?"

Patricia shrugged. "Not much. Just that the two of them never got along because Mary always put herself and her career first. And that like every child whose parents ignored them growing up, Lindsay Green will probably spend the rest of her adult life trying to get her mother's attention."

Julia was reminded of what Jonathan had said before she'd gone home the previous night—that for people like Mary's daughter, even negative attention is better than no attention.

"They're that desperate," he'd said.

Julia couldn't imagine being *that* desperate (assuming desperation was even quantifiable) for attention. But as the laughter upstairs died down and she imagined Peter snuggling with Leo, squished against the protective side guard rails, she was suddenly able to imagine herself doing lots of ridiculous and infantile things to win Leo back.

"I think I remember her shopping around a novel some time ago," Patricia said, handing Julia a videotape to slip into the machine. "But there were no takers. Maybe if it had been nonfiction she would have had better luck."

Julia turned the lights out, settled into the other corner of the couch, and pressed the Play button on the remote to start *What I Did for Love.*

"I remember when I first saw this," Patricia whispered while the opening credits were still rolling. "I was fourteen, in ninth grade, going to boy-girl make-out parties every weekend; learning how to smoke, how to French-kiss. One night my friends and I took the train from Greenwich into Manhattan to the Thalia on the Upper West Side, where they used to show old movies. It was so romantic and she was so beautiful. We all fell as hopelessly in love with Mary Ford as we did with Ray Milland."

An ill-fated romance set in England at the end of World War II and shot entirely in black-and-white, *What I Did for Love* was a star vehicle in the most classic sense of old studio pictures. Tall, willowy, and sophisticated, with luminous skin and a voice that was subtle and melodious and deeply affecting, Mary Ford, it appeared finally, was everything she had once been cracked up to be.

Later that night, after Julia got Patricia settled in the guest room, and after she'd done the dishes, since Peter had fallen asleep with

Leo while putting him to bed, and after she ejected the video from the VCR and slid it into its box and put the box in the new mudroom area in a basket marked *Out-Going,* Julia stood in the kitchen. It was quiet, and still, and except for the sound of the dishwasher heaving its way through its cycles there wasn't a sound in the whole house. Standing alone by the sink with everyone asleep upstairs, she felt both lonely and peaceful. This had always been her favorite part of the day—when it was dark and silent and she could sit at the table for a few minutes before bed and think about things—but the last few weeks since she'd returned to work had been such a blur of activity and anxiety and exhaustion that she hadn't had a moment to call her own.

Peter's digital camera was on the table, still out of its case from dinner, and she couldn't help smiling when she thought of him coming into the dining room with the camera to take a picture of the food he had prepared and Patricia thinking he wanted to take a picture of her. She turned on the camera and started to scroll through the photos he had just taken of the lasagna and the chocolate layer cake. Scrolling back beyond that, she started looking at all the other digital pictures Peter had taken during the days she'd been at work and the week she'd been out of town—a 1950s-worthy baked macaroni and cheese casserole topped with breadcrumbs for Leo, a deep brown pot roast surrounded with carrots and potatoes and laid out on a platter, a stack of pancakes with melted butter and warm syrup dripping down the sides. Had the photos been only of food, Julia might have started to feel as if Peter were in the throes of some strange and almost pornographic food fetish—creating mouthwatering dishes, posing and arranging them in sensual tableaus, and then photographing them for future enjoyment—but in all the pictures (except for

those taken that night and the one he'd made of the chicken potpie), there was Leo, beaming with pride:

*This was Daddy's food; this was food Daddy had made for him,
for the two of them to share.*

Julia dug deeper, searching for other clues to what Peter and
Leo had been doing without her. Back in the mudroom, she
found his little backpack (which was now, of course, in a deep
metal bin marked *Backpacks*) and, on the shelf above it, a large
black box marked *Leo's Artwork*. Inside it were all the little art
projects he had done at school since she'd been gone—hand-
prints and wax paper leaves; pumpkins cut out of orange construction paper and bats cut out of black paper—and she realized
suddenly half the fall was gone and Halloween was right around
the corner and she hadn't even thought about what Leo was going
to be, what he was going to wear.

Going through the box and looking at each piece of paper he
had brought home—pieces of paper with sometimes nothing
more than a single sparkle glued to it, or a single crayon mark, or
a single sticker stuck in the center of the page, but always with his
name at the bottom, written by one of the teachers in straight
block letters—she thought about how her parents had kept her
artwork in a drawer to the left of the refrigerator, in the house
they still lived in but in the drawer that wasn't there anymore, and
how, except for an occasional drawing on the refrigerator stuck on
with a tag of shiny, gummy Scotch tape, they almost never hung
any of her pictures up the way her friends' families did—their
sons' and daughters' drawings and paintings tacked onto cabinets,
the backs of doors, bedroom and bathroom walls; houses filled
with the sounds and activity and energy of happy children.

But the house she grew up in was different. It was quiet and
she was quiet and no one knew how to have fun.

Still looking through the pile of his efforts, she remembered reading in one of the child-rearing books that instead of hanging up every single piece of a child's artwork, parents should be selective—choosing, perhaps, one piece a week to display in order to preserve the sense of specialness. Unwilling to risk being stingy with her affections or withholding of her praise—and unable to pick a single favorite—Julia decided on three—one for every week she'd been at work—and hung them on the refrigerator door with two dinosaur magnets and one brightly colored interlocking-gear magnet.

Ready, finally, to leave the kitchen and call it a night, her attention once again was drawn to Peter's giant time chart. Staring at it this time, she couldn't help feeling an urge to change a few things. Making a handful of new orange squares from the supplies left over in the utility drawer, she placed them firmly on the current weekend and on the Friday of the following week when she would be back from the next leg of the Mary Ford tour. Standing back to admire her handiwork—a pointillist abstract picture that represented what their family life was like now—she couldn't help but feel better when she saw the orange squares breaking up the large blocks of blue *Julia at work* ones:

Julia home.
Julia home.
Julia home.

While Julia was entertaining Patricia, Lindsay Green had spent the weekend bad-mouthing her mother's perfume—or, rather, the maker of her mother's perfume—on *Entertainment Tonight, Access Hollywood, Inside Edition.*

And when she wasn't doing on-camera interviews, she was apparently on eBay selling her mother's underwear.

"Jesus, Jack," Julia said when he called her at home on Sunday afternoon. "Who told you?"

"No one."

"Then how did you find out?"

"Don't ask."

Given all the bad publicity, Bloomingdale's and Macy's had canceled both of Mary Ford's appearances scheduled for the end of that coming week—in Chicago and Detroit, respectively—and Jack said he expected Bloomingdale's to cancel their appearance in Boston and Macy's to cancel theirs in Orlando as well. All the retailers knew they would have enough to deal with at their flagship stores in Manhattan—the front line for demonstrations and protests by PETA activists (the Manhattan-based national entertainment, fashion, and business media always covered local protests)—let alone having to deal with actual live appearances by Mary Ford.

All for a perfume that didn't even smell good and wasn't even selling!

The cancellations were no surprise—especially to Jack, who had hoped this would happen the minute he hatched the plan in his mind months before. But there was a weird mix of satisfaction and annoyance in his voice.

"You sound disappointed," Julia said, relieved beyond belief to have two torturous cities cut off her tour of duty.

"I am. I thought more stores would cancel by now. But so far, Boston and Orlando and the West Coast are still on."

"I'm sure if you work a little more of your evil magic, the rest of the tour will fall in like a house of cards."

"Lindsay Green came across extremely well on television," he said. "Better than I'd expected, in fact. The perfect spokesperson. Articulate. Passionate. She even wore a bra, which is more than I can say for both times I met with her."

"I wouldn't know."

"Didn't you watch?"

No, she hadn't watched. Leo never let her watch anything she wanted to watch on television because he was under the strange impression that the television was all his.

Jack was silent. She could tell he was trying to figure out where he'd gone wrong: He'd devised the perfect strategy to obfuscate a failing product launch and celebrity comeback; he'd leaked the appropriate information to the appropriate media pawns; he'd done an especially poor job of crisis management by making himself unavailable for comment all day Friday. *Why wasn't this whole farce over yet?*

"Even if the stores didn't cancel, I was sure Mary would. I didn't think she'd still go. I mean, who the hell would willingly walk into such an explosive situation?"

Why, a desperate narcissistic has-been, that's who!

"Well, hopefully it won't be that explosive since I worked out the agreement with PETA. Our quick response to their concerns about Heaven Scent's animal-testing policies scored us some points—enough to at least buy us time to avoid any immediate protests and demonstrations."

She could swear she heard Jack scratching his chin. "Still, it's not the most optimal circumstances to be trying to sell yourself to a public that's all but forgotten you." He paused. "But Mary has too much pride to let her daughter get the better of her. I didn't figure that into the equation. Spite is a powerful motivator."

"She's a tough old bird."

"One that I wouldn't mind taking a shot at if I weren't afraid of those fucking PETA people."

A brief fantasy clip of a bunch of angry protesters chasing after Jack with homemade signs and cans of red spray paint danced through her head, but when it was gone Julia found herself wondering how he had convinced Mary's daughter to betray her in the first place.

"I convinced her to work with me because I didn't position her involvement as a *betrayal.* I positioned her involvement as a way to *help* her mother—as a way to *help protect* her mother from the shame of a very public failure. It's not Mary's fault that Heaven Scent couldn't afford to produce a decent fragrance. And it's not

Mary's fault that Heaven Scent performs irritability tests on the eyes of albino rabbits."

Julia laughed out loud. "So you're telling me that Lindsay Green agreed to help you sabotage her mother's comeback vehicle because she's a nice person?"

"No. I'm telling you that Lindsay Green agreed to do this because I knew that the only thing she wants more than attention from the media and from the public is attention from her mother. And I knew that this was the perfect way for her to get it."

She'd heard enough. "Go back to looking for celebrity underwear on eBay, Jack. I'll call you from the road."

This time, when she packed for the trip, Julia knew the drill—she knew all about Mary's luggage, Mary's comfort, Mary's meals; she knew about her schedules, her interviews, her hotel rooms, her Fresca, her breakfast menu orders, her Frick and Frack paranoia, her veal chops—so she didn't even bother with her small suitcase on wheels and all the little Container Store containers and zippered pouches. It wasn't worth it—using one arm to drag her own suitcase and the other arm to carry Mary Ford's heavy Louis Vuitton makeup case while her briefcase and her laptop hung from her shoulder. She'd worn the same black suit all three days because she barely had a minute to pee and brush her teeth, let alone unzip her garment bag and change her clothes.

Instead, she laid out a black suit that she would wear and not carry. Then she put two pairs of hose, two T-shirts, four pairs of underwear, and a small bag of toiletries into a black shoulder tote. She repacked her briefcase and made sure she had everything she needed—a wallet full of cash advanced by the company, her cell phone, her laptop, her files filled with airline tickets and paper schedules since she hadn't figured out how to use Peter's Palm Pilot, and all the other paperwork which was now essentially useless since so many of the arrangements had changed.

The next morning, Mary settled into her seat next to Julia on the plane, strapped herself in, and passed the next fifty-eight minutes of the flight north to Boston expressing her concerns and demands—Was an airline security person going to meet their flight and take them via golf cart to baggage claim? Had Julia confirmed that the Chestnut Hill Bloomingdale's had the proper equipment (a padded upholstered chair, a signing table draped with white linen and adorned with white flowers, an ample supply of Sharpie pens and, most importantly, cans of chilled Fresca and room-temperature Volvic water)? Were there any gossip or news items in the morning papers about her daughter's appearances on the entertainment shows over the weekend and was there any word on impending protests and demonstrations by PETA activists in connection with Heaven Scent and Legend?— which Julia tried her best to answer and address. But the hardest question by far to field was why there had been a change in their hotel accommodations.

"I thought we were staying at the Four Seasons."

"We are," Julia said.

"That's not what the new schedule says. The new schedule says we're staying at the Westin."

"The Westin?" Julia unfolded her copy of the revised schedule Jack had e-mailed her Sunday night at home and which she'd printed out but not yet looked closely at. "I don't know anything about this."

Mary rolled her eyes. "Another Frick and Frack situation. One hand doesn't know what the other one is doing."

Julia examined the accommodations page of the schedule for the first time and realized that Jack had downgraded their hotels from Ritz-Carltons and Four Seasons and other top hotels to Westins and Hyatts. He'd also switched their first-class flights to business class and coach. It was his way of trying to not only save some money but also give Mary further cause to become so incensed she'd play the star-treatment card and drop out of the tour.

But Mary Ford wasn't going anywhere.

"I hear good things about the Westin chain. They have something called 'the Heavenly Bed' and 'the Heavenly Shower,' with down comforters and pillows and special toiletries," she said, setting her jaw and fixing her hair. "I've seen their television ads. They're trying to compete with the more expensive hotels for the business traveler's business." Mary leaned across the armrest and stuck her finger into Julia's arm. "Don't think I don't know what that Jack Be Nimble is up to."

Poke.

"He's trying to smoke me out. But he's going to have to do a lot better than taking away my fancy hotels and my first-class airline tickets to get me to walk away from this so he can cut his losses."

Poke.

"My perfume might be tanking and my daughter might be trying to rain on my parade, but I'm washable. I didn't last in Hollywood for as long as I did because I was a quitter."

Poke.

She retracted her poking finger and sat back in her seat as the plane taxied down the runway and pushed its nose up into the air.

"Now what idiot at the *Boston Globe* is coming to my Heavenly Hotel Room to interview me?"

No idiot, it turned out, from the *Boston Globe* was coming to the hotel to interview her. That had been canceled, too, as Julia discovered upon check-in at the hotel, although for reasons having nothing to do with the PETA situation: George Clooney had been spotted in town, scouting locations for an upcoming film, and they'd put all their available entertainment reporters on that story. And so with only their five o'clock news segment to look forward to before their evening signing at the suburban Boston Bloomingdale's, Julia suggested they have lunch somewhere on Newbury Street and rest up for the latter part of the day.

After an uneventful meal at the recently updated Boston landmark the Locke-Ober Café, just across from the Boston Common (where Mary, who had been there years ago with "a gaggle of Kennedys," pronounced her Lobster Thermidor "fabulous"), and after Mary had poked and prodded at her teeth and Julia had paid the check, Mary announced that she wanted to go shopping.

"This is one of my favorite stores in the world," Mary said, as she led the way into Louis, Boston's equivalent of Barneys New York, which, like Barneys, had started out solely as a men's store. Gliding across the threshold of the converted nineteenth-century stone mansion and heading toward the elevator, Mary pushed the button for the fourth floor, where the women's department was.

Julia followed Mary off the elevator and through the quiet skylit and nearly empty store, around the racks of tiny Prada and Gucci sweaters and skirts and T-shirts that looked like they were sized for five-year-old girls, and over to the far side of the floor, a large part of which was devoted to a single designer.

"Jil Sander," Mary Ford purred as she pawed through the jackets and pants and blouses on their heavy wood hangers. "My favorite non-American designer." Julia watched as she pulled two suits—one black and one cream-colored—and two blouses off the rack and looked around for a salesperson. But before someone had the chance to spot her and lead her to a dressing room, Mary had taken off her blouse and had slipped one of the Jil Sander blouses on over her beige bra.

"This is fabulous," she said, buttoning the blouse and then reaching to slip on the black suit jacket. "No one knows fabric and fit like Jil. It's that German precision. Not even Donna can cut a suit to fit like this."

Julia looked around to see if anyone was watching the spectacle Mary was creating—taking off the jacket and blouse she'd just tried on and readying yet another blouse and jacket to try on, while standing there yet again in her bra—terrified at the thought that at any second Mary might even drop her pants in order to try on the suit trousers. But before that happened a small young man in an exquisitely tailored dark pin-striped suit with a florid purple shirt collar and cuffs poking out of the jacket appeared, blushing and bowing.

"Miss Ford," he said breathlessly and completely unsurprised by Mary's partial nudity. Has-beens must do this all the time, Julia realized—undressing in public as a way of getting noticed—she had just never been clothes shopping with a has-been before. "What an honor and a pleasure to serve you."

Instantly charmed, Mary turned toward him and gave him her classic grin, the one that had worked such magic that first day they met during the photo shoot.

"And who might you be, Little Well-Dressed Man?"

"Flint."

Mary raised an eyebrow. *"Flint?"*

He nodded.

"As in 'Lint' with an 'F' in front of it?"

He nodded again.

"What kind of a name is that?"

"A nighttime name."

She rolled her eyes at Julia. *I told you the gays love me.*

"Flint," Mary repeated dubiously.

He blushed again and curtseyed. "It's a stage name."

Mary rolled her eyes dramatically toward Julia. "An actor."

He smiled naughtily. "A performer."

As he led her away behind a wall into a dressing room with an armful of clothes for her to try on in private, Julia couldn't help being impressed by and a little jealous of how masterfully he was handling Mary. While she was momentarily distracted, Julia called the office.

Jack's phone went directly to voicemail, but Jonathan picked up their line on the second ring. The minute she heard his voice, she knew something was wrong.

"Lindsay Green's PETA news made the morning papers and columns," he said nervously, like a monkey that had been spanked and traumatized. Which she knew he must have been, having been left all alone with Jack during this crisis. "The *New York Post*, the *New York Times*, *USA Today*, the *Wall Street Journal*, *Variety*." He paused to catch his breath and she did the same. She'd only known about the *Post* and *USA Today* that she'd grabbed before getting on the shuttle.

"And it made all the morning shows."

"Fuck."

"There are two protests planned that we know about," he went on. "One in front of the Heaven Scent building on Fifth Avenue and the other at Bloomingdale's on Lexington."

"When?"

"Today. Late afternoon, around rush hour. They're going to start at Heaven Scent, then march crosstown to Bloomingdale's to maximize disruption. Jack thinks both are going to get wide coverage, both national and local, and that the story will move from entertainment to news."

"Fuck."

Julia glanced over at the dressing room. She could still hear Mary crowing about the fabulousness of whatever it was she was now trying on, so she turned back to the phone.

"What about the Bloomingdale's here in Boston?"

"So far it's quiet. No word of activists planning on showing up, no cancellation by the store."

Julia shook her head, completely flummoxed. "I don't understand. This is exactly what my conversation and agreement with PETA on Friday was intended to prevent."

"I think Jack overrode that agreement."

"What do you mean he overrode it?"

Jonathan paused and she could tell he was going into her office and closing the door for privacy. "I found a letter at the fax machine that he sent to PETA Friday night after you left." She could hear him shuffling some papers until he found what he was looking for—the letter itself, which, he confessed, he'd made a copy of and stowed in her office. "It said that 'despite the terms discussed with my associate regarding Mary Ford's participation in the making of a public service announcement denouncing cosmetics testing on animals, Miss Ford has declined to participate in your very worthy cause. While she loves animals and of course finds the cruel treatment and exploitation of them deplorable, she is otherwise currently committed to the promotion and marketing of her new fragrance, Legend.'"

"But that's a lie. Mary would have told me if Jack had called her. And she never would have gone back on her word. Especially on this. Even though she hates people, she loves animals." Before she could further deconstruct the counterintuitive negative-publicity-generating strategy and guerrilla tactics Jack was using to squash Legend, Mary emerged flushed from the dressing room, suits and blouses and Flint in tow.

Julia folded up her phone and slid it back into her jacket pocket. "Any luck?" she said with as much false cheer as she could muster.

Mary winked at Flint, who, on cue, gathered the clothes she was apparently planning to buy in his arms like little children. Then she winked at Julia.

"I think Jack DeMarco owes me a suit."

Julia stared at Mary, then at Flint, then at the suit's price tag, which she found tucked up inside the left jacket sleeve.

$3700.

"Excuse me?" Julia said.

"Combat pay. If not for his incompetence—and yours—I wouldn't be in this mess. For one thing, my perfume would smell good, and for another, I wouldn't be about to face the front lines of a rabid political movement."

Julia looked over at Flint but he shrugged helplessly. Not that she was surprised, since he obviously worked on commission and wasn't about to risk losing a sale like this.

"My little friend here told me about what's going on in New York today. And apparently he's heard through the grapevine that there's a very good chance we're going to run into some trouble at

Bloomingdale's tonight. Which is why I can't afford to look anything less than my absolute best."

She poked Julia and nudged her over toward the register.

"Take out your credit card, Einstein, and pony up. It's show-time."

If Julia thought she was prepared for what they would face that evening at Bloomingdale's, she realized, when their black sedan passed the store, because the throng of sign-carrying protesters was clogging both the front and rear entrances of the store, that she wasn't. She knew, from the quick research she'd done the previous Friday at the office, that PETA had a remarkable ability to organize protests all around the country on very short notice due to its e-mail network of eager and agile community activists, waiting by their computers for the call to arms, but she hadn't expected the crowd she saw gathered that night. With their signs and banners and their synchronized chants of *"Heaven Scent is a lie! Bunnies shouldn't have to die!"* Julia realized for the first time what they were up against: people who were going to look great on the eleven o'clock news.

Julia pressed her nose up to the glass of the passenger window and slid to the edge of her seat.

"Pull forward and behind that restaurant," she said, tapping the driver on the arm as she held on to the back of his headrest. When he put the car into park, Mary poked Julia.

"Where are we going?"

Julia pulled out her cell phone and her schedule and started dialing. "We're waiting here for a minute. I need to get a hold of my store contact and revise our game plan."

"What game plan? Clearly no one had a game plan, judging

from the size of that mob outside. I'd say there's at least two hundred people here. And three camera crews."

Julia glanced past Mary's head as she waited for the call to connect. There was a game plan. Extra security had been hired just in case; store personnel were supposed to have been in place in the back of the store to escort them in.

"The crowd is at least twice that size," Julia couldn't help correcting. "And there's only one camera crew. The other two are just giant SUVs."

As Julia pressed her cell phone to her right ear and stuck her finger in her left ear, Mary shifted nervously on the leather car seat. Up until seeing the rabid crowd lining the perimeter of the store and spilling out into the adjacent parking lot, she'd seemed up for a fight. But now it was obvious she was having second thoughts.

Not that Julia blamed her.

She didn't want to go out there either! Fight her way through an angry politically correct mob! Risk getting pushed, shoved, and spit on! And for what? To sell a few stupid bottles of perfume and forever tarnish Mary's reputation by having her comeback attempt marred by the perception of her being a bunny-blinder? If the store didn't cancel the event, she would.

Picking nonexistent lint off her brand-new crème-colored Jil Sander suit pants and sucking her teeth, Mary waited for Julia to finish her call.

"Well, there's been a change of plans, not surprisingly," Julia reported, then flipped her phone closed. "We're free to go."

Relieved, Mary was now free once again to complain loudly and proclaim with bravado her willingness to fight the good fight. "Why? Because of a little disturbance?" She looked out the window and poked Julia in the arm. "These soccer moms don't scare me."

"Well, they scare me. And they scare the store's lawyers. Bloomingdale's doesn't want to risk liability and litigation should you or anyone else get injured during the course of the demonstration."

"Chickenshits," Mary hissed.

Julia ignored her, then directed the driver to take them back downtown to the hotel. It wasn't even six o'clock. They could have dinner at The Palm next door to the Westin and get to bed early. Maybe by the time they got to Orlando she could straighten things out with PETA and this would all blow over.

"Get Jack Be Nimble on the phone," Mary barked.

Julia stared at her. "Jack has nothing to do with this."

"Get him on the phone anyway. I want an explanation."

Between Jack undermining the tour and Mary behaving like a diva instead of accepting her true has-been status and acting accordingly, Julia felt like her head was going to explode. "You want an explanation?" she snapped finally. "I'll give you an explanation. There are five hundred people out there ready to spray that thirty-seven-hundred-dollar Jil Sander suit with red spray paint because the company that makes your perfume sprays chemicals into the eyes of baby bunnies. And I need to protect my investment. There's not another suit where that one came from."

Like most bullies, the minute she was confronted, Mary backed down and shut up.

Julia turned away and wondered what the hell she was doing there—trapped in the backseat of a car with a has-been, racing away from a raging crowd of political activists. Wishing she had never taken the job to begin with but also wanting desperately to crush Jack DeMarco, she asked the driver without poking him this time (she was already behaving enough like Mary with the yelling and the bossiness) to take them back downtown to the hotel, and he did. She and Mary rode all the way there in silence.

When they got there, and when she and Mary had made their way back through the maze of the lobby toward the exit nearest The Palm, Mary stopped her.

"The explanation I wanted," she said firmly, but with surprising civility, "is why these protests were continuing when I agreed to make that public service announcement?"

Julia didn't know what—or how much—to say. She knew she should probably be politic and professional and not involve Mary in the internal struggle she and Jack were apparently engaging in, but she was tired of having him undermine her authority at every turn, tired of protecting him, and just plain tired of everything.

"I think Jack disagreed with that and with the terms of the agreement I tried to negotiate with PETA last week."

"What do you mean, he disagreed with it?"

Julia shrugged. "As far as I knew, that agreement—though merely verbal—was in place on Friday afternoon. An agreement that I was assured would prevent demonstrations like the one we just escaped from and the ones that took place in Manhattan today. In addition to your agreeing to shoot that public service announcement, Heaven Scent had opened a dialogue with them to find out what they could do to get off the 'bad list' of companies that test their products on animals and get onto their 'good list.' They'd agreed to begin what PETA calls a 'moratorium' on their current practices. All together, that was enough for PETA to call off the dogs and let us proceed. At least for now."

"So what happened?"

"Apparently, Jack told PETA late on Friday after I'd gone home that you didn't want to do a PSA because you needed to devote

all your energy to the marketing and promotion of your perfume."

Mary shook her head. "So what do we do now?"

"All I know for sure right now is what we can't do."

Mary scanned Julia's face. "And what's that?"

"Quit."

Because neither Julia nor Jonathan could get any intelligence later
that night about activists gathering at the Macy's in Orlando,
Julia decided to continue on with the tour. The last thing she
wanted to do was let Jack the Jackass win, and the last thing, too,
that she wanted to do was cause Mary's morale—and her own—
to sink any lower than it already had. In the face of such adversity—not only from the PETA protesters but also from Jack's
devious machinations—they needed all the strength they could
get. Which is why she decided forging ahead to Florida was the
best decision all around.

That night, sitting on her Heavenly Bed, having just gotten
out of her Heavenly Shower, she called Mary's room.

"So we're going ahead as planned."

"Good."

"You're sure you're ready for this?"

"I'm ready, Einstein. But the question is, are you ready?"

Julia fluffed up the pillows behind her and clicked off the television. "Oh, I'm ready."

Before going to sleep, she called Peter. She hadn't talked to him
all day and she wanted to tell him about the little dump truck and
cement mixer she'd picked up for Leo after the Jil Sander Incident

and before the Bloomingdale's Massacre. As she talked she could see the toys still in the bag on the floor next to the desk, and the sight of them made her ache to hug him. She couldn't wait to get home.

"So, did you finish the gingerbread house?" she asked. It was Monday, and Halloween was Wednesday, the day she was due home.

"Yes, I did, and I'm bringing it to school in the morning. They're going to put it in the block room so everyone can see it."

"That's great, Peter. And what about Leo's costume for the parade?"

"I'm just about finished with that, too."

"Amazing."

What had been her problem all those years? The sleepless nights wondering how she was going to get everything done and done well. Maybe she wasn't as cut out for the "job" as she'd always thought she was.

"You never did tell me what he's going to be."

"He's going to be an artichoke."

"An artichoke?" Julia said. "What do you mean, an artichoke?"

"I made these amazing artichokes last week when you were gone, for your parents, to thank them for babysitting and helping out so much," Peter said, "and I thought that would be a great idea for a costume—all the layers of green flaps with just his face showing."

Julia was quiet. Clearly he was spending too much time in the kitchen with his cookbooks and his food magazines, and while she didn't want to burst his bubble of deluded enthusiasm, she couldn't bear the thought of Leo marching down Larchmont Avenue on his first real Halloween dressed as a stupid vegetable.

"Why can't he just be a fireman? Or a pirate? Or Bob the

Builder? Or Superman? Or Scooby-Doo? That's usually what kids his age dress up as. I mean, you think Adam is going as anything other than Batman?"

"Actually," Peter said, trying to explain, "all his friends from school—Ali-Jon, Ian, Adam, Zanny, Deika, Mia, George—they're all going as vegetables, too. And we all agreed—all the moms—and, well, me—that the parents and kids would trick-or-treat together so we could be a salad."

Peter's handiwork was all over this one—the food-related theme, the organization of the plan, the coordination and cohesion of the parts (vegetables) into the whole (the salad)—and she couldn't help but see the humor in it. In fact, the more she thought about it, the more she couldn't wait to trail behind them all with the digital camera, documenting it all.

"What time are you going?"

"We're tossing around six. I figured if you got home on time, we could go as oil and vinegar. Or tongs."

— 20 —

Whatever respect Julia had earned by getting them through the Bloomingdale's Bloodbath and refusing to be intimidated by Jack into quitting the tour vanished the minute the driver who met their flight in Orlando in a giant white limousine announced that he was taking them to the Disney World Magic Kingdom Hotel.

Julia reached for her seatbelt and rolled her eyes at Mary.

"Funny."

"Can you imagine?" Mary said. "This white boat is bad enough."

Julia shook her head and thought about Meredith Baxter-Birney. "I would kill myself."

"You wouldn't have to kill yourself because I would have already killed you."

The driver, a large sixty-something dome-headed man with a gray comb-over and a heavy New York accent who looked like he either used to break legs or slice smoked fish for a living in his previous life, readjusted the rearview mirror and turned around to get a good look at them. He had a crater the size of a nickel in his neck, and Julia, though completely fascinated by the horror of such a thing (Was it from a bullet? A meat hook? An ice pick?), forced herself to look away from the crater and into his eyes. They twinkled with delight when he repeated himself.

"The Disney World Magic Kingdom Hotel."

Julia's face froze into a mask of fear and rage and she felt her mouth start to open and close. She hadn't felt this lost since that first time in the limousine with Mary on the way to Long Island, and she dreaded the return of the blowfish and all the poking that would come along with it. But for the moment, Mary ignored her. Instead, Mary calmly asked him what his name was.

"Nick."

"Nick what?"

He shrugged. "Just Nick," he said, as if that's what was officially on his birth certificate.

"Now listen here, Just Nick," Mary began, acutely aware that this was one driver who needed to be charmed. "Even though you don't appear to be the sort of man who is mistaken about anything, some other idiot must be mistaken. Because I'm sure you can see that we are two people who do not belong in the Magic Kingdom."

Julia felt her left eye start to twitch as she glanced down at her schedule. They were supposed to be staying at the Marriott Grande Vista—already a downgrade from what they were used to—but obviously Jack had pulled a fast one and switched the reservation just to torment them.

Which was working like a charm.

"Well, you know, Miss Ford," Just Nick said slowly, with a big grin spreading across his face, belying the fact that though he'd clearly been around the block a time or two, driving someone as famous—or someone who used to be as famous—as Mary Ford was still a big thrill for him. "I was thinking the same thing when the dispatcher told me that I was picking you up today. So I double-checked my orders with my car company and with the hotel and that's where you're staying."

Mary, whose patience and self-esteem had been severely tested the past few days—starting with the news that her daughter was sabotaging her comeback and then that Jack was sabotaging Julia's efforts to salvage that comeback—turned to Julia and, as she always did in moments of extreme stress—poked her.

"Get Jack Sprat on the phone," she whispered sharply.

"I'm trying to." Julia had already dialed halfway through Jack's office number when Just Nick pulled out into traffic.

"It must be tough for people like you," he said, flipping the visor down against the sun and taking his big hand off the steering wheel—a hand that had a gold pinky ring on it the size of the crater in his neck (Maybe that's what caused it? Somebody else's pinky ring?)—to talk. "Your careers go up and down. One minute you're on top and the next minute you're all finished. It goes in cycles, like a washing machine." He twisted his hand back and forth quickly to illustrate his point. "Today Disney's Magic Kingdom Hotel. Tomorrow the Ritz-Carlton Orlando Grande Lakes. Am I right?"

Mary grunted as Julia continued to speed-dial various numbers on her cell phone, but after not being able to reach Jack, or Jonathan—or even Vicky—and then losing her signal altogether—she folded up her phone and sat back in defeat.

Nick prattled on about how the hotel was actually one of his favorites; how he'd taken his eleven-year-old granddaughter there the previous April when she came down from Los Angeles for her spring break; how the hotel rooms were all themed to specific

Disney characters; and how they had great family-oriented activities.

"Have you ever heard of a Hidden Mickey?" he said, trying to catch Mary's eye in the rearview mirror.

"In my day, Just Nick, they were just called *mickeys*," Mary said firmly. "And I hope you weren't planning on putting one in my drink."

Nick laughed, turning his head again toward the backseat and lifting his big pinky-ringed hand off the steering wheel to explain how Hidden Mickeys—an image of Mickey Mouse concealed in the design of a Disney attraction (a ride, a resort, a scene in a film)—started out as an inside joke among the Walt Disney "Imagineers," and that in designing, constructing, or adding the final touches to an attraction, Imagineers subtly hide Mickey Mouse silhouettes in plain sight.

"Now, every time people go to Disney movies and theme parks, they hunt for Hidden Mickeys. Most of the hotels have some sort of contest."

"What's the prize?" Mary asked.

"You mean, if you win?"

Julia could tell that Mary was just dying to say *No, if you lose,* but it was clear that Nick scared her just enough for her to know she should watch her mouth.

"Yes. If you win."

"You get tickets for rides."

"Tickets for rides," Mary repeated, wholly unimpressed. "That's some prize."

"Haven't you ever been to Space Mountain? Or the Animal Kingdom?"

Mary looked away and out the window. "Long ago. With my children."

Julia had never been to Disney World and Peter had always talked about taking The Scoob the minute he was old enough to go—and she was curious about what Mary had thought about the whole experience.

"It was the worst week of my life," she said, checking her hair and lipstick in the mirror of a small black compact she'd slipped out of her purse. "Unrelenting heat and humidity; not being able to get a decent meal or a decent night's sleep; crowds wanting autographs. I never thought I'd have to go through it again, but here I am, headed back to the seventh circle of hell."

Nick pulled the sedan into the odd multi-circular driveway in front of the hotel, then turned to the backseat with a huge smile. "See? A Hidden Mickey!" he said, pointing out the window to the parking circle they were in (Mickey's head) and then to the two other, smaller adjacent parking circles (Mickey's ears) that were attached. As Mary reached into her bag for her big sunglasses and a scarf to tie over her hair—clearly, she did not want to risk getting recognized—Julia looked beyond the Hidden Mickey driveway and gasped: the hotel was a castle-shaped multicolored theme hotel with life-size costumed Disney characters everywhere.

Jack would pay for this if it was the last thing she did.

Nick popped the trunk, and before Julia could get out of the car, she saw Goofy opening Mary's door and reaching his huge paw in for her hand.

"Welcome to the Magic Kingdom!" a voice said from deep inside the Goofy suit.

Julia was confused. Hadn't she read somewhere that Disney characters weren't allowed to speak? Or was that just in the actual Magic Kingdom and not in the hotels?

Mary glared at the paw and then over her shoulder at Julia as she reluctantly got out of the car.

"This is a nightmare," Mary said.

Julia scrambled out of her side of the car to instruct Nick about how to handle Mary's luggage, but it was too late for that, too. Goofy, having escorted Mary into the capable hands of Sleeping Beauty, was now reaching into the trunk and handing the luggage off to Dumbo.

"Look at all these fucking bags," said a disgruntled voice inside the elephant suit.

"I'll get Sleepy and Grumpy to help," Goofy said, pointing and waving at two members of the Seven Dwarfs who were standing near the entrance of the hotel.

For an instant Julia felt herself leave her body and float up above the absurd scene, then look down. And during those few blissful dissociative seconds, she wished she had a camera— Goofy had just helped Mary Ford out of a tacky white stretch limousine; their driver had a huge hole in his neck—from what, she didn't know; Dumbo was pissed because there was so much luggage; and Sleepy and Grumpy were running over to the trunk of the car as fast as their little legs would carry them to help— and without proof no one would ever believe her. But when she floated back down and returned to the reality of her body, she knew that even if she did have a camera, there wasn't time to document the situation: things were quickly getting worse.

At the check-in desk, Mary was told she would be staying in the Minnie Mouse Suite and Julia was told she'd be staying across the hall in the Donald Duck Room. Mary shook her head with disgusted resignation and followed Dumbo and the Two Dwarfs to the elevator and off again and then down a long carpeted hallway to their rooms. Julia followed them. Disappearing into her suite without even saying goodbye, Mary barked orders at the three oversized costumed bellhops about their mishandling of her luggage. It was just another day, another city, another chapter in Mary Ford's life as a has-been, taking out a lifetime's worth of frustration on anyone unlucky enough to serve her.

Standing there in the hallway with her tote bag over her shoulder and her signal-less cell phone in her hand, Julia couldn't do anything to stop Jack from torturing them and she couldn't stop Mary from torturing the costumed bellhops (especially the Two Dwarfs, who, from what she could hear, were getting the worst of it) except reach into her bag for her wallet and the thick wad of twenties inside it. Even though there wasn't nearly enough money to compensate for the pain and suffering Mary caused wherever she went, when Dumbo came out with Sleepy and Grumpy behind him, she peeled a bill off for each of them anyway and whispered her apologies.

I'm sorry.

I'm sorry.

I'm sorry.

Knowing they had nothing to do until Nick came back to pick them up at five-thrty for the Macy's appearance at six o'clock, Julia went into her room and closed the door behind her. It was almost over, this tour, this farce—after today, after the Macy's event (assuming it wasn't overrun with protesters the way Bloomingdale's in Boston had been the night before), she'd be on a plane home tomorrow, back to New York and home to Larchmont to go trick-or-treating with Peter and the artichoke.

Since she had nothing to unpack and since she'd decided not to bother switching hotels unless Mary forced the issue, Julia put her tote bag and her laptop on the desk and sat down on the bed. It was quiet, and when she looked around the room she couldn't believe how far they'd come and how low they'd sunk.

A week ago they were at the Hay-Adams in Washington, and then the Ritz-Carlton in Atlanta; just yesterday they were at the Westin in Copley Square.

She bounced on the mattress once or twice to determine its quality (far from heavenly), ran her hand over the slick synthetic bedspread, then reached for the light—pressing the beak of the giant Donald Duck lamp next to the bed—and flipped through the room service menu. After almost fifteen minutes of distractedly staring at the two pages of offerings—it's a good thing they were going home tomorrow, otherwise Jack would probably book them into a Motel 6 or a Best Western or a Holiday Inn Express—she finally settled on the "Snow White Salad" with a side order of "Pinocchio Fries" and a pot of "Buzz Lightyear Coffee."

In the twenty minutes it took for Pluto to deliver her lunch, Julia had noticed at least four Deliberate Mickeys (Hidden Mickeys that were in plain view and used in décor)—the hand soap in the bathroom, the embossed toilet paper, the multicolored bedspread, and the alarm clock—and then three more on her room service tray: butter pats, sugar cubes, and corn chips. Looking down at the salad and picking briefly at the long, thin shoestring fries, she realized, though she hadn't eaten since the night before, she had no appetite. Shocked and amazed—she couldn't remember the last time she had lost her appetite, if ever—but too exhausted to be appropriately delighted by it, she put the tray on the floor outside her door. Then she called Jonathan to check in for messages and to make sure that all was quiet at the office (it was) and that there was no news of an ambush being planned at Macy's later that evening (there wasn't).

At the window she pulled back the curtains that matched the bedspread and thought she could see Main Street USA just past Cinderella's Castle. Though she'd never been there she knew that the Magic Kingdom was divided into five distinct "lands"—Tomorrowland, Fantasyland, Frontierland, Liberty Square, and Adventureland—and she remembered reading once that Walt Disney, being a complete control freak, had insisted that a huge network of underground tunnels be constructed to connect all the "lands" so guests wouldn't see any "behind the scenes" operations or costumed "cast members" walking "offstage" through one world (Tomorrowland) into another (Frontierland) and breaking the illusion of fantasy.

Julia suddenly felt sad that Leo wasn't with her now—she could just imagine his delight in the hotel room right then, with the Donald Duck lamps and wall sconces and the Mickey Mouse bedspread and the nonstop cartoons on TV—and she was crushed that there probably wouldn't be time for her to sneak away to the theme park itself before or after the event with a disposable camera and at least take pictures and buy souvenirs to bring home. Even if there were time, she knew Mary wouldn't want to go, given the terrible time she said she'd had there years ago.

But to Julia's shock and amazement they did go: first to the Magic Kingdom and then to the Animal Kingdom—after the Macy's appearance, which, though it had no protesters (even the staff hadn't really heard about the PETA situation), was grossly underattended. Despite newspaper ads and heavy in-store promotion, there were, at most, thirty women milling around the cosmetics department and only about half of them bought boxes of perfume for Mary to sign.

When Nick asked how it had gone as they crawled back into the car, Mary waved her hand at him dismissively.

"It was a bust," she said.

"It wasn't one of her better events," Julia said.

Mary rolled her eyes. "Einstein, here. The Queen of Relativity."

Julia nodded reluctantly.

It was a disaster.

In a moment of sheer celebrity-inspired exuberance, an over-eager Macy's saleswoman had sprayed the entire signing area with Legend just minutes before she and Mary had arrived, saturating the white linen skirted tablecloth and their upholstered wing-back chairs. Once she and Mary sat down with their noses crinkling and eyes watering, the saleswoman had returned, bottle in hand, ready for more spritzing. Which is when Mary almost attacked her.

"Get away from here with that bottle or I'll call store security," Mary barked, reaching across the signing table for Julia's cell phone to prove she was serious.

The saleswoman looked confused, then horrified, quickly checking the bottle in her hand to make sure it was Legend and not some other celebrity's fragrance. Relieved to see that she hadn't made some grotesque error, she smiled.

"But it's your perfume, Miss Ford! And we're so excited to have you!"

"I don't care how excited you are. Put that goddamn bottle down or I'll have you forcibly removed from this store."

Feeling a wave of perfume-induced nausea coming over her, Julia had smiled nervously. Then she sneezed. "It's just that I'm allergic," Julia lied, trying to make the saleswoman, who had tears coming out of her eyes, feel better, and to contain the public relations crisis already in full swing: the few customers who had been in line had overheard Mary's verbal threats and were now wondering why she, former star of stage and screen—and Hollywood legend—was bellowing at someone half her age and half her size. Julia wondered if she should fake a sneeze or two, but while she was deciding, she sneezed—for real—three times in quick succession.

Before Julia could get complete control of the situation, the saleswoman left the signing area in tears, and Mary sat back down at the table. The bottle of Legend was now in her hand, and Julia realized that while she'd been busy sneezing Mary must have wrestled it out of the poor woman's hand. Which was probably why the first three women in line had put their boxes of perfume down on the table and walked away, muttering the word "bitch" under their breath, without making their purchases. Clearly, things were going downhill fast.

Now, back in the car, waiting for some direction from either Julia or Mary, Nick finally started the engine and pulled out of the parking lot. And when his question of where they wanted to go now was met with a wall of silence, he suggested that they let him show them a good time.

"What kind of a good time did you have in mind?" Mary asked, with a raised eyebrow.

"Dinner at the Wilderness Lodge," he said. "Then the nighttime fireworks display at the Magic Kingdom. The perfect end to a not-so-perfect day." He turned around and told them he'd put some brochures in the side pockets on the doors for them to look at.

Julia picked up the brochure about the nighttime fireworks display and scanned the text:

Make a wish upon a star and then marvel as the nighttime sky comes to life. . . .

She turned to look at Mary, who had picked up and opened the same brochure.

Join Jiminy Cricket as he guides Pinocchio, Cinderella, Ariel, Peter Pan and other beloved Disney characters through this fantastic story told amongst the stars. . . . Discover that wishes do come true when you experience this story so big only the sky can hold it.

Mary put on her smart black glasses and read aloud, *"The show is presented as the park's good night kiss to its guests."*

"They think of everything," Nick said.

Mary took her glasses off. "Well, I don't kiss on the first date."

He laughed. "You said yourself that this is your second time here."

She smirked, then put the brochure back in the side pocket. "I'd rather go to the Animal Kingdom. I like animals. Despite what my daughter and her group of activists think. In fact, I like animals better than people."

When Nick told her that he had a friend who could get them special passes for the "Sundown Safari," she shrugged, as if still thinking about Lindsay and the PETA situation. Then she told him to slow down and keep it under sixty on the highway.

"Don't overdo it with the gas pedal."

Nick winked at Julia in the rearview mirror and pumped the brakes.

"Sounds like a yes to me."

It was after dinner at the Wilderness Lodge—after Nick had paid off a friend of his to get a golf-cart vehicle to drive Mary and Julia to a private nighttime ride across the savanna with their own special guide; after he had helped them both into the all-terrain–style vehicle with canvas awnings and bench seats high enough to see past the bushes; after Nick had sat down next to Mary in the seat just behind the driver and after Julia sat down in the seat behind them; after they passed two black rhinos and three reticulated giraffes—when Julia's cell phone rang.

The night air was chilly, especially for southern Florida in late October, and the park, bathed in its artificial simulated moonlight, appeared empty except for them. Mary, who seemed to actually be enjoying herself—no lines, no walking, first class all the way, finally—turned around briefly as Julia fished frantically through her big black tote bag for her phone.

When she saw the Caller ID number glowing—Patricia's office—and the time—well after ten o'clock, late even for Patricia to still be at work—Julia knew something was wrong.

"Can you talk?" Patricia asked, all business.

Julia looked past Mary and Nick in the front seat of the safari vehicle to the driver behind the wheel. He had just driven them past the rhinos and the giraffes and appeared to be headed for a herd of antelope foraging for food.

"Sort of." She turned her back on them so she couldn't be overheard and described the surrealistic scene for Patricia—strange and oddly humiliating as it was. "You know how it is."

"Unfortunately I do."

Julia shifted in the seat and stared at the antelope while she waited for Patricia to say whatever it was she had called to say. She assumed the animals were real, though she wasn't sure—this was a Disney theme park, after all, full of fantasy and illusion and the blurring of the lines between the two—and now, unable to ask the driver, she would have to spend the rest of the ride not knowing what was what.

"Look," Patricia said finally. "I'm calling to give you a heads-up on something."

Julia laughed nervously. "You've discovered something better than Thermage?"

Patricia didn't laugh. "Actually, I'm calling about Mary Ford's daughter."

"What about Mary Ford's daughter?"

"She has a book."

"Another novel?"

"No. It's nonfiction. A memoir. A tell-all book."

"Like a *Mommie Dearest* book?"

"It's called *Mary Dearest*. But yes. Same idea." Patricia paused awkwardly. "She's hired Pulse—and me specifically—to handle her and counteract all the bad-daughter press she's going to get when her agent sends it out." She paused again. "I know this makes your situation even more complicated but I thought you should hear it from me so you wouldn't get completely blindsided when the shit hits the fan in two days."

Julia blinked rapidly, trying to get her bearings. "How did she come to you?"

"Jack DeMarco sent her."

"Jack DeWack sent her?"

Julia shook her head in disbelief. This whole thing was going from bad to worse. First the perfume smelled terrible, then Jack and Lindsay sabotaged the promotional tour, and now they were coming in for the kill. The campaign was falling in with the timed precision of a house of cards. She'd never seen anything quite like it in all her years in the business.

"You've read it, I assume?" Julia asked, even though she didn't have to.

"Let's just say there are no surprises."

But her daughter was a nobody! And Mary Ford was a has-been! Who, besides Leeza Gibbons and Deborah Norville, would really be interested in either of them?

"Who cares? I'm not worried. When it comes out it'll disappear in a week." Julia knew she was doing a shitty job of pretending she wasn't flipping out but she did it anyway.

"It's not the book that will make headlines," Patricia said. "It's the film rights. This story has great female roles, one for an older actress. Material like this doesn't come along that often for women of a certain age, so they're expecting the submission to generate a lot of interest."

Julia knew she was right. Faye Dunaway, for all her great work in *Bonnie and Clyde* and *Chinatown* and *Network*, would always be best remembered for her viciously campy portrayal of Joan Crawford.

She stared at Mary in the front of the safari vehicle sitting next to Nick, and for the first time since she'd met her, Julia actually felt truly sorry for her. The two of them had discovered over dinner that they had grown up within blocks of each other in the Flatbush section of Brooklyn years ago and were still talking about the old neighborhood as the vehicle made its way across a twisted bumpy bridge over a turbulent crocodile pool. In the distance a group of hippos stood at the base of a cascading waterfall looking up briefly at the low headlights of their vehicle.

She had no idea how she was going to break the news to Mary, and she had no idea how she was going to position their side of the story to the media. She also knew she would have to tell Mary right away—she couldn't risk her hearing it from someone else. As the vehicle bounced and bumped along the rutted road, she asked Patricia what their time frame was.

"They're submitting the manuscript to publishers and film people on Friday—in time for them to take it home and read it over the weekend. By Monday we'll know more."

Julia folded up her phone and stared into the manufactured moonlight.

It was Tuesday night.

They'd get back to New York sometime the following afternoon.

Which would give her most of Thursday in the office to set up her end of a crisis-management response—Mary's official statement regarding her position on her daughter's book would have to be written and ready for immediate release; internal decisions would have to be made about who—Katie Couric? Diane Sawyer? Barbara Walters?—would get access to Mary for her first sit-down televised interview. Mary Ford might indeed be at the nadir of her fame, but there was nothing those ambulance-chaser shows loved more than someone—an actress, a mother, a has-been—under attack.

Just as she was trying to figure out when to break the news to Mary—Back at the hotel later that night? The following morning at breakfast before their flight home? Just outside Mary's apartment at the Ansonia while the car idled curbside, waiting to drop her off and take Julia out to Larchmont in time for Halloween?—Mary turned around and yelled out over the sound of the vehicle.

"Who called?"

Julia hesitated. "My friend Patricia."

"The one you told me about?"

Julia nodded.

"Why was she calling so late?"

Mary didn't miss a trick. Even with all the jungle noises and night-vision binoculars, nothing got past her.

Julia froze, wishing she could stop time, freeze the frame right there in order to be more prepared for what she had to do—tell Mary that her daughter had written a nasty book about her that was going to hit New York and Hollywood in about forty-eight hours—but deep down she knew that there was no way to spin the news of Lindsay Green's memoir into anything other than what it was: a public humiliation and the ultimate betrayal.

She also knew that delaying the inevitable wouldn't score her any points in the long run. Mary would be incensed if she learned that Julia had kept the news from her for any substantial length of time. And so, she leaned forward on the edge of her bench, tapped Nick on the shoulder, and pointed at the driver.

"Tell him to stop the ride."

The vehicle slowed down and came to rest right in the middle of a clearing of underbrush where a family of colobus monkeys was gathered. Their black and white fur glistened in the simulated moonlight and they looked remarkably peaceful on their little piece of fake wilderness, searching through the trees for leaves and berries.

"You've got more bad news for me, don't you, Einstein?" Mary said.

Julia nodded, then sighed.

"Well," she poked. "Spit it out already."

So she did.

And after she did they looked at each other and neither of them spoke.

Mary leaned over to Nick and politely asked him to sit up front next to the driver for a few minutes so she and Julia could talk. And once he'd moved she looked out into the forest at the towering canopy of overhanging trees and thick grass—vegetation which, Julia imagined, was probably a spectacularly lush shade of green in natural daylight.

"I'm sorry," Julia said.

"What are you sorry about?" Mary snapped. "You're not responsible for my daughter's behavior."

"I can fix this."

"No, you can't."

"Yes, I can. When I get back to the office I'll have a strategy and a plan in place. If we go on the offensive we can at least create a distraction with a counterattack."

But Mary shook her head slowly.

"Don't bother."

Julia sat forward again and began to talk rapidly about what could be done to spin the story in their favor—interviews Mary could grant; a press release they could issue disputing Lindsay Green's credibility; maybe even this time getting her son, Bruce, to finally speak out publicly on her behalf—but Mary put her hand up.

"I've had enough," she said wearily.

Julia was shocked to hear the deep defeat in Mary's voice.

"But we've come so far," Julia pleaded. "We can't just give up now."

"Yes, we can. There's no point trying to win a game I went in losing."

Julia thought about all the time and energy Mary had put into the Legend campaign long before she'd even started working for Jack—all the photo shoots and marketing meetings with Heaven Scent—and all the time and energy they had both put into it in the last months, especially the last two weeks of travel. After all Julia had been through—watching Mary steal the clothes; enduring her verbal abuse in the limousine back from Long Island; that first shuttle to Washington and the veal chop and all those evenings spent in Mary's hotel room watching Charlie Rose and helping her decide what to fill out on her breakfast room-service card when she could have been home with Leo—and after all the humiliation Mary had suffered—the inferior fragrance, the dwindling crowds, the PETA protests, and the Minnie Mouse Suite—she couldn't believe that Mary was willing to walk away in defeat.

"But you're letting Jack win," she argued.

"I couldn't care less about Jack DeMarco."

"Then you're letting Lindsay win."

"Maybe she deserves to win after everything I've put her through."

Mary ran her hand slowly through her hair and looked out at the animals. The family of monkeys preened each other and then huddled together as if in a group hug. As she stared she was collecting her thoughts, a lifetime of them, Julia knew—memories and incidents flashing behind her eyes like reels of home movies.

"I traded what should have been most precious to me—my children, my family—not for a wilderness of monkeys, but for just one stupid monkey. Fame. As short-lived and fleeting and fickle as it always was."

Julia stared at Mary, trying to place the reference, and when Mary realized that Julia had no idea what she was talking about, she shook her head.

"That stupid college of yours. Allowing you to graduate without making *The Merchant of Venice* required reading."

"Sorry," Julia said reflexively.

Mary shook her head again. "Have you ever heard of Shylock?"

Of course she had. She'd actually even read *The Merchant of Venice*, though clearly she'd forgotten it since the focus of the college seminar she'd taken—"Shakespeare from a Feminist Perspective"—was on feminism, not Shakespeare.

"Well, in the play, Shylock has a daughter who he loves more than anything in the world and he gives her a ring—the ring that had been her mother's. When he finds out that his daughter has married a Christian and traded the ring for some stupid monkey, he's devastated."

"*'That ring!'*" Mary bellowed, with great theatricality. "*'I would not have given it for a wilderness of monkeys!'*"

Julia nodded silently.

"I screwed up, Einstein. Everything—my acting career, my films, my fame, my fortune—it all came before my family."

"So you made some mistakes. Some errors in judgment. Every parent does."

"You don't understand. Your Leo is only a baby. He still loves you more than anything in the world. My daughter has spent most of her life trying to prove to me and everyone else in the world what a bad mother I was. And she has plenty of evidence to support her case."

Julia tried to make out the expression in Mary's eyes, but moonlight, artificial or otherwise, wasn't intended to illuminate such subtleties. All she could see clearly was that Mary's head was down, and that she was twisting the beautiful gem-encrusted yellow-gold stack of rings on her left hand.

"When I came here, years ago, with the children, it was terribly hot. Lindsay and Bruce were eating soft ice cream cones one afternoon and it was dripping down their chins and onto their shirts. What a mess." She forced a smile and tried to laugh. "I remember moving away from them into the shade for just an instant and looking around for restroom signs so I could get them cleaned up—it's not like today when mothers carry wipes everywhere they go—and when I looked back they were gone. Just like that. It took me a few seconds to realize in horror that they'd melted into the crowd, but once I did I screamed bloody murder."

Julia blinked. That was her worst nightmare, losing Leo in a mall, or on a beach, or anywhere at all.

"A guard took me to a nearby kiosk and within minutes they'd found them. They were both terrified. When I grabbed them and held them, Bruce clung to me, but Lindsay didn't hug me back. She wouldn't forgive me. But the guard tried to make me feel better. He told me, Julia, that in Disney World, there are no lost children. There are only lost parents. When children get separated from their family, their biggest fear besides actually being lost is that their parents will be angry with them when they get found. They shift the blame to the parents—where it belongs."

Julia felt a lump grow in the back of her throat. Mary had never called her by her first name.

"It's not Lindsay's fault," Mary said, her back straight, her jaw set, a single tear running down her cheek. "It never has been her fault. It's my fault. I'm to blame. I'm the one who was lost, and now it's finally time for me to pay the piper."

— 21 —

There wasn't much more to say or do after that except go home—back to the hotel, where this time Mary didn't tug on Julia's sleeve to get her to come into her room to watch Charlie Rose; back into the limousine the following morning with Just Nick, who took them to the airport; and back to LaGuardia and into Radu's black sedan, which was waiting to take them to the city.

But unlike all the other trips, Mary didn't seem to care much about anything this time—she didn't care that Sinbad and Tinker Bell dropped one of her bags while trying to fit all her luggage into the trunk of Nick's car; she didn't care that Nick had given her and Julia each a little Mickey Mouse stuffed animal as going-away presents with his homemade business card—*Just Nick—Just a Phone Call Away*—stapled to their ears; she didn't care that for once the airline escort was exactly where he was supposed to be and when—on the sidewalk in front of the airport's entrance, wearing an official red blazer, holding a working radio and with access to a golf-cart vehicle to take them through the airport, through security, and straight to the gate and onto the aircraft; she didn't care that Jack had downgraded their tickets to coach and that it took Julia twenty minutes of discussion with the head flight attendant—who was too young to have any idea who Mary once was and was trying to be again—to lose her battle to upgrade them to first class.

It was over—all over—and as Mary walked toward the Ansonia after the flight and the drive in from the airport and held up her hand to wave goodbye without turning around, Julia knew that something monumental was happening:

Mary Ford was quitting.

When Julia returned to work early that afternoon, she could barely look at Jack as she passed by his office—the Ultimate Cheeseball sitting there in the conversation pit, wearing another cheap suit, his arms outstretched across the top of one of the couches, meeting with Dennis Franz and his eager-beaver manager, auditioning for the part of career savior and master resuscitator with his usual unbearable pomposity. As she sat down at her desk and caught up with Jonathan, whose kindness and caring she'd missed out there on the cold hard road, she thought about the cold hard facts—the tight deadline she was under to manage her client's impending public relations crisis—and she swung into action, attacking the situation with the necessary logic and rationality by forming first an overall strategy (positioning Mary as the victim, the underdog, then attacking the attacker), and then proceeding to nail down and lay out the particulars (drafting Mary's statement, which would be e-mailed and faxed to the press Friday morning in advance of the story; formulating a wish list of media interviews for the following week; placing calls to or fielding calls from various producers and reporters for the remainder of Friday afternoon).

That was as far as she could plan things, she knew—the rest was unforeseeable. The reaction of New York publishers and Hollywood film people to Lindsay Green's manuscript, the response to the news of Lindsay Green's story by the entertainment media, and the continued attention to PETA's political action would remain a mystery until they unfolded in real time. All Julia could do was prepare herself as best she could—sketch out a to-do list for the following day, brief Jonathan on what was coming, have him cancel Mary's remaining appearances for the following week on the West Coast—then get home to Larchmont in time to toss the salad.

Racing from the train station to the corner of Larchmont Avenue and Putnam, where the parade always started from, she could see the collection of costumed characters gathered under a streetlight—a head of broccoli (Ali-Jon), a head of cauliflower (Adam), a red onion (Zanny), a spear of asparagus (George), a tomato (Deika), a carrot (Ian), a beet (Mia), and, of course, an artichoke (The Scoob)—posing for a group photo that Pinar, one of the mothers she hadn't seen since those first two weeks of preschool and whose last name she had forgotten, was taking with a tiny digital camera—Julia felt for a second that she was still in Disney World, or at an Anne Geddes photo shoot.

Making her way through the crowd with her nearly empty tote bag and her laptop case over her shoulder as the camera flashed and the children squirmed, she was amazed at what Peter had helped create out of cardboard, colored fabric, tinfoil, and colored cellophane: not just eight vegetables that weren't even primarily salad vegetables, but the group of parents dressed as large leaves of romaine lettuce, croutons, and a saltshaker and a pepper mill, which was led by the two of them wearing foil-covered tong-shaped hats—*and* by her parents, who were dressed as Oil and Vinegar.

As the crowd started to move and the salad formed a loose circle in the middle of the street—the parents watching as the children waddled in their costumes and waved proudly to the onlookers and to the other groups of costumed children passing by, all on their way to the firehouse for hot dogs and candied apples in the glow of huge jack-o'-lanterns—she looked over at her parents. They were wearing their usual sweatshirts and jeans and thick-soled Merrells, and they waved, their arms coming out from under the simple sandwich-board signs Peter had made for them. Leo was bursting with joy inside his green layers of artichoke leaves, and she grabbed his hand so she wouldn't lose him in the crowd.

Peter waved to her from the other side of the salad, over a gigantic leaf of romaine lettuce (Zanny's dad), and smiled a huge smile under his foil-covered tong-shaped hat.

"Isn't this fun?" he called out, pointing at all the parents and the kids and the parade marching all around him.

She squeezed Leo's hand tighter and waved back.

"Yes!" she yelled out even though she wasn't sure Peter could hear her. "This is fun! This is so much fun!"

Later that night—after they'd returned home and sorted through Leo's bag of candy; after he had fallen asleep, still in his artichoke costume, on the living room floor while Peter and Julia talked about the evening but not about the latest, and seemingly final, problem with the Mary Ford campaign and Julia ate two full-size Reese's cups and two small Kit Kat bars without the usual amount of massive guilt and self-loathing; after she and Peter had carried Leo up to his room—they went to bed, too, and, in a sugar-and-chocolate-induced haze, "did it" for the first time in weeks.

They'd turned the clocks back the previous weekend, and the room was black. Julia reached for Peter's hand in the dark, and when she found it, they laced their fingers together.

"What are you thinking?" she whispered.

He breathed deeply. "I'm thinking that for Thanksgiving, I'm going to brine a turkey. A big turkey. We'll have your parents, my parents, Patricia. We could have all the preschool moms over for dessert. I could make a few pies, some cookies, maybe a cake." He turned to her. "How does that sound?"

Slipping into sleep, she patted him on the arm. *It sounded great.*

— *22* —

The next morning, the answer to Mary's problems appeared in Julia's head—a little thought balloon, bubbling up from her sub-conscious like a dream. It was an elegant solution, one that would solve not only Mary's problems but Julia's, too—how she was going to handle the media crisis, how she would get revenge on Jack, and how she would show Patricia that even though she hadn't thought she was ready for anything more than a crappy job at John Glom Public Relations, she was back in the game.

Now all she had to do was convince Mary.

She took the train into the city and a cab uptown to the Ansonia, then collected herself in the lobby. Mary was expecting her—Julia had called from the cab on the way from Grand Central with the excuse about needing Mary's signature authorizing the firm to cancel all future promotional appearances for Legend—but Julia was certain that even if she hadn't called, Mary wouldn't have been that surprised to see her. Mary knew that her abrupt decision two nights before had shocked Julia and she knew she hadn't seen the last of her.

Mary opened the door and Julia walked into the cavernous, sprawling apartment that Mary had lived in for over thirty years—high-ceilinged rooms full of built-in bookshelves and beautiful furniture and old black-and-white framed photographs on the fireplace mantels. Hollywood film memorabilia—old movie posters from *All the While* and *What I Did for Love*—hung on the walls in the hallway, as did an impressive collection of modern art that included, among other things, an enormous Andy Warhol silk-screen portrait of Mary's face of the sort that had been so popular in the 1970s. Leading Julia over to two facing couches in the living room, she motioned for her to sit down.

"So," Mary said.

"So," Julia said back.

"I assume you're here to talk me into not quitting."

She nodded.

"I have to say, Einstein, I admire your tenacity. I didn't think you had it in you."

Of all the left-handed compliments and direct insults Mary had flung at her over the weeks, this one bothered Julia the least. Probably because it was true. She didn't know she had it in her, either.

Mary stared at her. "It's over. You know that. There's no way to get around the damage Lindsay's book is going to do to me."

Julia raised an eyebrow. "I think that there *is* a way."

"You do," Mary said dubiously. "And what way is that?"

Knowing how counterintuitive what she was about to say might sound, Julia leaned forward on the couch and took a deep breath.

"Embrace the book."

Mary laughed out loud. "Embrace the book?"

Julia nodded. "For lack of a better way to phrase it. Yes."

"You're joking."

Julia shook her head. "I'm not."

"Then you're an idiot," Mary pronounced. "Why else would you tell me to support something that's going to humiliate and embarrass me?"

Julia sat back on the couch and clasped her hands in front of her. "Because it's the right decision. And because you have no other choice."

Mary ran her hand through her hair. Her brow was furrowed and her lips were pursed. She didn't like being told what to do and she certainly didn't like being backed into a corner.

"The right decision, says who?"

"Says me."

Mary waved her away and made a face. "Like you know anything about anything. Up until a month ago you were home watching *Barney* with little Jimmy Durante."

Julia bristled. She knew Mary was going to get personal and mean—she always did when she felt she was being attacked or when she was on the defensive—but Julia still couldn't help feeling a surge of murderous maternal rage whenever Mary picked on Leo.

"First of all," Julia started, "I wasn't even around when Jack made the deal with Heaven Scent. Secondly, Lindsay didn't offer her services to PETA. Jack did. And thirdly, Leo and I never watch *Barney*. We watch *Tom and Jerry*." She narrowed her eyes and crossed her arms in front of her chest. She wasn't going to dignify the Jimmy Durante reference with a response.

Mary blinked, confused, and Julia realized that this wasn't the time or the place to defend herself—and her child—against accusations of idiocy, so she forced herself to return to the subject at hand, explaining how Jack had leaked the information about Heaven Scent to PETA, and how he'd then contacted Lindsay and put her in touch with PETA, knowing she would welcome the opportunity to get involved with a high-profile political cause that would put her in the public eye.

Mary shook her head. She couldn't understand why Jack would sabotage his own client, why he would purposely torpedo a project—Legend—he himself had helped create.

"Because he knew long before he told you that there was a problem with the perfume itself. He knew that Heaven Scent had had to cut corners in the production of the fragrance and that it didn't smell right and that because of that, Legend was going to be more of a hindrance than a help to you. In order to shift attention away from the lousy perfume and back to you, he decided to try to get publicity for you any way he could. Creating bad publicity for Heaven Scent was his strategy for keeping your name in the press while distracting everybody's attention away from the fact that your perfume—your comeback vehicle—was destined to be a failure."

Mary sucked her teeth.

"But once I started negotiating with PETA to scale back their protests, Jack's plan was in jeopardy: the focus was going to go back on the perfume, which he didn't want, so he tried to shut down the whole campaign as quickly as possible and cut his losses."

"Hence the Minnie Mouse Suite."

"Exactly. As for Lindsay, once she'd gotten attention from the media, Jack gave her the means and opportunity to sell her book in exchange for helping him bury Legend."

"Jack may have given her means and opportunity," Mary said

slowly. "But he didn't give her motive. She had enough of that on her own."

Julia stopped.

Motive.

Maybe what Jack had said was true.

"What if Lindsay actually wanted to *help* you by getting involved with his plan instead of wanting to hurt you?" Julia said. "What if, by signing on with PETA to attack Heaven Scent, she did it to try to *protect* you from the public humiliation of having your perfume fail by taking the focus off you and putting it onto the issue of animal rights?"

"That's absurd," Mary said.

"No. It isn't." Julia sat forward again on the couch. "Look. Obviously, Lindsay has issues with you and with your mother-daughter relationship," she argued. "And obviously she was 'acting out,' trying to get your attention by taking a public position against your perfume. But what if she was also conflicted? What if the other part of her—the part of her that loves you and wants you two to be closer—was also acting out? What if she saw her participation in Jack's scheme—and the writing of a memoir—as the ultimate way to connect with you?"

Mary stared at Julia without blinking. "That's quite a stretch."

"Maybe. And maybe not. But whatever Lindsay's intentions were doesn't even matter at this point. All that matters is how you're going to handle the situation she's created—how you're going to behave under the worst possible circumstances and come out of this whole thing a winner."

Mary looked around the room and sighed again, then sat back against the cushions. "And you're telling me that the only way to do that is by not fighting the memoir? By letting Lindsay say anything she wants about me—whether or not it's even true? Even though most of it probably is."

"That's only part of what I'm advising you to do."

"And what's the other part?"

The other part was the key to everything—the strategy Julia believed would not only save Mary's reputation, but would achieve the comeback they'd been trying for all along:

"Lobby to play yourself in the movie."

Mary's mouth dropped open. For the first time since Julia had known her, it seemed the impossible had happened:

Mary Ford was speechless.

"I know you think I'm crazy," Julia said, "but I'm absolutely certain this will work. By going along with the book and the movie you'll deflate Lindsay's accusations against you and show everyone that you're human, and that you have a sense of humor and a sense of irony about yourself and about the whole institution of parenthood: Yes, of course your daughter 'hates' you. But all daughters 'hate' their mothers sometimes. Because all mothers make mistakes—even big, famous movie stars like Mary Ford. All parents, no matter what they do and how hard they try, can never win."

Mary said nothing, so Julia continued.

"It's the opportunity to play the role of a lifetime—*yourself*—as you are now—an older, wiser Mary Ford. A role that is the ultimate comeback vehicle and that is virtually guaranteed to put your movie career back on track."

Mary still said nothing, so Julia pushed forward to the end of her argument.

"And perhaps most importantly—you get a chance at building a whole new relationship with Lindsay. You told me yourself that you have regrets about some of the decisions you made when your children were growing up," Julia said quietly. "How you feel you put your own needs before theirs. Well, if that's true, then now's your chance to make it right. Now's your chance to connect with Lindsay in a completely different way. On her terms, collaborating on a creative project you both have a huge stake in."

Mary swallowed, and just like two nights ago on the moonlit savanna, a tear made its way down her cheek.

"What if she doesn't want me?" she said, her voice, for once, weak and tentative.

"She needs you, and you need her. Everything else will fall into place."

Mary pulled a tissue out of the sleeve of her sweater and wiped her nose, taking one last moment to decide whether or not to trust Julia with what was left of her career.

"It's a jungle out there, Einstein," Mary said, keeping her eyes trained on Julia's face.

"I know."

"Are you sure you can handle it?"

Julia didn't flinch. "I've been there before," she said. "And I think I still know my way around."

Now that she had Mary's approval, all Julia had to do was not fuck it up.

Racing back down to midtown in a cab, she knew that she would have to act quickly in order to line everything up before Lindsay Green's manuscripts started going out the next day. She walked past Jack's office on the way to her own and saw him sitting at his desk, talking on the phone, but she ignored him. Instead, she called Jonathan into her office, closed the door behind

him, and told him about her strategy to turn the Mary Ford situation around.

Jonathan's eyes widened and then he slowly started to nod.
"Cool!"

"You think?" Julia said, desperate for reassurance, albeit from
an assistant half her age who wore love beads and whose pants
were so big on him they were practically falling off.

He nodded furiously, unequivocally supportive. "Who would
ever expect her to support her daughter's nasty book? It's a total
shock. It turns the whole thing on its head."

She breathed for what felt like the first time all day, or all week.

I ♥ Jonathan.

"Then why am I so scared to call Patricia?" She couldn't believe
she was asking him this.

"Because."

"Because why?"

"Because from what you've told me about her," Jonathan
started, "Patricia is—well—she's kind of into herself."

"You're so right," Julia said.

"Though probably not deeply narcissistic, one might go so far
as to say that she has a rather healthy ego."

"Right again."

"Also from what you've told me, Patricia sounds like she's all
about control."

"So, *so* right." She nodded till her neck hurt. Everyone except
for Jonathan and herself—Mary, Jack, Peter, The Scoob, Walt
Disney—and everything—the Container Store, *Cook's Illustrated*—seemed to be about control. "But why am I afraid?" Julia
said, hoping he would connect the dots for her.

"You're afraid because it's a really good idea and you're worried that Patricia is going to be jealous that you thought of it and she didn't."

"Then what do I do?"

He considered the equation and the solution. "When you call her, you need to do two things: play to her ego and distract her from the fact that you're trying to control her. She's going to have to think that letting Mary glom onto Lindsay's film deal is her own brilliant idea."

Twenty minutes later, Jonathan came back with coffee and a Krispy Kreme donut so perfectly and translucently glazed it looked like plastic. Then he closed the door and sat down across from her as she'd asked him to.

Jonathan Leibowitz: copilot. Wingman. Friend.

Julia took out a fresh yellow legal pad and one of the crappy supply-drawer ballpoint pens that she was actually starting to like, and picked up her cordless phone headset. She dialed Patricia's office number, got past her assistant, and, after a little small talk with Patricia herself, got down to business.

"So how's the submission going?"

"So far, so good, I hear."

"A lot of interest out there?"

"Yes."

"You know that for a fact?"

"I sure do."

They both paused, then Patricia sighed loudly. "Julia?"

"Yes, Patricia?"

"Did you call for a reason or are you just killing time?"

"Of course I called you for a reason."

"I'm listening."

Julia paused one last moment to collect her thoughts.

"What if I told you that Mary Ford is prepared to support her daughter's book?"

Patricia was silent. "What do you mean, 'support'?"

"Meaning, she won't publicly denounce it; she won't speak ill of it or ill of her daughter to the press when the sale is announced or at the time of publication."

"Look, Julia, I'm not sure you understand what this book is. It's an unflattering portrait of a selfish woman who cared more about her own ego and public image than she did about the well-being of her daughter, let alone her son. It's not a pretty picture and I can't imagine it's something she—or you as her publicist—would want to endorse."

For the second time that day, Julia bristled. "I understand what the book is, Patricia," she said with arch assurance, then stuck out her tongue. Jonathan stifled a giggle.

"Then how can you tell me that Mary Ford will support it?"

"Because that's what she's decided to do."

"But why?"

"Because she thinks her daughter deserves to have her say."

"But what's the catch?"

"There is no catch."

"There's always a catch."

Julia smirked. *Duh.*

"Look," Julia said, as fortified by sugar and caffeine as she was by her desire to win this last and final round. "You're about to go out with a highly subjective memoir about a Hollywood mother who's a has-been, by a daughter who's a loser and an ingrate. Right?"

Patricia didn't answer.

"Wouldn't it be great if the has-been mother supported the

loser daughter's right to speak her mind? Wouldn't it be great if the has-been mother was willing, in fact, to accompany her loser-ingrate daughter later on television appearances and interviews when the book is published in order to demonstrate to the world how one mother and daughter can resolve their differences and live to tell the tale?"

Patricia was completely silent now but Julia knew her mind was working—Julia knew she could see the Oprah interview; the Diane Sawyer sit-down; the conversation with Larry King and the hour-long session with Dr. Phil—she could see Mary and Lindsay discussing their problems and how they healed their troubled relationship.

"It would certainly help humanize Lindsay Green, who's going to come off badly when she hangs her mother out to dry and cashes in on all the family secrets," Julia said. "Wouldn't it?"

"It would," Patricia conceded.

"Because then there would be a really great story to sell—not just the story of the angry adult daughter of a former movie star, but the story of failure and redemption and the power of people to come together despite years of emotional injury."

Julia was ready to barf, with all the psychobabble language she was using—words that Jonathan had written down on a legal pad in big bold letters behind which he was shaking with laughter—buzzwords and phrases for her to throw in to make it all sound official. He'd howled as he'd written them all down, and as her eyes scanned toward the bottom of the pad and she saw CYCLE OF PAIN and WORLD OF HURT she almost lost it.

Patricia paused. "Like I said before, Julia. What's the catch?"

Julia drew a giant fishhook on her pad and swiveled in her cheap shabby chair until it squeaked, and flashed Jonathan the drawing. "Like *I* said before, Patricia, there isn't one."

Patricia laughed. "Well, I don't believe you."

"Fine," Julia said as matter-of-factly as she could. "That's your prerogative."

"I know it is."

"I know you know."

"Good."

"Good."

Julia sighed loudly for effect, as if, out of bargaining chips, there was nothing else for her to do but hang up.

Patricia didn't flinch.

"Well, okay then," Julia said, as if this time she was really serious and was about to hang up. She closed her eyes, held her breath, and started counting.

"Wait," Patricia said right before Julia got to three, with just enough urgency in her voice for Julia to know that the balance of the power equation had suddenly shifted to where she wanted it.

"So let's just say for the sake of argument that you're telling me the truth," Patricia hedged.

"Which I am."

Sort of.

"And let's just say for the sake of argument that Mary Ford really *is* genuine about supporting her daughter's story. Or, at least, genuine about creating the illusion that she is supporting her daughter's story."

"Which she is."

Kind of.

"Then what? What's the quid pro quo?"

She was all set to dance around the answer for another minute or two until Patricia figured it out, but she was tired of walking on eggshells with everyone. Julia sat forward in her chair and stared at Jonathan.

"A part in the movie."

"A part in the movie?" Patricia laughed nervously, and if Julia hadn't known her as well as she did, she would have thought Patricia really was nervous, instead of just getting a handle on the strategy and trying to figure out how to work it to her advantage. "She's a little old to play herself, don't you think?"

"Of course she's too old to play her younger self. There isn't enough makeup or Botox or Thermage in the world. But she's not too old to play her older self."

Patricia was silent but Julia could hear the wheels turning in her head.

"So Mary Ford wants to play herself in the movie based on her daughter's unflattering memoir."

Julia felt herself start to sweat.

"So she can have one last chance at immortalization in the role of *Mary Dearest.*"

More sweating. "Think of Faye Dunaway."

"Yes, but Faye Dunaway wasn't Christina Crawford's actual mother."

Julia wiped her forehead and stood up. "Listen, Patricia. With Mary Ford behind the film, studios and producers and directors who will be considering the project will be much more likely to sign on since they'll know that she won't try to get the whole thing tied up in a big legal battle. And being able to offer Mary Ford along with the property makes the property much more interesting and thus infinitely more valuable both as a book and as a movie."

She waited a beat, then heard the squeak of Patricia's chair.

"Jules?"

"Yes, Patricia?"

"Whose idea was this?"

Julia hesitated, trying to figure out what to say. But when she saw Jonathan looking at her with pride, as if, whatever the outcome, she had won the bigger fight, she closed her eyes.

"Yours."

Patricia laughed out loud and the two of them dissolved into hysterics.

"I knew there was a reason I liked this idea so much."

— 23 —

Her mission accomplished, Julia decided to take the rest of the day off and leave early. She told Jonathan that he could leave early, too, and after sending a quick e-mail to Jack's computer next door informing him of the fact without even bothering to make up a lie, she packed up her bag, left a message for Peter on his cell phone, and rode down in the elevator with Jonathan. When they got outside, Jonathan looked up at the sky.

"Wow," he said. "It's light out. I don't think I've left the office before dark since I started."

"Me either," Julia said.

Jonathan lifted his big black messenger bag so the strap went diagonally across his body. While they waited at a crosswalk, he turned to her and smiled.

"Wouldn't it be cool," he said, "if we never had to go back?"

*   *   *

It was just after noon when she got on the train, and she knew that if there were no delays she'd get to the station and into her car and to the preschool in time to pick up Leo. She couldn't wait to surprise him and to be back in the cramped little foyer, squished in with all the other mothers waiting for their children to be released, one by one, after lunch.

When she arrived, just a minute or two before one, Lisa was there. So were Pinar and Monika and Hilary, and in the few brief moments before the children appeared with their coats and their lunchboxes and their little masterpieces of artwork in their paint-stained hands, her long-lost mom-group surrounded her, asking her all about her job and her trip and everything else they hadn't had a chance to talk about the night before at the Ragamuffin parade when they were all dressed up in salad attire. Shocked that they seemed so happy to see her and thrilled that her brief re-entry into the preschool routine was so pleasant and painless, Julia couldn't help wishing she could do pick-up more often, just to keep her hand in things. She also couldn't help noticing that each of them was carrying a black three-ring notebook: their very own Family Binders.

Monika rolled her eyes with relief. "Your husband has totally taken over the preschool parent-involvement situation, organizing everything to within an inch of its life. Instead of wasting our time in meetings once a week trying to figure out who's going to do what and when—meetings which inevitably devolve into discussions about recipes and laundry—we just wait for Peter to e-mail us with our job and our deadline."

When the door finally opened and the children started spilling out into the foyer and into the arms of their waiting mothers, Julia made her way to the front of the line and looked past the teachers and into the block room where the kids were dressed in their down jackets and their backpacks, looking like little astronauts about to blast off. And there, in the middle of it all, was Leo. His back was to her and all she could see was that he was talking excitedly to Adam—who was wearing his cape again—and pointing at something in the corner of the room. As she moved closer to the doorway and stood on her tiptoes, she saw that what he was pointing at was the huge gingerbread mansion that Peter had made—on display on a table and all lit up from the inside by a string of little white Christmas lights. From where she was standing, it looked amazing, and she had no doubt that it was even more amazing up close. Leo couldn't have looked prouder.

"My daddy made this!" she could hear him say over the dismissal din to Batman and to the teachers and to anyone else who would listen—including Julia herself, who had, by now, slid past the teachers and was only inches away from him. When Leo saw her he screamed and pointed, first at her legs and then at her.

"Hey! That's my mommy! That's my mommy!"

Kneeling down and hugging her Scoob, she was almost embarrassed by how happy he was to see her. But she wasn't embarrassed about how happy she was to see him. She felt impossibly lucky and incredibly grateful: her world had shifted and turned, but she was still in it, still a part of it, still holding on for dear life.

Epilogue

By Monday afternoon, Lindsay Green's half-completed manuscript sold to a publisher for a high-six-figure sum, and then it sold in a dozen or so other countries for more than a book like that—a child-of-a-celebrity memoir, destined for instant remainderhood—usually sold for. Which was *bupkes.*

But the big news was the film sale of *Mary Dearest* for a cool $2 million, which *Variety* reported on the following week, deeming it "one property worth its price tag since the star attached to the star vehicle is none other than Mary Dearest herself."

As Julia expected, Patricia got her name in the trades a lot, but to her credit she credited "Julia Einstein, publicist and spokesperson for Mary Ford, for bringing the two parties—mother and daughter—to the table."

When the time came for contracts and monies and pay-or-play options to be discussed, Julia stepped aside and handed over the reins of the project to the phalanx of managers and agents and lawyers that Mary Ford had underemployed for years, but who were now fielding offers for product endorsements, movie roles, print interviews, and talk show appearances. It was one of the most dramatic reversals of fortune Julia had ever seen and she couldn't believe that the whole project was now almost entirely out of her hands.

But what she really couldn't believe was that during the four gruelingly stressful weeks she'd been back at work she'd lost ten pounds. Which, as any woman who had ever had a baby and never quite lost "the weight" knew, was the true measure of any successful professional comeback.

After raining down on Lindsay Green, Mary Ford, and Patricia, the success of the sale of *Mary Dearest* trickled down next to John Glom Public Relations.

Has-beens from far and wide flocked to their New York and Los Angeles offices with managers and agents in tow, in search of answers for how to revive their own dormant careers, and for the next week it was all Jack and Julia and Jonathan and Vicky could do to keep up on their end with scheduling new-client meetings, attending new-client meetings, serving bottled water, drawing up new-client contracts, and collecting the retainer checks. Everyone wanted to sign on with the "Extreme Career Makeover Dream Team" (as she and Jack were dubbed in the trades, which annoyed her no end since in her opinion he'd had nothing to do with Mary Ford's resuscitation—unless placing the pillow over Mary's face for Julia to later remove could be considered "helping"); everyone wanted another shot, a second (or third) chance at a successful comeback. And who could blame them.

Legend was the next beneficiary. Sales of the failing perfume had almost instantly increased dramatically, forcing Mary to reconsider her earlier decision to abandon the promotional tour. With the PETA problem back under control and Heaven Scent reforming their research and testing practices as well as starting production on a new and improved version of the perfume to hit stores in time for the Christmas rush, all of the appearances that had been canceled were rescheduled, with Julia and Jonathan working overtime to reconstruct the campaign that had originally been in place before it went so off track. Back on the itinerary were the five-star hotels and the first-class airline tickets; back were the fans and customers lined up in stores, sometimes out to the handbag and shoe departments; back were the television crews and the newspaper reporters with their cameras and their tape recorders, waiting to get a glimpse of the legend behind Legend; waiting to get a word with Mary Ford, former star of stage and screen and "It" girl once again.

This time, though, when the new schedule was complete and it was time to hit the road, Julia stepped aside and turned the reins over to Vicky. Despite the fact that Julia had finally mastered the art and science of traveling with Mary, it was time for someone younger, hungrier, and without a husband and a Scooby-Doo waiting at home to take over and reap the benefits of all her hard-earned wisdom from the set of Identity Assumption notes outlining "What to Do and What Not to Do When Traveling with Mary Ford" that she prepared.

Jack, unfortunately, was next in line, waiting for his own unearned, undeserved manna from heaven to drop out of the sky and into his manipulative, opportunistic hands.

Up to his eyeballs now in rabid has-beens who had come back begging—Tony Danza, Morgan Fairchild, Joan Lunden, Joan

Collins, Carol Burnett, Phil Donahue, Alec Baldwin, Richard Chamberlain, and David Cassidy, to name only a few—and without an assistant (except for the few times he would get up the courage to ask Julia if he could borrow Jonathan and she would let him), he felt overwhelmed by the task at hand and under-whelmed by a sense of purpose. He knew he'd have to start ramp-ing up the agency as soon as possible to handle all the new business; he knew that he'd have to hire staff and get them trained and up to speed on the special art of has-been handling, and that he'd need to spend at least six months killing himself with long hours and late nights in order to keep up with the demand for their services. And for what? To connive and lie and manipulate his way to another meaningless promotion and insufficient raise at a loser firm?

So when he got Lindsay Green's call from the West Coast, he couldn't have been happier.

Deluged with attention after the sale of her book—interview requests from magazines, articles to write, fashion magazine photo spreads to do, not to mention the fact that she still had to finish writing the book so that she herself could start adapting it for the screenplay, as had been negotiated—she begged him to be her own personal media advisor and career manager.

Given the salary she was offering (double what he was making, which she could easily afford, given the book and film advances that would soon be coming in), the accommodations she was making available (the guest cottage on her property in Beverly Hills, which was empty since her last advisor slash manager slash boyfriend moved out), the first-class prepaid ticket she was pre-pared to FedEx to him (which was one-way and open-ended), and the fact that they were so obviously compatible in and out of bed—two inveterate narcissists who shared a passion for getting attention and getting their own way—it was an offer he couldn't refuse.

Jack was nimble.

Jack was a dick.

Jack got over his divorce real quick.

And finally it was Julia's turn.

Not more than a week had passed from the time of the *Mary Dearest* book and film sale before her own phone started ringing, too, and after several interesting offers from various public relations firms and talent agencies, the one call she'd been secretly waiting and hoping for all along finally came in—from her former boss, Marjorie, at Creative Talent Management.

Listening to her offer—Vice President of Media Relations— the promotion and title change she'd never stuck around long enough to receive four years ago, the promotion she always wondered whether she ever would have gotten even if she'd stayed— she couldn't help feeling like she was hearing from a long-lost boyfriend who wanted her back. Half of her wished she could, simply on principle, resist the tug of the past trying to reclaim her, but the other half of her—the half full of latent venality and repressed lust for financial security and career advancement— had no desire to resist.

But because she had come to feel that working with has-beens was infinitely more interesting, challenging, and rewarding than working with non–has-beens—they were the Special Olympics of the public relations world, a parallel universe of outsiders she herself had come to feel a kinship with—and because she couldn't bear the thought of seeing Jonathan in such a corporate setting—an enormous office filled with assistants who would eat him for breakfast his first week there and make fun of his love beads—and mainly because a big job like that filled with stress and dress codes and back-to-back meetings and a presumed level of animalistic ambition that would suck the life out of her and rob her of what she wanted most—time and energy left over for Peter and Leo—she turned down CTM's extremely generous offer.

But not before negotiating a competitive contract with John Glom himself over the phone to manage the New York office. Though he didn't match the salary CTM had offered, he'd come close enough, which gave Julia some leverage to negotiate a few other things she wanted: a four-day workweek twice a month so she could have two Fridays off to be with Leo, a raise and promotion for Jonathan, and one perquisite she was deeply ashamed of herself for insisting on—a car and driver just like Patricia had.

Just as Peter had done and just as she'd advised Mary to do, Julia was determined not only to make the best of the situation but to succeed in any way she could, so on the train ride home that night she decided that her first executive decision would be to prove that a new management style and sensibility was now firmly in place in the land of the has-beens: calling in the Container Store to outfit a supply closet with built-in shelves and drawers and keeping it constantly filled to capacity with a vast array of high-quality office supplies and organizing equipment.

Jack left just before Thanksgiving, and shortly after that, in early December, Mary called Julia to tell her that she was leaving, too. It seemed that the interest in her for film roles had remained steady since the initial onslaught, and now that the promotional tour for Legend was pretty much finished, Hollywood was where she needed to be for her career. It was also where she wanted to be now for Lindsay, who was, apparently, struggling to finish the book and start on the screenplay.

Though Mary didn't intend on moving out there lock, stock, and barrel, her plan was to stay with Lindsay ("despite the fact that that insufferable Jack Be Nimble who I hate is living in her guest-house") until she found her own house to rent and shuttle back and forth to Manhattan whenever she had time. And without having to say as much, Julia knew that the other reason Mary was so willing to make herself available to "help" Lindsay with the manuscript was so that she could try to soften some of the anecdotes and rewrite history just a little to take some of the sting out of the book.

"So since I knew you wouldn't come along to help me get set-tled," Mary said, "I called Just Nick to see if he knew of a driver out there who wasn't a complete idiot."

Thinking about how Mary must have pulled off the business card that he'd stapled to the stuffed Mickey's ear with a mixture of annoyance and amusement and how thrilled he must have been to hear from her, Julia smiled.

"And let me guess. Just Nick recommended Just Nick."

Mary laughed—a deep, throaty, smart-alecky laugh that Julia realized she'd never heard before—and sighed. "Now don't go getting any ideas, Einstein. He has a son who lives in Newport Beach who he wants to spend some time with over the winter."

"Or so he says," Julia said.

"Or so he says," Mary said, laughing again. "He told me he's going to take me to Disneyland and show me some more Hidden Mickeys. I said to him, 'Listen, Just Nick. Don't overdo it with the Hidden Mickeys.' But I don't think he heard me since by then he was already packing."

In the cold, snowy weeks before the break between Christmas and New Year's, Julia rode to and from the office in the comfort of Radu's black sedan and tried to adjust to all the changes that had occurred since September and all the changes that were going to occur over the coming months.

Though Peter still hadn't found a job, he had picked up some consulting work that would start in January, and Leo would be increasing his days at the preschool from three to four. Nothing, it seemed, was staying the same—the updated family schedule now reflected in the new time board that Peter made for the kitchen; the fact that she couldn't pin Patricia down for a cele-bratory lunch date because she was too busy dating Lindsay Green's film agent, whom she had met on a recent trip of his to New York; Leo, whose interest in trains was just starting to give way to an obsession with dinosaurs and superheroes; and even her mother, who had, at Peter's suggestion which came in the form of a prepaid Hanukkah gift certificate, signed up for a cooking class—albeit at the local Jewish Community Center—everyone and everything was up for grabs.

Months before, when it had all started—when she had first been forced to go out and get a job and Peter had first been forced to stay home—he'd promised her one night that things would eventually go back to the way they were, the way they'd planned them, the way they'd wanted them. And though she could never have imagined it or admitted it then, the world hadn't come to an end when she'd gone back to work. Of course she missed Leo and he missed her and of course Peter hoped he would someday get his career back on track. But they'd survived, even flourished. Not knowing what would happen over the next few months or years, she returned to the office after the holidays with a whole new set of pictures for her desk and her computer, feeling like she was heading into the wilderness toward a destination still unknown.

It was a jungle out there, she knew. But she'd been there before. And she figured she'd find her way.

About the Author

LAURA ZIGMAN grew up in Newton, Massachusetts, and graduated from the University of Massachusetts at Amherst and the Radcliffe Publishing Procedures Course. She spent ten years working in New York City as a book publicist, then moved to Washington, D.C. After working briefly for The Smithsonian Associates and Share Our Strength, she finished her first novel. *Animal Husbandry* was published in 1998 and became a national bestseller, and in 2001 the film based on the book, *Someone Like You,* starring Ashley Judd and Hugh Jackman, was released by Fox 2000. Her second novel, *Dating Big Bird,* came out in 2000, and her third novel, *Her,* followed in 2002. She currently lives outside Boston with her husband and young son.